"THEIR CREST," the Revived Man said, pointing to the ruins below. *"THE CREST OF THE SECOND INTERPLANETARY CONFEDERATION."*

In spite of the passing of centuries it had survived. Three sunbursts still glowed along one intact radiation shield, the proud emblem of the ancient Empire.

"One for each of the planets they held," said the Brigadier.

"They ruined this one," Khalia said. "See what it says about the legend." She felt the cold edge of menace.

The Brigadier read out the words with a connoisseur's pride. "Powerful words! Listen! It's just a line, but it's survived for a thousand years. A promise and a threat:

> "The Regiments of Night
> shall come at the end."

The Regiments
of Night

BRIAN N. BALL

DAW BOOKS, INC.
DONALD A. WOLLHEIM, PUBLISHER

1301 Avenue of the Americas
New York, N. Y.   10019

COPYRIGHT ©, 1972, BY BRIAN N. BALL

ALL RIGHTS RESERVED.

COVER ART BY KELLY FREAS.

Dedication:
*For my daughters
Jane and Amanda*

PRINTED IN U.S.A.

The Regiments of Night

CHAPTER

★ 1 ★

A dim yellow sun shimmered for moments in the space that still shook with the eerie trailing dance of the hypercubes. The girl tensed.

"I don't know why you bother," Mrs. Zulkifar said over her shoulder. "One sun's much like another. This one is quite undistinguished. I don't think I'll trouble to leave the ship at all."

Khalia smiled politely. "I expect you're right," she said.

But she still looked out into the blankness, waiting for the moment of transition from the weird phenomenon of Phase, when the ship would break loose from the coils of the unreal dimensions and slip into a tenable structure of space-time.

She wanted to see the sun. The Sun. And Earth.

Corridors of unholy power spun before her. There was a momentary blankness beyond belief as the ship pulsated with energy.

"No," said Mrs. Zulkifar. "I don't think I'm up to another excursion."

"Nonsense!" Brigadier Wardle said heartily. "You must come with me—I promise you won't be disappointed! Splendid ruins down there! You can't miss Earth!"

Mrs. Zulkifar shook her handsome head. "I may take one of the other trips," she said. "But a whole day in the weather just isn't for me, Brigadier."

They talked on, Wardle pursuing the attractive widow with a hearty enthusiasm that had been comic during the first part of the long voyage. It bored Khalia now. She wanted to see the planet.

The entire ship was invested with a disagreeable rippling of power. The sharp angles of walls and seats blurred for a tiny fraction of time.

Then the moment of transition from hyperspace to the comprehensible dimensions was accomplished. Khalia looked about her.

The ship was riding smoothly alongside a belt of asteroids. The passengers could look at one another and not have to hide a secret fear of the gulfs between the stellar systems. They could leave the protective couches and look at the reassuring solidity of the planets, sure that they could make an easy planetfall if they wished.

Time and space had been forced aside, so that the voyagers could add one more excursion to their itinerary. Galactic center never lost a ship.

Suddenly the vessel lurched; Mrs. Zulkifar yelped.

"What the devil—" began Wardle.

"This is not an emergency!" a smooth metallic voice said at once. "Your captain apologizes for the discomfort. A small adjustment of course was necessary to avoid a vessel in the immediate vicinity. There is no cause for alarm. Thank you!"

"It's too much!" Mrs. Zulkifar complained. "Anyway, I thought there wasn't a captain."

The retired soldier was happy to explain. "No more, my dear—ah—Emma! It's a polite fiction, like pretending that the food comes from real grains and vegetables and animals. Galactic Center hasn't used a crewed ship for a couple of centuries! Why should it?"

"What's another ship doing here?" the middle-aged woman with the firm figure and exquisite clothes wanted to know. "I thought the whole planet was derelict!"

"Not altogether," said Wardle, with a gleam of excitement. "What was the ship?" he asked the humanoid handing around drinks.

"The captain believes it was a private vessel, sir," said the automaton. "It didn't respond to signals. Of course it could be the famous Dr. Dross's supply vessel—the archaeologist, sir, you know."

"I know," said Wardle.

"Of course, sir! Perhaps Dr. Dross is exhibiting signs of his well-known eccentricity. Maybe he buzzed us deliberately, sir!"

"Why?" asked Khalia.

"The Doctor is averse to visitors," explained the robot. "But don't let that deter you from visiting the famous ruins, miss. The Doctor is obliged, by the terms of his contract with Galactic Center, to act as host to our passengers."

It spoke with a degree of satisfaction that Khalia found repellent. It chuckled. It was a laughing little robot. Khalia had heard its poor jokes halfway across the Galaxy.

Wardle was launched on a lecture. "It must have been badly-handled to make us take evasive action. I don't like to think there's some incompetent blasting around just as we're coming out of Phase."

"The captain said we're not to worry," Mrs. Zulkifar said firmly. "He should know!"

"Damn it, there isn't a captain!" growled Wardle.

Mrs. Zulkifar pointedly ignored him.

"The robots take too much on themselves!" he added, but no one was listening now.

Khalia was looking through the scanners at the green planet. It would not be long before the big tourist ship sent out its fleet of excursion-craft to the various local attractions.

Khalia was going to Earth. She was as excited as she could ever remember. Her face was calm enough, but inwardly she was brimming with eagerness. The rest of the long, slow haul through the Galaxy had been interesting enough. There had been a succession of often bewildering new sights. None had stirred her as the thought of the ancient planet that swam greenly about its red-yellow sun. There was little to see as yet.

Probably the excursion would be a disappointment. According to the guidebooks, most of the land-surface was unapproachable. The deep radiation of the Third Millennium and its Mad Wars still gnawed into the planetary crust. Nothing grew on the twin continents that straddled the globe. The Southern landmass was a fiercer waste than when the human race had invented space-time travel. Parts of what had been Europe remained green.

The scanners at last began to pick out detail. Forests and lakes under drifting white cloud made the planet a welcoming place. Here and there the remains of a tower-city thrust through the clouds, still supported on thin stilts. One blue city caught her attention. It parted the white mist like a needle in wool. Would it be on the itinerary? It wasn't.

Then the city was obscured by a raging storm. Khalia flicked the scanner away. Before it moved on, she saw a tiny ship hang like a fish in the clouds. And then another.

"There were two ships!" she exclaimed.

"What?" said the Brigadier, all bustling energy.

"I saw them—two ships! Just before I moved the scanner on. I can't find them now."

"Couldn't be!" said Wardle heartily. "One, yes. Not two. Maybe you saw the same ship twice. Optical illusion—aftereffect on the retina."

"Maybe I did," said the girl.

Wardle caught the tone of dissatisfaction in her voice. "There just can't be!" he went on. "One ship, yes—that would be Dr. Dross's vessel. He'll need supplies from Center from time to time. But there's no reason for another ship. Not a real ship, that is, not this sort of ship. The dig down there is the only official settlement."

He paused. "Of course, there'd be a few hoboes," he continued. "Eccentrics. People who've stranded themselves deliberately years ago. The sort of people who'd come to live on Earth out of sentiment."

"It doesn't matter," said Khalia. She was too happy to resent his patronizing.

He began to talk about the planet, quite interestingly at first. He knew an amazing amount about the oldest known planet of all. He spoiled the effect by trying to impress his circle of female listeners with his knowledge of the theories about the origin of human life. Khalia moved away when he began the familiar recital. The business of mythical accounts of a settlement by extra-Terrestrials was worn-out, tedious stuff.

Yet when the ship had slipped out of the curious and frightening effect called Phase, she had become unbelievably excited. Had she been able to look at herself, she would have been deeply ashamed of the flushed cheeks, the wide open eyes, and the furious throbbing of her neck arteries. She had been totally absorbed in the moment of revelation. It hadn't been in the least dull.

She looked what she was, a young woman undergoing a profound sense of wonder at feelings she had not guessed could exist. She sensed the mystery of the ancient spinning globe, and it moved her strangely.

Mrs. Zulkifar said something caustically to Wardle. The older woman regarded Khalia's slim but well-rounded body with some dislike. Khalia knew she was talking about her.

"—flaunting herself—" Khalia made out.

Khalia pushed the short skirt over her legs. What made Mrs. Zulkifar such a disagreeable bitch? Khalia hoped she would not make the trip to Earth. "And I did see two ships," she said, but under her breath. Why provoke another lecture from the Brigadier?

When Danecki's ship cut across the whirlpools of vortexes set up by the huge cruiser, he realized that he might have a chance. The two fresh-faced boys who had flicked their dainty scout with contemptuous ease amongst the dimensional storms of hyperspace could, just conceivably, be confused. They had followed him, turning, twisting, sinking along the mazes of the continuums, always able to pick up his trail.

And why not, thought Danecki grimly. They had the better ship, the keener sensors, the bigger screens. And the lash of outrage. Not all his years of hard-won expertise in the mysterious wastes of the gaps between the planets of his own system would save him, for, in the end, the odds were against him. Deliberately so.

Danecki had picked on this little-used sector because it was almost as far as you could go towards the rim of the Galaxy. Here, the inexperienced boys might lose themselves in the complex of star-systems.

Twice he had flung his little ship—the customary robust vessel allowed to the offender—out of Phase. But they had followed. The second time, a sudden gobbetting of incandescence had sheared away the auxiliary power units of his little ship, a neat chopping away of all but the big engines. A failure that occurred at any distance from a planet with a breathable atmosphere meant death.

All he had of the ship's once considerable emergency equipment was the simplest kind of power-glide pod. He had improvised manually for hours, desperately fighting the banks of controls so that they would not falter. He had somehow kept them working. Reaching the space-time unit of the sector that held Sol was the limit of his ship's capacity.

The big ship came out of hyperspace just as his own stubby little vessel jangled out of the phenomenon of Phase. For a moment he had thought it was the pursuing ship, but it was far too powerful for that. Only ships from Center had the mighty thrust of those engines which had tossed his own craft aside. What ships would visit this sector? It's habitable planets had been poisoned a thousand years ago. Except for Earth!

"Tourists." Danecki muttered. "A tourist ship." The boys would be confused. They would keep their ship in the strange peripheries of hyperspace, like a hunting beast, its sensors confused by the turmoil of the huge ship's passing. But for how long?

He saw a ruined city below him. Then the clamor of warning systems sent him reeling to the controls. "Tourists?" he said aloud.

The robot evaluator answered promptly. "Yes, Danecki. This is Earth. Tourist ships visit regularly. Certain areas are clear of radiation. We should move, Danecki. The ship's getting hot. The screens are at only three percent efficiency."

"Earth?" he asked.

"You asked for the nearest breathable atmosphere, Danecki."

"And this is it?"

"Yes."

"What's down there?"

"Most of the land areas are unusable without a radiation suit."

"Which I haven't got."

"Which the ship can't provide."

"The Jacobis?"

"Breaking out of Phase, Danecki."

"Power!"

Above the ruins of a city that hung poised on its still-active stilts of force-fields, the ship hung blackly for a moment and then flashed through the sunrise and out across a blanket of high clouds. The pursuing vessel burst through the confines of the dimensional cage that protected it in hyperspace.

"There!" called Danecki.

The sit-rep chart focused on a landmass that was bland. No violent radioactivity shimmered evilly on the screen. The ship responded and plunged through the clouds to what had once been the plains of Kent. Danecki caught a glimpse of himself in the smooth metal of the ship. His face was unshaven. The eyes were deep in the already-deep sockets. He looked like a criminal, a hunted man that had become a *thing* to the last of the Jacobi clan. He made his preparations. Really, there was no decision to make.

He was already punching a series of instructions into the manual controls. He could not trust the robot to follow his orders. The Jacobis were near—perhaps they were watching him even now, though he thought they might still be chasing one of the thousands of false trails set up by the big vessel's shock waves.

The robot interrupted. "Orders, Danecki?"

"Abort yourself."

The cone of metal grunted and then began to give off a thin vapor. Danecki shouldered the heavy pod and made for the big port. Behind him the robot controller splashed into a pool of running metal. When the ship's speed suddenly decreased Danecki opened the port. He looked down through the clouds. It was all to end there, where, for the human race, it had begun.

"A race!" Danecki said aloud.

The pod hurtled him head over heels twenty times before he found the trick of planing. When he was within two hundred feet of the ground he cut in the drive.

It jerked him abruptly. He tried to see the ship but the clouds had long since closed over it.

A year ago, thought Danecki, I couldn't have done this. Now I think like an animal. I need food. Cover. A weapon. Then I can kill the last two of the Jacobis and —and what?

"Dr. Dross, you can't do that! Damn it, Doctor, you're not handling mildewed corpse-wrappings or rusty bits of iron from the Steam Age. This is sophisticated machinery. Put it down!"

Dross blinked at the speaker. He settled his massive paunch against a particularly interesting piece of Third Confederation robotic architecture. The carapace was in his hands. He had been trying to remove the flat humanoid face so that he could examine the brainbox. He dropped the head into the yellow mud.

Knaggs was the kind of man you couldn't argue with. His qualifications were the highest; Knaggs was the best in his field. Whatever antique piece of hardware came out of the ruined fort, he would run his fingers over it and say, "Yes, it might be, it's about right for the location we found it in, Doctor, it's a simple fusor system." Or, "This isn't right, Doctor, don't forget this place has been a ruin for a thousand years and other teams have picked it over—this thing is probably an early Galactic Team's burrow-bug directioner. Interesting, but you could pick up one in a museum at Center."

Knaggs examined the robotic head again. "And don't let those things fall, Doctor," Knaggs added. "They've always got a complete memory-track from that period! I could maybe get us a rundown on the last days of the fort with that!"

Knaggs was a puny figure of a man. He was short and painfully thin. His nose poked out at the level of Dross's broad, fat chest.

"Mr. Knaggs, haven't I always passed on such finds to you?" Dross spoke with a pleasant calmness.

"Not always, Doctor, not always!"

"And don't I give you a free hand with anything that's in your field?" Dross asked.

"So far, Doctor, so far," said Knaggs. "But I don't trust you when you get your hands on these defense systems —you can't help fiddling, Doctor, and that's when there'll be trouble. That and the tourists! Why can't you all leave me to get on with my work. Doctor, it's a miserable life when the place is crawling with inquisitive women who clutter my workshops up with the bits of gewgaws they leave behind!"

Dross still looked calmly down at the fuming little engineer. Though he smiled, his eyes were slits. "Mr. Knaggs, I too have my difficulties. One is the problem you mention. No more than you do I like to have my diggings overrun by ignorant visitors who come to gape and leave their rubbish behind. Another of my problems is the way we have to work here. Instead of the modern equipment I'd choose, we have to employ an antiquated robot to sift through the remains of the largest single defensive installation produced in the ancient world. Both of these problems, Mr. Knaggs—" and here Knaggs recognized the subtle shift in emphasis as Dross ground out his name so that it sounded like a snarl—"are dwarfed by the presence of a—" and Knaggs moved back, but not sharply enough, for Dross had placed two enormous bulky hands on his shoulders and lifted him clean off his feet— "self-opinionated, conceited, over-bearing—"

With each word, Dross raised the little struggling figure higher. "—totally unreasonable—" Now Dross shifted his grip and caught Knaggs against the vastness of his paunch. "—manikin who cannot let the greatest archaeologist in the entire Galaxy get on with his work."

Now Dross had tipped Knaggs upside down, so that he was staring in fright at the yellow mud which had so recently covered the perimeter installation where the decapitated robot lay.

Knaggs yelled and bawled to be put down, for the mud was peculiarly uninviting, and Dross's intention clear. "A ship!" gurgled Knaggs into the mud. He emerged to see Dross chuckling fatly.

"Tourists!" burbled Dross. "Our tourists."

Knaggs glared at him. "Look at me. It'll take me an hour to get clean. You're mad, Dross, mad! You should be recalled! You're completely unbalanced! You'll never find the—" He stopped, for Dross was looking at him with a glaring intensity. Knaggs squelched to his feet. "It didn't sound like a tourist ship," he said.

Danecki heaved the pod into a rain-ditch.

He recognized it as such in spite of the silt and the small trees which almost concealed it. The depression ran along what had once been a large field, now a coppice of beech and willow. This place had never been subjected to radiation bombardment. It was an unlikely spot in which to die.

The end should have come in one appalling cataclysm of white-hot vapor as a sungun tore his ship into its component molecules. Not here, not in this friendly place where even the rain was soft and warm.

Earth.

He had never thought of visiting it, though it had been the ambition of a number of his friends to make planetfall on that shattered place. They spoke of the remains of a hundred empires which a man could investigate. But somehow they never went. He could not recall a single instance of anyone he had known having been to Earth.

It was a focus-point for a dream. A place you would always say to yourself you'd make the effort of visiting when you had time. Meanwhile the Totex gave you an approximation of what it was like. And you never troubled to put the total-experience simulators on either.

He ate what could be his last meal. The heavy pod had contained little that would help an officially licensed criminal. Enough canned air to take him to the surface of a planet if his ship blew up under him, and enough canned food to give him a day's grace. Nothing else. Nothing that could even remotely help him to hinder his officially licensed pursuers.

If they followed the ship and destroyed it without investigating what it held, he had escaped. But the Jacobis wouldn't do that. They had made a binding and solemn oath that they would return with him. Or enough of him to show that they had completed their grim task.

A beetle inspected the synthetic crumbs at his feet. It raised antennae at him as he changed position to give it a clear run to the sodden flecks of food. Danecki realized he hadn't thought of things like fields and the beetles in them for over twenty years. There hadn't been time. A good practical navigator who could also do some quick fixing of the systems that powered the hyperspace ships was always in demand.

"Not my field," he said to the beetle.

It brought a friend to evaluate the crumbs.

Thus Danecki missed the long, quiet, looping flight of the searching vessel. Its heat sensors picked him out unerringly. He watched a consultation between the two black shiny insects. It was they that picked out the alien slurred sound.

Danecki saw the ship. He had spent the few precious minutes of anonymity looking at this patch of greenness. The Jacobis were playing with him. They could have finished him off with any one of a dozen minor holocausts.

The beetles went back to the crumbs. The last Danecki saw of them as he made his run was a puzzled wiggling of antennae. A land-bug whistled out from a port in the side of the black scout.

Danecki ran.

Why? asked Danecki, lungs bursting and heart smashing at his rib cage as it sought to cope with the huge exertions the body demanded.

"I never wanted anything like this!" he gasped aloud.

"Danecki!"

He jinked across the ditch, between clutching branches which whipped wetly across his face, over tussocks that sent him from side to side like a crippled spider; and the land-bug sawed its way through the undergrowth, keeping in station behind him in grim and relentless pursuit.

"You're nearly finished, Danecki!"

And he had seen only one Jacobi face to face, one of the dozen or more pursuers who had hunted him clear across the Galaxy, and who had left their distended corpses or their ringing dust-motes in four different planetary complexes. Not one of them had been prepared to listen.

The boys wouldn't. And now they were hunting him to his death.

Danecki knew his trouble. Quite suddenly it came to him that he was tired of using that edge of honed skill to destroy the others. And yet he couldn't stop and turn to face the little craft. Not yet.

"I do hope you enjoyed your lunch, Miss?"

Khalia thanked the attendant robot. She liked the excursion ship. It spun down through the gaseous envelope of Earth in a bright ring of flames. Small, fast, somehow quite antique. She reached for the guidebook.

"Would you like me to hook you into a sensory frame?" the robot asked deferentially.

"I'd rather read," she said. Again, it was more appropriate to read than to use the machines. She opened the book.

Mrs. Zulkifar's voice rang out in the small cabin: "I'm not sure this is a good idea, Brigadier! Are you positive this is a suitable excursion?"

"Quite—ah—Emma!"

In a loud whisper, the woman went on: "I wonder *he's* allowed to come!"

Khalia sighed. Mrs. Zulkifar was nodding her firm jaw at the strange figure of Mr. Moonman. She herself had never quite overcome her dread of the long, gaunt figure. It wasn't enough to be reassured by Wardle that he was a perfectly normal human being; not when the face was slightly luminous, when the eyes were like round white pebbles, and the long hands like something out of a grave.

She tried, however. In the loose union that kept some sort of order in the Galaxy, there was room even for the Revived. They, as much as anyone else, were entitled to use the tourist ships.

Mrs. Zulkifar thought not. "It isn't *nice!*" she said. "He should stay on the ship."

Mr. Moonman could not ignore the woman. When he spoke, it was like listening to a voice from a hole in the ground. "Madam, I hear you. I understand your attitude. You fear me, I know." He inspected his ghastly hands. "You know what it is to see me. I *am* me!" Then he called: "Steward!"

The attendant robot rushed forward. "Anything you require, sir? The trip takes another few minutes. We serve drinks. Your comfort is assured. Dr. Dross has been informed of your impending arrival."

"Put a screen round me," Mr. Moonman said.

Mrs. Zulkifar glowered. "I should think so too." She had expressed her detestation of the Revived Man across the Galaxy.

To some extent Khalia could understand it. The Revived constituted a minority group that all could sympathize with, but whose appearance aroused only deep, half-submerged feelings of horror. They were the zombies of myth, the dead brought back from the grave into which unhappy chance had thrown them.

"They should be decently buried," Mrs. Zulkifar had once grated to the Brigadier. "I shouldn't be expected to travel—eat—breathe the same air—as a dead man!"

On that occasion Khalia had answered the woman: "Leave Mr. Moonman alone," she had snapped, amazed at herself. "He's every right to be here. And you've no right at all to say that about him!" She had wanted to ask the Revived Man to sit with her. But she had seen the cold, dead hands. He had understood, she thought. Mrs. Zulkifar had ignored her after that.

Khalia dismissed the others from her mind. The excursion brought her to a feeling of delicious anticipation—of a kind that she could not remember since she was a child. Why?

The guidebook was almost banal: "You have chosen to visit one of the wonders of *All Time!* You will not be disappointed with your excursion! You will see the ruins of the mightiest fortification conceived in those far-off days when the entire empire of the Second Interplanetary Confederation stood like a proud ship amongst the storms of war and riot. A thousand years have gone by since the fort was sundered by fire and fission. Once there, the eminent archaeologist, Dr. Dross, will personally conduct you around the ruins. You will be thrilled by your contact with the great civilization that was to perish in such appalling instantaneous catastrophe! You will thrill to hear of the legend of the Lost Fort, and the even stranger legend of the infamous Black Army!"

In spite of the over-enthusiastic prose, Khalia again sensed the excitement that had gripped her so strongly when Sol and its attendant planets had appeared from among the jangling hypercubes of the unreal dimensions. Was it fear that made her tingle so, she wondered? Was it the frightened, zany pleasure of a child's nightmares that excited her?

"Your tour will be conducted in perfect safety," the prose glowed. "Although most of the land-surfaces may not be visited without protection, the ruins were subject to short-lived radiation only. There is positively no danger for a hundred miles around the Ancient Monument."

Mrs. Zulkifar's voice cut in on her thoughts: "I can't say I've ever heard of this Dross before, whatever you say, Brigadier."

"Perhaps not, madam," the soldier answered, somewhat put out. "Nevertheless, I happen to believe that the Doctor is the proponent of the most exciting of all theories in connection with the Second Interplanetary Confederation and the way it met its end!"

He caught Khalia's eye. "Remarkable man, young lady! Foremost authority in the Galaxy! Not everyone agrees with him—I'd go so far as to say that in some quarters he's regarded as a crank—but he has his followers."

"You among them, I see," Mr. Moonman put in.

"Yes—ah—sir, yes!" the Brigadier wheezed. He had barely acknowledged the presence of the Revived Man during the long voyage. Yet he could hardly avoid him in the confined space of the small craft.

He turned back to Khalia. "Lot of blah in the guide-books. They don't tell you anything of the real mystery, my dear. They don't!"

He had engaged the girl's interest. "No?" she asked.

"No! Not a bit. Greatest exponents of the art of manufacturing robots ever! Remarkable people! They lived, breathed, warred, loved for all I know, with robots. Supreme cyberneticists. And if Dr. Dross says there's a hidden fort somewhere hereabouts, I'm prepared to believe him!"

Mrs. Zulkifar chirped up disdainfully: "I thought you'd had enough of playing soldiers, Brigadier! Wasn't your little army disbanded?"

Wardle was quietly furious: "It was! It was! Put out to grass! Thought we'd seen enough of action! A mistake! I told them—my planetary system isn't ready for peace yet!"

"Aren't you?" asked Khalia.

Wardle stared at her. He seemed to be considering her as a person for the first time, instead of a background phenomenon. "Never thought of it," he said. "Never thought of it."

"You're still playing soldiers," said Mrs. Zulkifar.

Wardle could say nothing to ease the situation. He smiled his familiar ingratiating smile, the one that Khalia found so pitiful after it had ceased to be amusing.

Mr. Moonman pointed to the ruins below. "Their emblem," he said. "The Crest of the Second Interplanetary Confederation."

In spite of the passing of the centuries, it had survived. Three sunbursts still glowed along one intact radiation shield, the proud emblem of the ancient Empire.

"One for each of the planets they held," said Wardle.

"They ruined this one," Khalia said. "See what it says about the legend." She felt a cold edge of menace in the warm craft. It chilled her.

Wardle read out the words with a connoisseur's pride. "Powerful words! Listen! It's just a line, but it's survived for a thousand years. A promise and a threat: 'The Regiments of Night shall come at the end.' "

The little ship hovered over the ancient base.

CHAPTER

★ 2 ★

"I refuse!" Dross bawled. "Emphatically, no! No!"

The green-bronze robot eyed him placidly. "It's in our contract, sir. Center might believe you were too busy to attend to the last party. And the one before that, Doctor. But not three in a row."

"I'm sick, Batty!"

"Yes, sir."

"Sick of interruptions. Sick of malicious pedants in their tight, tiny offices at Center! And sick beyond measure of the buffoons and meddlers! Look at that young fool who came with his asinine parents—was it three months ago? Early summer. The one who found the landbug we'd sealed off. Why, he could have wiped us all out with that machine! It was still working—a thousand years gone, and it still could have blown us all apart!"

The gnomish thin little man behind the robot grinned. "Don't worry, Doctor," Knaggs said. "I've defused all the active stuff. How would you like me to show our visitors the remains of the war-robot we found? The prototype you got so excited about, Doctor. Three times the size of Batty, and all weapons and armor—nasty bit of work! Shall we let them see it—give them an extra thrill?" He smiled innocently at Dross, but Dross did not rise to the bait.

"You'll be ready, sir?" the robot asked.

"I'm sure Dr. Dross will," said Knaggs.

"Then I'll escort the visitors to the reception lounge, sir," mumbled the robot.

"No!" grunted Dross. "Take them straight to the main

observation deck. Let's get it over." To Knaggs he said, "Have you got that humanoid apart yet?"

Knaggs raised his hands in mock shame. "I forgot it. I had to clean up, Doctor, so that our guests wouldn't be offended. I'll pick the head-piece up later. Another hour or two won't hurt, anyway. It's been lying there for a thousand years."

Danecki was finished. But still he kept to his feet, and still he moved instinctively towards shelter. The trees here were heavier, stronger growth, the ground was carpeted with the first fallen leaves of autumn. And there might be hollows where a man might hide for a few moments, not with any idea of escaping the sensors that could follow any warm-blooded life across whole worlds, but with the instinctive urge to conserve energy—to gain a breathing-space so that he could manage one more stumbling run.

"We're coming, Danecki!" called the light young voice.

How old were the last men of the Jacobi clan? Twenty? Eighteen? They were the best, regardless of their age. They gave him no chance.

The bug snapped trees aside. And then it ground to a halt.

Danecki moved again, for the boys would come out now. They were allowed personal arms, but they would probably want to finish him by hand. He caught at a dead branch but it flaked away in his hand, too rotten to support its own weight. And the unending plunging run continued, though now the trees were hazy and outlined in red. It wasn't the morning sun, however, that caused the film of redness about the trees and undergrowth. It was blood in his eyes from the scratches on his face.

He stopped, unable to move. It seemed right to wait.

There was no noise of pursuit. The familiar crashings of the powerful bug had not resumed. And there was nothing but the quiet murmur of raindrops in the trees.

A bird yipped at him and startled a flock of woodpigeons which whirred away in fright. Then Danecki looked back. Still the Jacobis had not left the bug.

He found fresh strength in his lean body. He ran towards the blackness of the woods with long thrusting strides. One of the Jacobi boys yelled out angrily, though Danecki could not hear what he said. For the second time since leaving the wildness of hyperspace, he began to hope. There was a fault in the bug. Only that could explain its immobility, for the Jacobis should have been out of it and at his heels by now.

He pitched into a heap of soft black earth as a root caught him. Ignoring the wrench of pain in his right ankle, he bored through nettles and brambles until he was deep in the gloom of the big trees—at the top of the steep escarpment he had been making for. And still the Jacobis were not behind him.

Over the rise he stopped, for the woods were at an end. He stared in despair and amazement at the vast bowl that lay beyond the woods. Before and below him was the ruin of a titanic military base. Its towers were tangled black skeletons of metal. Open to the sky, its series of layered decks were split apart in heaps. A few pockets of stunted trees had somehow contrived an existence here and there amongst the ruins, but most of the fort lay as it must have been left when the last of the colossal bombs had sent it juddering into chaos.

A weapon, was his next thought. And where should you look for a weapon but in an armory?

"You'd think they'd have some sort of shelter," complained Mrs. Zulkifar. "I mean, it's not as though there's any pleasure in waiting around with weather being hurled at you from all directions. I wish I'd gone out to the asteroids."

"Most inconsiderate," agreed Brigadier Wardle. "As an old campaigner, you know, I'm used to roughing it. But you ladies should have some protection."

"I like the rain," said Khalia.

"And I," the Revived Man said. But no one looked his way.

Brigadier Wardle looked at his watch. "There should be a guide or something," he announced. "We've been here for five minutes already."

"What time is it?" asked Mrs. Zulkifar.

Khalia remembered that the middle-aged woman was a creature of habit. She segmented her day into stretches of useful endeavors.

"Time?" The Brigadier was happy to answer. "Ten-zero-one, local time. Galactic Time's taken from a spot not far from here. Now, on your planet, dear lady, it would be—let me see—zero-two-four-one." He began a lecture on Terran Time. The lost days. Sidereal periods. The Julian Calendar.

Khalia found it fascinating. The concept of time held them still, while the rain tumbled in gusts over their bare heads. They caught the eeriness of the deserted fort as Wardle went on to describe the time-keeping procedures of Earth.

No ships raced across the sky, no flicker of light showed the passage of high-speed land-craft; the only sounds were birdcalls and, once, a crashing in the woods that could have been a clumsy animal.

"That's all very well," said Mrs. Zulkifar, "but when I come to see an official Ancient Monument, I expect service."

"And you shall have it, if I've anything to do with it!" said Wardle.

Mr. Moonman turned to Khalia. "Why did you come?" he asked, as the Brigadier and Mrs. Zulkifar talked about other excursions.

Khalia hid her instinctive horror. What had happened to the colony in the Sirian System was not the fault of the people themselves. Caught in a freak temporal effect, they had hung for two centuries in an unhappy half-life, neither living nor dead. The few that had the resilience to survive that bizarre and traumatic experience had been saved by a chance visit when a Galactic Center ship had called in. Mr. Moonman was one of the survivors.

Khalia tried to answer honestly. "It was here, or the asteroids, or the base on the Moon. I wanted to be in the open again, I suppose. But the main thing was the way it all ended down here—the Confederation. I mean, if it hadn't, we wouldn't live in our loose Galactic Union. There'd still be empires."

Mr. Moonman nodded and looked out at the ruins.

Khalia recalled eerie tales about the Revived. She had heard an old tutor talk about their strange metabolism: they could not *age*, he had said. Was it true? "Why did you come?" she asked, on impulse.

"You really want to know?" he replied.

"Yes," said Khalia. She meant it.

"I had this fancy, to visit the beginnings of it all. In a way, like yourself. It's like visiting the grave of the oldest person you remember from your own childhood. That person's memories would reach back over the whole of a century. The oldest person he could remember in his childhood would take him back through another century." He gestured to the ruins. "Machines lying here in the mud will have memories of the days of the Confederation. I hope it doesn't sound too morbid."

It did, suddenly. The little group felt the pressures of the past in cold surges. There was too much space.

Danecki found the going easier. A track had been pounded through the scrub, downhill to the ruin. Whether animals or men had made it he couldn't be sure. Probably animals, for he had to stoop at times to get through tunnels in the thick bushes. He tried to remember what had happened to animal life on Earth after the Mad Wars. Mutants? Carnivores? He shrugged the idea aside.

The Jacobis were the danger.

And then he was through a ravine-like gash in the perimeter defenses, shambling eagerly towards a complex of disordered bays. One whole deck of the fort had been turned on its axis so that vast slits lay open to the rain. Danecki looked down into the black waters of a lake.

"Here, Danecki," a voice said softly.

Danecki lurched around with a speed that always was insufficient. The Jacobi boy was laughing at him ten yards away. He was a short, well-made youth with curling black hair and white teeth. He looked as happy as a boy seeing his first space-flivver. His only response as Danecki tried to avoid the needle-dart was to smile.

It caught Danecki in the calf, paralyzing his left leg. He knew that the next one would be into his right leg. The Jacobis had fooled him completely. Whilst the bug guarded the rear, they had circled from opposite directions—one on each flank, as the terrain had pushed him, inevitably, toward the fort. They had known that he would try for the high ground where the trees grew thickly. It was the natural course for a hunted animal.

"You die here, Danecki," the boy smiled.

Where was the other one? "You're wrong," Danecki said, as he had tried to say to older and sterner Jacobis. "There's no reason for this. I wasn't responsible for them. It was an accident that could have happened to any ship."

The boy was wildly angry behind the smile. "You killed my sister," he said. "And her children."

"An error of judgment I'll give you," Danecki said in a tired voice. "Who hasn't made a mistake?"

"Me."

Danecki fell into the mud. In this the boy was right. They had hunted him like a pair of professionals. But where was the other Jacobi?

"I think you've kept them waiting long enough, Doctor," said Knaggs.

"Hasn't it occurred to you, Mr. Knaggs, that our visitors may wish to commune with nature for a few minutes before my guided tour?"

"You're a horrible fat old bastard," said Knaggs "You're keeping them waiting in the rain so they'll be too wet to do anything but drink in the reception hall."

"Announce my impending arrival," ordered Dross.

The green-bronze robot creaked off slowly.

The boy had the glittering gun at his head. Danecki watched the struggle as he aimed at one eye then another. So he was waiting for his brother. They must have worked out how it would be. And if they had had time to plan the manner of his death, it was certain to be peculiarly unpleasant. For no reason at all, he remembered pleading with one of the oldest of the Jacobis, a man of over seventy. That one had the same haunted eyes. He had given Danecki more trouble than any other of the clan—more, oddly, than the boys had been able to give him. Until now. The old man had pursued him with a fierce cunning that took them both spinning across time and space, crossing and recrossing the Galaxy in its entirety until both were worn out. Danecki had sheltered in a whirlpool of dimensional forces.

Too tired to hold his spinning ship, the old man had been taken down into the maelstorm, away from Danecki, and with no thoughts of vengeance—nothing in his tired old head but the wish for rest.

Danecki put his hand to his leg.

"Tired, Danecki?" asked the boy. "Hurting?" *Hurt,* his eyes said. *Feel pain.*

There was supposed to be a code of conduct for the licensed victim as well as his hunter. The kill had to be quick and painless. Danecki shuddered.

The boy liked this. He came closer, the gun poised in his brown hand. Danecki clutched at the ground, feeling for the security of the solid ground. His right hand closed on something in the mud. There was no weighing up of chances, no thought whatsoever. The thing bulked in his hand, and it was immediately the weapon he had wished for and not found—as the fort proved to be a desolate ruin where the waters had closed over what might have been an armory. It was heavy, and it came noisily out of the yellow mud.

The boy saw it and he did not shoot.

Danecki saw the metal carapace spinning off the boy's head, and in a flash of recognition he knew why there had been a total incomprehension on the part of his enemy. He had picked a head out of the mud and smashed the boy's forehead open with it.

The boy jerked epileptically for a full minute while Danecki tried to get to his feet. The rain swept down on the boy's limbs and his gray contorted face. What had the blow done to him? His eyes met Danecki's without recognition. Blood came in a slow trickle from a gash in his head, and in a black flood from his nose and ears.

"Again," said Danecki to the tormented boy. The old trick of winning had not deserted him. He began to crawl toward the boy to finish him as he had been forced to kill so many of his clansmen. But he stopped. Why harm the youth? More to the point, where was his brother?

Danecki found the leg's power returning. The pain had diminished, turning to a slow center of grinding corrosion. He crawled to the youth and watched him for a few seconds. Death grew on the wet white face. Then he turned the boy's head so that he lay face upward to the sky. As he began the slow anguished crawl away from the place of blood, he noticed that the rain was sluicing the dead face.

He had gone a hundred yards when the footsteps splashed behind him. Immediately he tensed. The mud-streaked robot head was in his hand, ready to strike.

"Visitors may not remove artifacts from the Ancient Monument!" the newcomer said severely.

A robot. Danecki flinched and then realized what he was talking to. Ancient Monument . . . visitors . . . artifact. They added up to one thing. He was talking to a robotic guide.

"You should not leave your group at any time during the excursion," the robot chided. "Galactic Center expressly forbids it. Dr. Dross will be here shortly to conduct you to the main observation post."

The Jacobi youth would not be far behind.

"I hurt my leg. I was resting," Danecki said.

The robot nodded. "Tourists meet with minor accidents if they stray." It confirmed his beliefs.

Danecki considered its humanoid face. Green-bronze, like its elegant body, smooth and well-sculpted. He wondered how he could best explain its presence. And that of the Jacobi. How aware was the robot of human motives, and the extent of human deceit? He had made up his mind. There was a way of turning its presence to advantage. The old skill of decision, instant and unthinking, had not left him. "Another member of the party has also strayed," Danecki said. "He is a young man called Danecki."

The robot was of considerable age itself, but it was a sophisticated piece of hardware. Surely it would be able to pick up the heat-emissions of Jacobi's body? Danecki needed warning of the youth's approach.

It paused and seemed to sniff the air. It had the appearance of abstractedness, characteristic of humanoids. "Your friend is not in the neighborhood," it said at last. "And no one of that name is included in the visiting party."

Danecki rapidly changed the subject. "See to my leg."

It slit the material with one deft movement and located the dart with a tiny probe.

"I felt a pain," said Danecki.

"You've been shot, sir."

Danecki's self-possession barely faltered. "Tell me about the ruin," he ordered.

The robot would not allow itself to be diverted. "I must report this, sir."

"Take me to my party," Danecki countered.

"What is your name, sir?" the robot asked.

"List the names of the party visiting this Ancient Monument."

"Very well, sir. Mrs. Emma Zulkifar. Mr. Moonman. Miss Khalia Burns. And Brigadier Wardle."

Danecki felt the strength returning to his leg. The dart had been a limited-duration paralyzing needle. The Jacobi boy had been very sure of himself. "I am Brigadier Wardle," Danecki said.

"Can you walk, Brigadier?"

"Help me."

It levered him to his feet. "May I take the artifact, Brigadier?" it asked.

Danecki handed over the mud-streaked robotic head.

"Dr. Dross will want to see this, sir. He may also wish to speak to you about it."

Danecki thought of the dead youth who lay in the mud. The ghastly carapace had been the only weapon offered by the ancient fort. And now it was to be a museumpiece. He wondered if the robot had sensed the presence of the cold Jacobi boy. Probably not. But there was still the other murderous clansman. "Inform me should a young man with a body-weight of about one-sixty enters the area. He will be my friend Danecki, an unlisted member of the party to visit the Ancient Monument."

"Very good, sir." The robot waited. It was clear that it would not permit him to go to any place but the party's destination. There was the matter of the artifact. And the dart in his leg.

Dross? thought Danecki. *I've heard of a Dross.* He tried not to hurry, but he kept the robot between himself and the threatening greenery of the forest. What else could he do now, but try to find shelter inside the ancient fortification? A visiting party meant an excursion vessel from the big ship that had jinked him out of his orbit. A vessel meant escape. Food, at least. And Dross. *The archaeologist!*

"You asked about the fortification, sir."

"So I did."

The robot began to talk.

"Here's someone coming now," said Mrs. Zulkifar.

"Hello. Come out of the rain!" Knaggs called, as he approached the group. "Hasn't Batty turned up yet?"

"No!" said Wardle sharply. "No one's come. We've been here for a half hour—bad organization, that's what it is!"

"Are you responsible?" Mrs. Zulkifar inquired.

"Not really," said Knaggs. "Batty, our pet robot, should have been along before this."

"Well, he hasn't!" Wardle snapped.

Khalia was happily wet.

The fort had lost some of its eeriness now that they had waited around for half an hour. But the sensation of awe remained. The vast ruins had mouldered and rusted for ten centuries. It was, as the guidebook had pointed out, a colossal feat of human engineering. Ruins, though, were ruins. They were distant from the terrible wars that had rolled over the planet; they could be approached with a tinge of sentimental awe. Harmless, but inspiring; vaguely threatening, without being specifically dangerous.

Khalia began to realize that this was why she was so excited. It was like seeing the caged tiger. It peered back but it had no power to harm. The fort was only the shadow of its once-terrible self.

And now a charming little man had come to show her around. It was entirely appropriate that on this planet the tour should have got off to a disorganized start. Mr. Knaggs introduced himself.

"The Doctor should be here soon," he said. "Old Batibasaga—Batty, we call him—was sent to take you down below, but he must have had a lapse of memory. I'm just Knaggs the systems engineer, so the Doctor uses me as a messenger when Batty breaks down. All ready?"

"I'm not sure I want to go anywhere else," Mrs. Zulkifar said. "These do-it-yourself tours are all very well, but how do we know what's going on? At least when we did the Zero-Alpha Complex, there was a fully automatic strip right through it. And a commentary."

"Not many tourists come here," said Knaggs. "It wouldn't pay to automate fully."

"Come, Mrs. Zulkifar," said the Brigadier. "You must press on now. It's the most perfectly preserved military installation of all. And, you never know, there might be a bit of excitement—there's the legend—ah—Emma."

Khalia found Knaggs catching her eye. He winked. "You'll find the Doctor exciting enough," he said.

Danecki allowed the robot to stutter out the whole history of the fort. He learned about the Second Interplanetary Confederation and Dross's researches into its greatest fortification. He and the robot trudged through mud and over a carpet of brilliant yellow flowers.

"So there won't be a ship here for days," Danecki was saying when they reached a relatively untouched building amongst a mass of black, twisted fallen towers.

"Very doubtful, sir. Dr. Dross receives supplies from time to time, but it might be that the Center vessel will not call here this trip."

Danecki maintained a flow of questions. He was not surprised when the robot told him that there were no weapons among Dross's equipment, and that when ancient but still operative weapons were turned up in the dig, they were immediately rendered harmless by Dross's engineer, Knaggs.

"I need a hot drink," he said to the robot. "I've had a shock. It is necessary for a man who has been hurt."

The robot was uneasy. "I really think we should meet the Doctor now. He will have taken the rest of the party to the main observation deck. You, of course, have been very flattering both in your interest in the dig and in my capabilities. I fear, Brigadier, that I may have overstepped the mark in remaining with you for so long. I should have given the party a message by now."

"Weren't you ordered always to consider the comfort of official guests?" Danecki parried.

"Oh, yes, sir!"

"Then get me coffee. And whatever food there is."

"Very well, sir."

There might not be an opportunity to eat in the immediate future. And, by keeping the robot in conversation, Danecki wished to gain more information about the resources of the archaeological base. It might be that there was a land-craft tucked away.

The robot brought food and coffee. Danecki ate and drank. He had been at the controls of the little hyperspace ship for hours. It was almost a whole day—nearly twenty-four hours—since he had slept. Curiously, he felt no fatigue. That would come later, when reaction set in.

Things had gone amazingly well, though he could not be grateful for his good fortune. It had meant yet another in the long series of violent deaths. The face of the Jacobi boy would stay with him, awake and asleep, for months. He would remember the clear eyes and the rain on the boy's face.

Danecki drank more rapidly. For over a year now he had been developing the skill of reacting instantly to desperate situations. He had learned the trick of staying alive. It was not a trick you could glow with pride about.

"How about personal transportation?" he asked. "I expect the Doctor must spend a good deal of time surveying the area?" Danecki was afraid he had gone too far.

The robot was poised, still, frozen.

"Well?" Danecki said.

The robot turned. "You must ask Dr. Dross yourself, sir. It would be in order for us to go to meet him at the main observation deck in the fortification below. It is approached by means of a spin-shaft. It is fortunate that your friend can join us, Brigadier."

Danecki stared and then remembered that he had told the robot he was a Brigadier Wardle. And that another member of the party was somewhere in the ruins. "Friend?" he asked, deadpan.

"You requested me to locate a young man, sir. Body weight one-six-five. Would that be a Mr. Danecki, Brigadier?"

CHAPTER

* 3 *

Dross thrust his bulk ahead of him so that Khalia wondered if his big chest and vast belly would cause him to topple forward. He was infuriated with Mrs. Zulkifar.

"Madam, I am Dr. Dross!" he boomed. "Not your guide, as you call it. And if you've been kept waiting here for a mere half hour, you should regard yourself as fortunate! You have the opportunity of experiencing the finest piece of archaeological scholarshp in the modern Galaxy, Madam. And I, Dross, am in the process of showing it to you."

"Are you coming?" Khalia asked Knaggs quietly.

He hesitated. "If you like."

"Please," she said.

"This way!" Dross bellowed in an unnecessarily loud voice. He had effectively quieted Mrs. Zulkifar. "We go to my principal discovery, the main observation deck of this unique fortification." He led the way through the swirling rain to a hole in the ground. Khalia looked. The hole contained a shifting, colored whirlpool of force-fields.

"And what, may I ask, is that?" demanded Mrs. Zulkifar.

"That, Madam," announced Dross, "is a spin-shaft."

"Very interesting," said Mrs. Zulkifar.

Her sarcasm escaped Wardle. "One of the original systems, eh, Doctor? Is it? In good shape if it is!"

"No," said Dross. "A recently installed system. My engineer, Mr. Knaggs, had it sent out by Center. He put it in. It saves a good deal of physical exertion."

"Quite safe," Knaggs said to Mrs. Zulkifar. "Serviced

regularly. All Ancient Monuments have fixed service schedules for this kind of installation."

"You may prefer to find your own way through the various levels," invited Dross, "or you may remain here in the rain. Your decision is of no importance whatever to me." He was coldly furious at what he took to be Mrs. Zulkifar's impertinence.

Mrs. Zulkifar followed the direction of Dross's big hand. A gash in the side of a cliff-like wall of metal was the only opening. There may or may not have been handholds. It looked sinister and dangerous.

"I wouldn't try it," said Knaggs. "I've been working here for years and it would take me a quarter of an hour to find my way down."

Mrs. Zulkifar flicked rain from her elegant nose. "I wasn't complaining," she said. She stepped towards the shaft. "I just like to know where I'm going. Ugh!"

Mr. Moonman refused to acknowledge that an accidental brush against him was the cause of the woman's exclamation.

Danecki plunged into the vast gap smashed through the deck of the surface installation. He felt rotting vegetation beneath his feet, and then he was in deep darkness falling forward and flailing his arms about in a desperate effort to find a handhold. He fell into a shallow muddy pool which broke his fall.

"Tourists may not enter this area, sir!" The robot, for all its creaking antiquity, moved fast.

"Where's the other man," Danecki asked.

"My sensors are impaired at this depth, sir. My last reading placed him near the reception area. You must return there, Brigadier. Come, sir." It took his arm firmly.

"No!" Bones grated in his arm as he tore himself free. He ran again without thought. The remaining Jacobi clansman was closing. And still he had no weapon. The lower decks of the fort were suffused by a dim light. Some of it came from above, where the weak daylight filtered through gashes in the upper decks. But as much again would be from the fort's own energy system, still functioning after its ruin; little independent lighting units alerted by his presence.

"Danecki!" screamed a high-pitched voice. It was a terrible cry of rage and bewilderment. "Danecki, you killed my brother!"

"Mr. Danecki! Brigadier Wardle!" called the robot. It

halted in its pursuit, electrons spinning madly about its old cortex. "You must go to Dr. Dross!"

Danecki, the robot, and the youth raced through the echoing corridors, across warped decks, past vast coiled machines that had been halted in the act of pouring gobbets of incandescence against the enemy.

Danecki caught a glimpse of the agile youth, who had suddenly appeared around a ten-foot-high cylinder. He ducked and skittered away as the long weapon came up. Molten metal splashed the ground where he had momentarily paused.

"Firearms are not permitted!" shouted the robot, sorely puzzled.

"Disarm him!" yelled Danecki.

The robot set up an outburst of high-pitched electronic nonsense, gibbering into the echoing vaults of the ruined fort. It stopped abruptly as Jacobi ranged the powerful weapon at its dull-green body.

"Danecki!" screamed Jacobi.

But Danecki had found a sloping corridor in a hidden recess and he was pounding along gray ashy floors—down and down into the bowels of the ruin.

A stray gust of wind reached into the sheltering cliff of metal. It flicked Khalia's skirts aside showing her firm, white thighs. Brigadier Wardle grunted appreciatively.

"I'm not sure I shouldn't go back," said Mrs. Zulkifar, noting the direction of Wardle's interest.

"Stay up here if you wish!" Dross said.

Before the first faint squeaks and odd sparks of light indicated that the tunnel was moving them through the upper layers of the fort, a hard squall of rain sent a few drops to splash Khalia's upturned face. For no reason at all she felt apprehensive. She noticed that Mr. Moonman too was afraid. It showed in the careful way he measured the distance between the black shaft of the tunnel and the flowering tiny gobbets of light where the shaft was operating. It showed too in a tiny movement he made to watch the sullen sky.

"Cold, Miss?" asked Knaggs.

"Not really. But it is a bit mysterious and goose-pimply. Eerie, that is."

"I'm sure it's safe," said Brigadier Wardle.

"I hope so," Mrs. Zulkifar said. "What I've always wondered is what exactly happens when these things break down." She poked a jewel-laden hand at the almost incandescent sides of the shaft.

Dross considered her carefully. Suddenly he said "Boom!"

Wardle regarded Dr. Dross in astonishment. Khalia found herself liking the irate big-bellied archaeologist.

"I beg your pardon?" Mrs. Zulkifar rasped.

"Boom!" Dross said louder.

"I really don't know what you can mean!"

"I think he means 'Boom!'" Khalia giggled. "Boom!"

"Really!"

"Yes," said Knaggs. He winked openly at Khalia. "I'm the technical man. I'll explain. At the moment we're displacing the constituents of matter for a tiny fragment of time. Before the next bit is moved away, we displace the next section equivalent to our mass and energy. We have to move at precisely 'n' to maintain our equilibrium."

"It isn't a speed," the Brigadier inserted in the voice that had bored Khalia for weeks, "it's more of a—an—"

"Orbital movement," continued Knaggs. "An orbital spin imparted to the molecules in the mass we fill."

"Oh." Mrs. Zulkifar persisted. "And if it stops?"

"We have two lots of mass trying to fill the same space."

"Boom!" boomed Dross again, raising his big arms to encompass the group.

"Now I know I shouldn't have come," said Mrs. Zulkifar. "Brigadier, don't you have a nasty premonition about this tour?"

Wardle laughed. "Yes! A premonition, yes. I heard about this fort when I was stationed in the Vandersberg Complex, and I've waited ten years to see it. I have a premonition—but only of excitement and the satisfaction of intellectual curiosity!"

"Is that so?" said Knaggs.

The mysterious play of the lights ceased at that moment.

"Safely down," Dross intoned. "And now I am appointed to entertain you. We walk now to the main observation deck."

They followed the course of the fighting as they stepped over shattered weapons and pulverized heaps of material, horribly suggestive of the long-dead men who had died there. Above them a jagged hole had been ripped through the honeycombed tiers of offices. Huge banks of control panels lay twisted fantastically; great fibered girders were strewn about, smashed into wreckage; living quarters gaped, their bright furnishings still hanging. Three immense halls were fused into one block of basalt-like residue. Dross talked of a battery of rockets spinning out of control: of a sudden blistering surge of power from a portable sungun; and the hand-to-hand fighting which had left the black heaps of solidified matter where groups of men and women perished.

"Hand-to-hand fighting, Doctor?" Wardle spoke with no arrogance whatsoever. Khalia realized that there was a basic solidness beneath his pedantic manner and, stripped of his tiresome gallantry, Wardle was a decent human being.

"That's what I said," droned Dross.

"Why does that surprise you?" asked Mr. Moonman.

"The object of any attack is to destroy the enemy," Wardle said. "There would be no point in committing forces within this kind of installation, except for a particular purpose. Certainly it was unnecessary to send them in to complete the destruction of the fort."

They passed a weapons store that was split neatly into two sections. Ruptured storage tanks lay in rows beyond.

Eventually Dross answered the Brigadier: "The Confederation forces wanted the fort's equipment intact. Had they so wished, they could have obliterated the fort. They felt it worth the sacrifice of eight crack regiments in a massive assault to reach the ultimate weapon."

Khalia sensed the archaeologist's obsessive interest. Dross's fluting voice trembled slightly. The Brigadier noticed too. "The Hidden Fort, Dr. Dross?"

"Indeed, Brigadier. The Hidden Fort!"

"I don't know what you're talking about," said Mrs. Zulkifar. "Have we much farther to go? And I can't say I'm interested in seeing any more military bases. One's very much like another, isn't it?"

"No, Madam," Dross said. "Not this one."

"You mean there's another fort here? *Another* one?"

"Quite possibly, Madam."

"More than that," said Wardle. "More than possible, eh, Doctor? There wouldn't be the legend without some substance would there?"

Dross recognized a fellow-enthusiast and responded. "The legend is too strong for pure chance to have placed the Hidden Fort here. No matter how garbled a recollection the legend is of the true facts. I can't escape the conclusion that there is a lost army of robots hereabouts."

"What about the other reference, eh, Doctor?" asked Wardle eagerly. "The Pit, sir. Underground silo, wouldn't you say?"

"In all probability," Dross said.

"Now I am lost," said Mrs. Zulkifar.

They passed into a smallish room that was little more than adequate to house the party. Even here, the violence of the centuries-gone conflict was evident. Dross's own equipment was in the middle of the room.

"Incredible!" said Wardle.

"The complete war room," Dross said with pride. "We found it only this year. From here the entire interplanetary situation can be monitored. All three planets."

"Yet it fell," said Mr. Moonman.

Dross looked at the Revived Man. "Yes, sir," he said with formal politeness, "it did."

"With the legendary army intact," Khalia put in.

Dross's eyes gleamed. "Yes, my dear! I see you have more than the usual shallow interest in the Confederation!"

"It's a terrible story," she said. "And this is a haunting place."

"But full of interest!" Wardle enthused. "What was it again? Ah! 'The Regiments of Night shall come at the end!'"

"They didn't, though," sniffed Mrs. Zulkifar.

"The greatest mystery of all!" Dross intoned. "Yes—'The Regiments of Night shall come at the end!' And then, as the Brigadier says, there's a weak source that refers to their falling into the 'Pit.'"

"I thought that had been effectively shown to be false, Doctor!" said Wardle. "Surely it referred to a silo—an underground hangar, or whatever?"

"That, Brigadier, is the object of my researches! I appreciate your interest, sir! Perhaps we might discuss this further after the tour?"

"With pleasure!" Wardle beamed.

"There'll hardly be time," said Mrs. Zulkifar. "I expect you to see that the excursion ship leaves at the appointed hour, Brigadier!"

"Ah, yes—ah—Emma!"

Dross looked coldly once more at the woman. "As I was saying, sir. Mr. Knaggs and I are taking the ruin apart piece by piece to establish the truth about the end of the Confederation. I have hopes of solving—"

They all heard the robot's high-pitched yell. It halted Dross's speech.

"What's troubling Batty?" said Knaggs.

Jacobi had made the mistake of bringing too heavy a weapon. Its power was entirely disproportionate to the task at hand. Where a simple stun-gun would have been sufficient—it could have been carried feather-light in one hand—Jacobi had encumbered himself with a long heat projector more suitable for encounters in the free-fall of space. But he was young and agile, while Danecki felt his thirty-three years, and the long slog through the mud of the tracks.

The weapon had to be pointed with some accuracy, but there again, thought Danecki, the terrain was against it. Trees, rocks, even deep-space armor, would have given way to its rolling shock waves of heat. Time and time again, though, he had been able to shelter himself in the massive ruined installations of the ancient fort; it had been built to absorb such onslaughts.

"Brigadier, can you explain what is happening!" jerked the robot. "Sir, I am completely confused. First *this*," it said, holding out the antique carapace with its mud-streaked patina, "then *that!*"

Danecki nodded, poised to move as the remaining clansman tried to outflank him where he lay safely protected in a narrow fissure between two sections of a computer system. No wonder the robot was confused. The Jacobi youth had reduced it to a one-sided wreck. More than half of the robot's right side had boiled off on to the gray ash of the floor as the heat-gun blasted out.

"I think my friend has become psychotic," Danecki said. "To protect yourself and me you should get us to a safe place."

The trouble was that the robot had lost some of its memory banks as well as a good deal of its locomotive power.

"I am confused," admitted the robot.

"Isn't there some way of getting to safety? We have to get out of the fort without Danecki knowing it. That, or find a weapon for me."

"No weapons, sir," the robot whined. "Absolutely no firearms permitted!"

Jacobi's aim improved and a section of the computer fell wetly beside Danecki. He watched as a pool of red metal crept downhill away from him.

"Then find a way out," ordered Danecki.

The robot gained its surviving foot and hopped out of the fissure towards an almost-hidden archway. Jacobi sensed the movement and shot off another splash of steaming liquid metal. Danecki jumped over it, barely avoiding the glowing pool. "Dr. Dross!" bellowed the robot. "Dr. Dross!

Danecki plunged after the crazily hopping automaton. He saw the face of the age-old head staring at him from the green-bronze robot's remaining hand. It glared like some distraught spectator deprived of the power to follow the terrible game.

It seemed days since the tourist ship had flipped his own little vessel aside as it spun about the untenable regions of Phase.

At times the robot spun dizzily on its one leg; it halted, considered the blasted green-bronze body, and then jumped into the air. Then it attempted an end-over-end motion, whirling noisily through the echoing corridors, disturbing a colony of bats that had taken possession of a vast domed place.

In a moment of near-sanity it called to him: "I regret the lack of a commentary on the tour, sir! No doubt Dr. Dross will—" It realized its complete inability to cope with the situation. It began to howl—a fearful tremulous, high-pitched quavering that rang down the long, dimly lit corridor. The howls were taken up by distant echoes and the shrill answers of frightened bats.

The robot made for a doorway. Danecki followed.

A small group of people stared back at him in bewildered astonishment.

CHAPTER

★ 4 ★

Knaggs was the first to speak: "You Outlanders aren't supposed to come down here! How the hell did you get through the fort?"

"Kindly explain your presence," added Dross.

"Batty!" Knaggs shouted, seeing the robot properly. "How in blazes—"

Batibasaga pegged his way noisily to Dross and Knaggs. Mr. Moonman cowered back as the robot raised the ancient head towards Dross. Mrs. Zulkifar screamed and hid behind the Brigadier. Khalia, who had been staring at the blood and mud-stained Danecki, felt hysterical laughter rising up in her throat. Knaggs stuttered in incredulity at the sight of the grotesque robot. Dross was similarly unable to express his amazement.

"Dr. Dross?" Danecki inquired, taking advantage of the inability of the others to get out a comprehensible question. Had the situation not been so desperate, he might have found it amusing. His clothing hung in muddy shreds. There was blood from half a dozen scratches on his arms and legs; his hair was plastered to his head by the rain, and he knew that his eyes were bright with the fear of the hunt. Altogether he must present a desperate sight.

Knaggs stuttered at the automaton. "B-B-Batty! What the devil's happened?"

Dross, however, took control. "Who are you?" he demanded. "And how has this happened?"

It was no time for evasions. Danecki decided that he could trust the archaeologist. "Danecki. Licensed victim. I have to get out of here."

"Victim!"

Khalia was hysterical now. She screamed once, twice, and then Knaggs was holding her, telling her quietly that she was safe.

She had heard of the barbarous customs of the Antiran Sector. The licensed vendetta was tolerated only in such primitive societies. She stared at Danecki, seeing now the fatigue in the slope of his wide shoulders. This man had been forced to become an animal. He had the aura of a cornered but still dangerous beast.

Knaggs burst out: "You're not one of the Outlanders! Then how did you get here?"

Dross looked thoughtfully at the doorway. "That doesn't really matter at the moment, Mr. Knaggs. I think this gentleman has some explaining to do, but it can wait. What's more to the point just now is that he is being hunted."

"Yes," interrupted Wardle. "Explains the state of the robot! Heat-gun of some sort?"

"I think that can wait too, Brigadier," Dross put in. To Danecki he said, "Where is your licensed executioner?"

Danecki could see by the intent, half-frightened stares, that the men and women in the small room knew they were rubbing shoulders with a killer. They knew too that he was a marked man, one that might himself be killed before them. They were deliciously thrilled by the presence of impending violence. He had an impulse to explain.

But how could he hope to convince them in a minute or two that he had been, until a year ago, an ordinary man, much like themselves. A man with a secure, pleasant enough life. Until the grim accident that had begun as a little interruption to the chore of ferrying the annual ship across the Sector. *Accident?* It hadn't been that. Not on the Jacobis' part. But you couldn't explain, because no one could understand, not unless they took part in the ritual of the hunt. Once you became a licensed victim, you stopped living as a human being. You learned to exist. What could the little man with his arm around the beautiful girl know of the mindless rage that swept you when you saw yet another Jacobi challenger flashing toward your ship? What could this stout old soldier understand of a man on his own, always against superior odds? And did it matter that no one here could possibly know how he felt?

Danecki watched Dross. He knew that he had been right to trust him. Batibasaga revolved slowly on his remaining leg.

"Where is he?" asked Dross. "The man you're running from."

"Near," replied Danecki.

Mrs. Zulkifar squealed angrily: "You're putting us all in danger! I know about these hunts. You're supposed to do it all in deep space. Not where there are innocent bystanders! You've no right to endanger our lives!"

Dross ignored her. "You've put us all in danger," he said. "But the personal vendetta is a vile outrage to human decency, and you shall have our help."

Batibasaga hopped to the doorway. The clatter of his progress distracted them all. Danecki was relieved when the staring eyes were withdrawn. He had felt like some grotesque specimen in a peep show while they were weighing him up.

The robot was poised, listening. "Weight about one-six-two," it said. It pivoted slowly like some sentient gyroscope. "Nearing."

Danecki understood at once, Dross fractionally later. Of the others, only Wardle picked out the robot's meaning.

Mrs. Zulkifar asked for information as Danecki leapt for the doorway. "What is it?" she asked. "What's happening? It's an outrage!" The robot answered her with considerable politeness: "The missing member of your party is here, Madam."

That was how the last of the Jacobis saw them: an onrush of figures towards him as he readied the long heat-gun. He must have been completely distraught at that moment; or perhaps he was as amazed by the numbers rushing toward him as Mrs. Zulkifar was to see him. Whatever was responsible, however, he failed altogether to notice the presence of the robot at the side of the entrance.

"Murderer!" he yelled, seeing Danecki's lunging figure.

The weapon came down. Danecki saw the pinpoint of incandescence at its end. In the smallest unit of time, it would flower into a raging blast and take him into charred blackness. He heard one of the women sequealing horribly. Dross's voice boomed out.

The robot acted. Batibasaga swept upward in a grotesque and frighteningly quick movement. It took the incipient blast of the fusor on what was left of its chest. In the same instant of time, the robot shot out a skeletal appendage and flicked the youth's feet from under him.

Noise rolled in Danecki's ears. Screams. His own voice in a bull-roaring. Wardle and Dross bellowing too. Cries of terror. And then the thin whistling of the vicious weapon.

The long fusor rolled across the floor, seemingly of its own volition. Then the room was suffused in the eerie light of the weapon's blast. Noise and light seemed to lift the room into another plane of existence altogether, one where there could be no end to the gobbetting fury of the heatgun, and the terror of the people there.

"Get it, Batty!" yelled Knaggs.

But the robot was gibbering nonsense, adding its own high-pitched whinings to the confusion.

"Good God, Doctor, look there!" bawled Wardle in Danecki's ear.

The heat and blast had shattered the far wall of the already battered room. Metal ran redly and a hole suddenly gaped through the wall. Dross answered Wardle, but his voice was lost in the noise. Danecki saw an array of levers through the hole. Then these too glowed red, then white and splashed down out of sight.

"Controls!" screamed Knaggs. "Get the gun, Batty! *Get it!*"

And still the terrible weapon spun its web of fury.

The crippled robot acted at last. It became a whirling metal scarecrow as it hopped over both Dross and the little engineer. Khalia felt the skin on her face tightening as the molten wall radiated a fierce heat into the room. She saw Danecki follow the robot as it smashed downward on to the juddering, slender shaft of the fusor. Then Danecki had the half-conscious Jacobi in his big hands, and the robot had the weapon.

Worse happened.

Danecki, the terrified Mr. Moonman, Dross, Wardle, and even the still-dazed Jacobi—all remained still, hypnotized by the bizarre result of the wrecking of the controls. Mrs. Zulkifar inquired in a chilling voice what Danecki had done now.

Khalia knew that something uncanny and inevitable was taking place in the ancient observation deck. The older woman's complaint was pitifully inadequate as a response to the eerie happening.

For, among the molten debris and the shattered machinery beyond the wall, a new squat structure was taking shape. It built itself up, a cube of iron-black force-fields. Rough, whirling, spinning, grinding forces began to shake the room; the cube began outside the little observation deck, and almost at once it was within it, surrounding the amazed group of men and women. To the watchers it seemed that some evil being was asserting its power in the ruins of the titanic military base.

Knaggs recognized it for what it was. "Back!" he snapped. "Through the doorway!" He pushed Khalia violently toward the entrance of the chamber. She jerked forward, but there was no entrance now. The cube was not only in the room: it was the room. "Come on!" implored Knaggs uselessly, but the girl could not move nearer the grinding, smashing sides of the cube.

"It's a force-field!" Wardle shouted. "Doctor, damn me if there aren't machines working here!"

The cube held them in a threshing fog of black light now. Within the network of forces, they struggled for understanding.

"Try to get out!" Knaggs shouted. "It's a spin-shaft! Not one of ours!"

"Yes it is!" Dross was beside himself with excitement. "A primitive artifact," he called, trembling. "Yes!"

Knaggs hurled himself at the cube. It seemed to bend and sway under his impact, and then brute forces smashed him with incredible violence hard into the youth. Danecki heard the sound of bones snapping; the screams of bewilderment and shock came.

The noise was unbearable—worse, if that could be, than the earlier uproar. There was a grinding rush of spinning molecules at the edges of the cube. The floor tilted beneath them. Jacobi yelled in fear and pain, while Knaggs's thin screams told how badly he had been hurt. Khalia contrived to keep her mouth closed; she watched as Mrs. Zulkifar set up a howl of terrified protest.

Danecki saw Dross smile. Dross knew what had happened. As the grip of the spin-shaft tightened and they began the plunging descent, Danecki knew that one man at least had been successful in his quest.

Khalia saw the youth's arm snap. It was entangled in the tumbling heap of bodies; and when Knaggs violently catapulted across the space within the mesh of force-fields, the arm took the full force of his onrush. It gave way with a dull cracking sound. In the turmoil of the moment, it was one more sickening element, another fragment of horror. She saw Knaggs collapsed on the tilting floor in a heap, Dross flung into the squirming pile of bodies, Mrs. Zulkifar fallen backwards with an expression of acute embarrassment on her face. Only the grim-faced man with the wild eyes kept his balance against the forces that locked them into the confines of the grinding spin-shaft. Then she too felt the subtle and powerful sway of the tunnel. She put an arm out instinctively and felt it taken.

Above the cries and the colossal roarings of the primitive installation she heard Danecki reassuring her. "Relax. It doesn't matter if you don't keep upright. Relax! This is almost free-fall."

Danecki marveled at the calmness in his own voice. Naturally the girl was in a state of terror. Even more naturally, the hurt and dazed party were yelling to one another, to him, to their gods, to the controllers at Galactic Center who had set up the excursion, and to the attendant robots that should have been on hand to rescue them. The girl trembled, but she kept control of herself. She was watching him. He kept her hand and pressed it firmly. The skin was smooth and warm against his palm. He tried to remember the last woman he had had. The girl was talking.

"What is it? What's happened? Have you done this?"

He couldn't hear the words but he could see the shape of her questions. "The fort," he mouthed. "Spin-shaft. It's got us. It's taking us!"

"Where?"

Danecki shrugged and fell off-balance. The girl came with him, still holding onto his hand in a timid display of strength. When he could watch her lips, and when she wriggled into a position from which she could see him too, he shouted: "Underground! Down!"

He saw that she understood. She obviously had a dozen other questions, but she did not trouble with them. Instead she was edging toward Knaggs. The little engineer's face had a waxen look about it that Danecki knew well.

Danecki half-pushed the girl, using the quivering body of Mr. Moonman as a platform. She reached Knaggs and tried to separate him from Dross's bulk. Dross bellowed something, his first response to the situation. Danecki saw the girl's mouth open to shout back angrily—but then the rough sides of the tunnel let out such a roar of grinding noise that all the stunned occupants desperately tried to block it out with hands and arms.

Mind reeling, Danecki watched vast sheets of energy build up in the tunnel. Black shocks of power smashed at the cage that held them. Rococo picture frames of energy formed and dissolved as molecular spin shook the mass of the space they occupied. A wild blast of sound and splintering shards of molecules rocked the tiny cage; those that were conscious knew at once that this was the climactic moment of the plunging descent. The force-fields that contained them were battling in the structure of the ancient spin-shaft. Danecki reached out to the girl, but she was holding the lax body of the systems engineer. He saw the gratitude in her eyes as the roaring built up into a blinding, brain-shattering crescendo—where tiny universes of molecules flashed into being and disappeared in pinpoints of immense sunbursts.

And then they were through the fault in the tunnel and quite suddenly at rest on a hard glittering metal floor.

Danecki was on his feet almost instantly. The habits of the past year gripped him in an unshakable routine. His eyes swept the new hunting ground, looking for the location of the enemy.

Khalia felt a stab of pity for him. Here, in this ancient cave of blued steel—even here, in a deserted, abandoned, lifeless place—Danecki was first and foremost a hunted animal. Then she saw what made the others gasp in awe and amazement. Dross, as usual, was the first to recover.

His voice rang with reverent delight. "Dross promised you marvels! And here is the greatest! This is the find of a lifetime, ladies and gentlemen—the Hidden Fort!"

CHAPTER

★ 5 ★

They were in a control room, so much was apparent.
In the low-ceilinged, blue-steel cavern, the entire length of one wall was filled with sensor-pads, control seats, a huge, pale, dead screen, directional sensors—in fact, the whole apparatus of a powerful and gigantic military installation. The great room was on a far bigger scale than the wrecked observation deck above. Clearly, this had been the nerve center of the grand armies of the long-dead Second Interplanetary Confederation. It was here that their military genius had been lavished, rather than on the conventional fortress which had fallen to the crack regiments of the enemy.

Danecki automatically checked his escape route. Three corridors radiated from one end of the underground vault. Another opening nearby might or might not be an exit. At the other end of the control room was a pair of great black doors.

But of the spin-shaft that had deposited them so unceremoniously on the steel floor, there was no sign. It had appeared in the ruins like some long-asleep beast—flung them downwards—and, its duty completed, vanished.

Wardle and Dross were dazed with wonder.

"What a find! Congratulations, Doctor," Wardle burst out. "Undamaged—untouched. Amazing! Exactly as it stood a thousand years ago!"

Dross drank in the sight of the glittering controls. "Perfect!" He advanced with shaking hands to a seat that clearly had belonged to some long-dead commander: the battle-direct chair.

The Jacobi youth was staring at his wrecked arm, apparently unable to let a single sound escape his lips; he looked no more than a schoolboy. He lay propped up on his good arm with the other at an impossible angle. Danecki let him lie in his universe of pain. He was no threat.

Mr. Moonman lay dazed beside the shattered robot. Face to face, they looked like some strange flotsam sluiced down into the cave of blue steel.

Khalia was afraid for the little engineer, and it was she who broke the spell of the two ecstatic men: "Can't one of you do something for Mr. Knaggs?" Her voice rang around the clean, brightly-lit cavern. It bounced off crisp, blue-steel walls—setting up tiny echoes that flicked around the functional chamber like winged things. "He's badly hurt. Can't you see?"

Knaggs heard her. His lips moved slowly in his gray-white face.

Dross was at Knaggs's side with a speed surprising for a man of his bulk. His large, perspiring face was contorted with agonized pity. "Mr. Knaggs," he called. Dross shook his head, still unable to believe what he could read in the engineer's eyes. His trance of glory slipped away, and he was suddenly a broken, aging man who sees a friend dying. "How bad?" he whispered.

"It's bad," said Danecki. "See?"

Dross wrung his fat hands helplessly. Mr. Moonman watched as Danecki stripped the engineer's shirt back.

Mrs. Zulkifar would not look at the little, crushed figure. "I'm going back," she said firmly. "I didn't want to come in the first place. Brigadier! It's your duty to do something for a lady!" She stared defiantly at Dross. Still she refused to look at Knaggs, who was breathing raggedly in Danecki's careful arms.

His rib cage had been crushed. Down the left side, the normally convex curve had been pushed inwards. There was only a slight reddening of the skin to indicate the force of the blows he had received when the spin-shaft formed, but the bones below the surface had the pulpy feel of multiple fractures. No man could live long with those injuries.

"He needs expert attention if he's to live," said Danecki. "The bones are in his lungs and there'll be other internal punctures."

Yet, with an incredible effort of will, the little man was forcing himself to speak.

"Don't!" Dross implored him. "We'll get you to the

surface—I've a full surgical unit," he added to Danecki.

But Knaggs wouldn't be denied. Dross watched the thin lips in the gray face become blotched with frothy blood.

Knaggs's voice bubbled through the redness: "Controls?" he whispered. In vain, he tried to repeat what he had said.

Dross looked to Danecki. "I must act, get him out. The shaft—the spin-shaft! Where are the controls?" His eye fell on the robot. "Batty! Up. Locate the spin-shaft controls. Get us out—Mr. Knaggs needs attention urgently!"

"Yes," Wardle called. "Let's get him to the surface. Quickly, now! Damn it, the robot's not stirring!"

Dross touched the blasted frame of the robot with his foot. He stared at it helplessly. There was no sign of movement from the automaton. As he kicked it again, his foot knocked against the ancient robot head that Batty had been carrying since intercepting Danecki in the ruins above. "Wrecked!" Dross said helplessly. "It must have been put out of action by the fusor. Batty!"

Mrs. Zulkifar's icy voice rang out again: "I believe you planned this, Doctor. Really, it's too much! You and that ruffian! I'm going to report you all to Galactic Center. Now, what are you going to do about getting us out of here? Can't you use the controls? You're supposed to be an expert, Doctor!"

Knaggs was listening.

Danecki said in a fast urgent voice: "Be quiet! All of you!"

"—touch—controls—" Knaggs's voice was a feeble croak.

Dross bent down. "Please don't talk, Mr. Knaggs. We'll find how to operate the controls—yes, they're here! The whole Hidden Fort is here. We've found it, you and I, Mr. Knaggs!"

But Knaggs would not allow himself to relapse into the peace of unconsciousness. He was struggling against the pain of a score of bone fragments grinding into damaged organs; struggling, too, against the blood welling up into his mouth.

"Then get to work!" Mrs. Zulkifar ordered. She saw Danecki's eyes and was quiet. They were the eyes of an animal, slits of fiery menace. She shivered visibly.

"He's your systems man, isn't he?" asked Danecki. "Your engineer?"

"He is. My friend, too," replied Dross.

"Then listen. He's trying to tell us something about the systems down here."

Knaggs's clouded but still-bright blue eyes widened. He could hear and understand. When he did manage to speak, after an agonizing minute of effort, his voice was distinct. "Don't touch the controls. . . don't touch the controls!"

"I got that," said Danecki. "Don't touch the controls. Why not? We want to get you to a surgical unit."

"Leave him!" Khalia said fiercely. "It's torture for him to breathe!"

Danecki pitied her for her youthful innocence. "Why not?" he said again.

"Des. . . des. . ." the little man muttered. And then: "Destruct circuits. Unauthorized personnel. Ab. . . ab. . ."

"Abort?" said Danecki. "The fort is on a destruct circuit if unauthorized personnel use the controls?"

Knaggs whispered, "Yes." His eyes closed and he was in a kind of peace.

The Jacobi youth began to moan.

Khalia saw the hardening in Danecki's hooded eyes. The look of the hunter was in his face again as he glanced at the wounded youth.

"Please," she said. "He's hurt badly too."

But Danecki was uninterested in the youth now. He got to his feet. "He'll die without immediate help," Danecki told Dross. They both turned to the inviting banks of controls.

"No robot. No systems engineer. The spin-shaft gone. No way of knowing how to get out of here," said Dross slowly. "What am I to do?"

"I should think that's obvious," Mrs. Zulkifar said, with all of her former venom. "You managed to get us down here. Now get us out!"

"I wish I knew how," said Dross.

Wardle was becoming impatient with the irate, splendidly-handsome woman. "Have patience, Emma!" he said firmly. "We'll do all we can. Myself. . . . the Doctor here. . . . and—ah—Mr. Danecki. It may take time. But we'll see that poor Mr. Knaggs has medical attention. And soon. Soon!"

He looked quickly at the raggedly-breathing little figure, with its blood-stained lips. Khalia was wiping Knaggs's mouth frequently. It was obvious by Wardle's look that he knew Knaggs was dying.

They all knew.

Mrs. Zulkifar was close to screaming: *"Do* something! Find a way out! Use the controls!"

"I'm afraid, Madam, that it would be an act of criminal irresponsibility to do that," Dross told her coldly.

"What the Doctor means—ah—Emma," Wardle explained, "is that if we try to use the installation's systems, it will destroy itself."

"Then what *can* we do!" At last the woman was beginning to realize the extent of their predicament.

Khalia watched her for a moment. Then she said: "Who can set a broken arm?"

Danecki took the boy's own dagger. He sliced through the material of his tunic, revealing the shattered arm.

Jacobi was crying as the first shock waves of pain flooded around his grating bones; Danecki saw him recognize who it was that stood over him, and, incredibly, the boy conquered his agony. It was a pitiful gesture, but one that was sufficient to recall Danecki to a state of distant terror. The long year of pursuit, violent death and nightmare fears came back.

The boy saw him standing next to Mr. Moonman. He lurched up onto his good arm and tried to take the dagger from Danecki. Almost at once, the screaming nerves in his broken arm jolted him into unconsciousness, but the movement had been made, and Danecki was the licensed victim again. The boy's throat lay exposed.

One foot on that slack neck, a crushing heave, and there would be no more nightmares.

Mrs. Zulkifar stopped him. She shrieked: "Just where are we, Doctor! I mean, I don't like to be kept in one place for long! I don't like it here!"

Danecki restrained himself as Dross explained what had happened to them since the fury of the iron-black cube had taken them from the ruin above. "Madam, like it or not, you're here. An accident of incredible importance has resulted in our being sent down the entrance to a long-lost military fortification dating from the days of the Second Interplanetary Confederation. It is known through legend. Some called it the Hidden Fort. Others, the Lost Fort. Now, it is neither hidden nor lost. You, Madam, and the rest of us, including my unfortunate colleague Mr. Knaggs, have been permitted to see what has not been seen by the eye of a single human being since the last battle of the Mad Wars!"

They all looked about them to see the smooth surfaces. The walls, floor, and ceiling had a bright, clean deadliness that thrust itself upon the imagination with a grim and glittering force. The great chamber might have been polished only that hour.

Danecki looked back to the youth as Mrs. Zulkifar gobbled her incredulity. He shut her out of his mind. "He'll need splints," he told Dross. "A pain-killer would help, but you haven't one?"

"No, nothing! Nothing for Mr. Knaggs or the youth. I haven't any experience with this sort of thing. Batty knows where everything is. Can't you do something for him?"

Danecki made his decision. The boy reminded him of the rain-streaked face on the surface, the face with its eyes open to the steel-gray sky. "I'll splint the arm."

Khalia began to understand the effort it had taken Danecki to make the decision.

CHAPTER

★ 6 ★

Wardle watched Danecki's quick hands. Then he pointed to the control banks. "The fort could save Mr. Knaggs," he said. "This is a very big installation. There'll be a fully-equipped casualty station somewhere about here. Why not? There'll be food, medical supplies, all the equipment for a garrison of hundreds. Damn it, surely we should try. We have to try! And what about the spin-shaft? Where is it? Gone! Not a sign of it. Dr. Dross," he called. "We could search for hospital facilities!"

Danecki paused in the act of forcing fragments of bone together. For a moment he thought that Wardle would not be able to resist the urge to find out more about the incredible underground redoubt.

Dross halted the Brigadier. "Everything here will be controlled by automatic systems," he said heavily. "Somehow we have been allowed to enter the fort without causing it to become active. Should we do anything that would activate the control systems, I am sure that the fort would recognize us as unauthorized intruders. I have to rely on Mr. Knaggs's judgment, and my own researches into the period. No, Brigadier, we may not investigate the fort at all! For, if we do, the fort, as well as ourselves, will certainly be destroyed."

Danecki heard the bones click and Jacobi shriek in his pain-filled delirium. He splinted the joint with the scabbard of the ceremonial hunting knife the boy carried at his belt. He bound the arm.

Wardle was talking, almost to himself. "It was the ultimate weapon. A Hidden Fort that could last for a thousand years! Self-perpetuating—completely automatic—the final undiscoverable fortress! And fully efficient after a thousand years. Even the spin-shaft worked!"

Mrs. Zulkifar said angrily: "Do you mean that I've been traveling down a spin-tunnel that's a thousand years old? Why, that's illegal. It's madly dangerous!"

"You have, Madam, and it certainly is. Illegal, dangerous and mad," Dross assured her.

"Then where are all the people?" she said, quietly now.

Dross was almost amused. "People?"

It was obvious that no human had trod this bright, polished floor for centuries. No one had died down there. There were no bones, no little heaps of ancient dust, no sense of human intrusion for year after year after year.

Mr. Moonman spoke to Mrs. Zulkifar. "We are the first to see this fortress in ten centuries, Madam. One thousand years."

"Precisely!" Wardle said. He turned to face Dross. His eye fell on the shuddering figure of Mr. Knaggs, and, though the Brigadier flinched with pity, he went on with a subdued air of excitement, "We're the first! The assault regiments didn't reach here! Can it be possible, Doctor? That somewhere down here—"

They understood one another.

Khalia knew too. "'The Regiments of Night,'" she quoted. "Is that what we'll find?"

"Oh, goodness," said Mrs. Zulkifar. "You're all so *calm* about it. Why, it's an outrage—isn't it?"

"I suppose it is," said Khalia.

"But you're so calm yourself!"

"That doesn't mean I'm not scared."

Danecki was glad to hear the girl's confession. There was no hysteria in her voice, nor any sign of fear on her face. She was a self-contained, resolute, and beautiful young woman. Yet it would have been wrong for her to claim the hard fearlessness that he had molded himself into.

"I don't understand you," Mrs. Zulkifar said. "Really, I don't! It isn't feminine to be so quiet! It isn't natural. I'm not sure that it's even decent!"

The girl smiled, a slight crinkling of the features that tore at Danecki's heart. He smiled back at her.

Dross turned to Danecki. "What are we to do?"

Danecki asked Mrs. Zulkifar's unasked question. When Dross had turned to him, she had glared viciously. But she remained in her angry, hurt silence. "You're asking me?" Danecki said. "You're the expert, Doctor. And the Brigadier knows about military installations."

"So I do," strutted Wardle. "Studied ancient fortifications for years!"

"I know a good deal," Dross said quietly. "I expect to know more should we conclude this adventure satisfactorily. The Brigadier, unless I'm much mistaken, shares my interest in this remarkable find."

"What? Certainly!" put in Wardle.

"I am the foremost authority on the Second Interplanetary Confederation, Mr. Danecki. Yet I still have sufficient humility to recognize my own limitations. You're a qualified hyperspace navigator?"

"I was," said Danecki, "in another life."

"Worked your own ship?"

"Yes."

"Small planetary system—remote from Center?"

Danecki appreciated the archaeologist's shrewdness. "Yes. Not such a small system, though. But remote. You'd call it primitive."

"I'd call it barbaric," said Dross with complete sincerity. "And yet you've survived—for how long?"

Danecki thought of the months and weeks and days of tumbling about the eddying whirlpools of hyperspace; of the sudden desperate encounters that lasted for fifteen seconds or, once, for seventeen long days and nights. "A year. Just a year."

Khalia sensed the utter weariness of spirit in the man. But he was not broken.

Dross went on: "Then you are an expert in precisely the skills we need here and now, Mr. Danecki!"

Danecki nodded.

Dross glanced at Wardle. "I know you held field rank, sir, but you commanded armies. We need a man who can adapt instantly to any bizarre set of circumstances. An expert, Brigadier, in the art of survival!"

Dross turned to Danecki. "How do we survive, Mr. Danecki?"

Invulnerable, massive, the ultimate in defensive fortification building, the ancient fort glinted in the bright lights. The control panels waited for long-gone officers. The great black doors at one end of the cavern pressed stiflingly in on Khalia. She began to fear their massive presence. She began to notice the structure of the fort.

There were corridors she had glimpsed only vaguely before.

There were three great corridors, wide tunnels, but not high. They would allow easy passage for a considerable number. How many? A hundred? A thousand? Khalia wondered what sort of people the long-dead builders had been. What sort of future had they imagined for the Galaxy? Had they seen their own place in the long series of frantic Mad Wars as that of a civilized minority keeping at bay the forces of wild, black revolution? And why was the fortification *deserted?* Danecki was thinking about the fort too. "How good is Mr. Knaggs?" he said, surprising Dross as well as Khalia.

She had watched him surveying the bleak banks of controls with a close, detailed scrutiny—as if he would wring out their secret knowledge by hypnotizing the bare screens. And yet she could see the inevitable logic of his question. After all, Knaggs had almost condemned himself to a miserable death by his warning.

"He was the best," said Dross. "I've never known him to be wrong. He holds qualifications few at Center could match. I've seen him take robotic systems to pieces and put them together again with a skill that I can only describe as uncanny. But that's not what you mean, is it, Mr. Danecki?"

"What?" Wardle put in. "What do you mean, then?"

"It's a matter of judgment," said Dross. "Can we rely on the judgment of a man who is as badly hurt as my engineer. Can we, Mr. Danecki?"

It rested on Knaggs, Danecki knew. It was becoming increasingly obvious that the little systems engineer could not last much longer; even skilled surgery might not save him, and it might be that the fort itself was not equipped to handle such severe cases.

But it might!

For a moment Khalia caught herself wondering what life could be like on Danecki's own iron world—where a savage justice was still permitted that had long since been abandoned in her own advanced system. The men she knew were safe, self-contained, tender. Danecki radiated an energetic despair that shocked, yet thrilled, her.

Danecki crossed to the large, functional chair where a Confederation battle commander might have sat. Mrs. Zulkifar saw him touch the smooth, elegant back of the chair.

"Don't!" she yelled. "Don't touch anything. It might be

dangerous. Leave it all to the proper authorities when we get out! Just think what happened when that madman came in with the fusor! We might all be killed—in this place. It's horrible! Didn't the engineer say that we'll all die if we touch anything?"

Khalia caught the infection of terror from the woman; she had a moment of pure horror as she imagined herself remaining in the bright, blue-steel pit until the air failed, or some nameless enemy contrived a lingering death. She was shocked to realize that she was ready to believe Knaggs. And it was because of the fear of death in the underground fort.

Danecki shrugged. "We have to trust him," he said. "He knows more than any of us about the engineering systems of the Confederation. Another thing—" he said, indicating the banks of controls. "The fort is becoming active."

Wardle was again the keen student of military affairs. He bustled about the control room with a professional stride, as if he were about to take charge of the great fortification.

"Should have guessed!" he said. "Eh, Doctor? Mr. Danecki? Here we are, intruders, and the installation recognizes that it must provide the essentials to keep life moving—light, heat, air! Fuel cells to power the place. Ah! Thought at first we were going to have a surprise—find the descendants of Second Confederation survivors. But no!"

Dross half-listened. Like Danecki, he was staring at the control panels. A single sensor-pad, part of the control mechanisms in front of the battle commander's chair, began to waver blindly. It sought a human hand to begin pumping out information about the state of the Confederation empire.

Khalia saw the sensor-pad. She willed Danecki to move away from it, and she felt sweat break out all over her body as he did so.

"It's happened before!" Wardle went on jerkily. "Heard about the odd affair on Cygnus VII? Tribe of primitives thought they'd be wiped out. Went to earth. Lasted more than three hundred years. Moles! Came out blind. Could have happened here—Confederation survivors stranded down here—maybe a few ignorant soldiers or lower-grade base personnel—they could have bred down here. But no! No sign of life. Not till we came down!"

He stopped. Khalia realized that Wardle, as much as Dross and the others, was waiting for Danecki.

The wide shoulders were erect, and the face was set in a grim mold when at last he completed his survey of the control room. "We don't dare try to get out," he said quietly. "Your engineer is probably right. That means trying to call for help before we try anything else."

"Anything else?" asked Mrs. Zulkifar. "What else *can* we do? You must report our danger to the ship. I'll certainly have you turned over to the proper authorities if you don't!"

Danecki found the woman's defiant hostility wearing. But he merely said: "So far as you are concerned, I am the proper authorities."

"No! The Brigadier here—he should take charge! He's an older man. He's a person of position, not a criminal on the run! Doctor, I demand that you ask this man to show a proper respect for me. I demand it!"

Dross said wearily: "Please, Madam, try to be realistic! Try to have some understanding of other viewpoints than your own. We have a man who may be dying in our midst—have some respect yourself, Mrs. Zulkifar. Leave matters to me, at least for the moment. I know that Mr. Danecki is the proper person to make our plans!"

"It might help the lady if I consulted with the Brigadier," Danecki offered, "and with the Doctor."

The woman inclined her head.

Khalia unclenched her fist. She wished she dared strike the crass middle-aged woman, who was adding another strand of tension to the situation.

"Well, Mr. Danecki?" asked Dross. "What can we do to save Mr. Knaggs?"

"Get help from your ship," Danecki answered at once. "Even at the risk of activating some of the fort's systems."

"You think that will happen?"

Danecki pointed to a faintly-glowing screen that seemed to be the centerpiece of the great control panel before the armchair. Its gray blankness had gradually changed into a faded, light-blue, glowing haze. It seemed to be waiting to be called into life. "Minor systems are beginning to function," he said. "If we start to use any kind of electrical impulse down here, other systems are going to be alerted. It won't take much of that kind of activity to get the major systems working."

"Then why aren't they in action already?" Khalia found herself asking. "Why isn't the fort on the alert now? As the Brigadier says, we're intruders. Why haven't we been asked to account for our intrusion?"

It was, Danecki realized, a question that he had already put to himself and discarded. But not explicitly. He had found a situation and accepted it.

"Been asking myself that!" said Wardle. "Surprising, eh, Doctor?"

Dross shook his head. "The thought had passed through my mind too," he told the others. "I dismissed it. You see, the Second Interplanetary Confederation was obsessively security-minded. They lived by the robot. Cybernetics was their way of life. Apparently, the robotic systems that have sensed our presence consider that we are here by right. The Brigadier has pointed out that light, heat, and air are provided. Therefore we are legitimate entrants. There is also the fact that we entered the fort by the customary means—we did use the Confederation's own spin-shaft, remember. I believe, along with Mr. Knaggs, that it's only if we should attempt to *use* the control systems, that we will be recognized as intruders. Until that time, we are, in effect, members of the Second Interplanetary Confederation."

"And it's all a thousand years old." said Khalia. She was bewildered now by the idea.

"And working as efficiently as ever!" Wardle assured her.

Something was troubling Danecki. "That may be so," he said. "But a thousand years is a long time for any set of machinery to remain unchanged. And when the major systems are activated, we'll have trouble."

Knaggs groaned in agony.

"Time isn't on our side, whichever way you regard matters," said Mr. Moonman. "Isn't it a question of weighing up the certainty of Mr. Knaggs's condition against the relative uncertainties of the installation's systems?"

The others turned to look at him. He smiled back. His thin gaunt face creased into a caricature of apology. It was like watching a shadow in a sepulcher.

"You have a personal communicator?" Danecki asked Dross.

"No," said Dross. "And how I regret it now! Mr. Knaggs and I agreed never to carry the wretched things—we abandoned them after several disagreements about working methods."

Mrs. Zulkifar was not completely put down. She had been following the discussion, carefully avoiding looking in Danecki's direction. Now, she addressed herself to Wardle: "Brigadier!"

Wardle responded to the icy tone of command.

"Yes, Emma?"

"Isn't this what you would call the command area? Of the fortification, I mean?"

Wardle was pleasantly surprised by the handsome woman's appraisal of the cavern. "Yes. Undoubtedly."

Khalia knew that it was true. The batteries of controls that were faintly stirring with returning life demanded the presence of a dozen sets of guiding hands. The huge blue screen that now rippled with life was waiting to show a battle commander how his enemy's dispositions lay. There was an air of functional menace about the cavern that had not been present when they were hurled onto the steel floor. The fort awaited a commander.

"And is the machine operational?" Mrs. Zulkifar went on. "Are its communicators effective?"

Khalia realized that Mrs. Zulkifar still hadn't grasped the point of it all.

Dross said: "Everything seems to be in superb order, Madam. So far as we can see."

"Then why not use the machine's own communicators?" Mrs. Zulkifar demanded.

"I thought I'd explained," said Dross wearily. "If we try to operate any of the systems, we blow ourselves up."

"Surely not! No!" Mrs. Zulkifar shouted. "I know quite well that you're wrong, Doctor! Isn't it true that all robots are subject to the Laws of Robotics? Don't they carry a program stressing the sanctity of human life?"

Dross shook his head. "You have to believe this, Madam," he said. "Laws of Robotics! You might as well talk about the love-life of the robot! And the sanctity of human life? No! Mr. Knaggs and I found the prototype of a Confederation robot a few weeks ago. Do you know what was numbered amongst its duties?" He glared at the self-possessed, immaculately-dressed woman. "It was a perimeter guard. It was designed to sniff out all living things that tried to enter the surface base. Everything, humans included. And then kill."

Wardle coughed. "I think the Doctor's right," he said. "We have to assume that the fort is hostile."

"Only if we alert it," added Danecki. "And that we must do to get help."

Khalia heard the dry, racking sounds in Knaggs's throat. She thought he was dying. "Mr. Knaggs!" she cried out.

He was looking at Dross. His eyes were dull gray-black pools; they stood out against the gray of his face, pools of anguish. Knaggs was trying to speak.

They all heard the bubbling words.

". . . try the robot. . . try. . ."

"Knaggs! Mr. Knaggs!" Dross cried. He was down on his knees beside the small figure. "If I'd known—you've been listening! You know what we're talking about!"

"You know we have to get help?" Danecki stared into Knaggs's pain-filled eyes. He was beside Dross. Khalia tried to stop him talking to Knaggs, but he pushed her carefully away. "You know we have to get help before the fort becomes active?"

"Don't speak!" Khalia cried.

A look of compassion and command from Danecki quieted her. The others craned forward to catch the slightest sound from the dying systems engineer. Even Jacobi, rising for a few moments of anguished consciousness, moved toward the group, affected by their concentration.

"Keep back," Wardle ordered.

They did so reluctantly.

Knaggs closed his eyes. Formless words bubbled through the froth, too low and too slight for anyone to hear.

"You said 'try the robot,'" Danecki prompted. "Before that you told us not to touch the controls. Move your head if that's right."

Mrs. Zulkifar shuddered uncontrollably. Khalia held herself against Danecki's big shoulder, her hands in Knaggs's feebly clutching fingers. His eyes opened for a moment, and she could see them surge with life. Then they closed.

He nodded, a slight, barely perceptible movement. More words bubbled through. A moan of pure anguish trailed behind the words as Knaggs strove to draw air into his wrecked lungs; Khalia wondered how long his slight frame could stand the torment. She stared in helpless pity and admiration at the little man. He was desperately trying to put out an understandable sequence of sounds.

Seconds passed without any further attempt at communication. The eyes opened again.

Danecki waited until Knaggs appeared able to focus.

"No," he said. "I couldn't understand. 'Try the robot.' Which robot?"

The lips moved.

Mrs. Zulkifar began to whimper.

"What do we do?" whispered Khalia.

There was no movement on the dying face. Knaggs was in a region of pain that cut him off from the straining attention of the trapped party. They waited in utter silence. But they could all see the intelligence in the pain-darkened eyes.

He breathed two syllables. Then he was unconscious.

"Well?" Wardle snapped, unable to restrain himself. "What did he say, man?"

Danecki stood up. He looked away from the systems engineer. Khalia followed his look. He was staring at the wrecked green-bronze length of the guide-robot.

"Batty," Danecki said at last. "Mr. Knaggs said 'Batty.'"

CHAPTER

★ 7 ★

"But, damn it, the robot's ruined," wailed Wardle. "Wrecked! Dead!"

"Nevertheless," Dross told him, "it makes a convincing kind of sense. At least, Mr. Danecki convinces me. I take it that you propose to attempt to restore Batibasaga to some kind of functioning capacity, Mr. Danecki?"

"If I can," said Danecki.

Wardle touched the inert robot. "It looks a write off to me."

Dross regarded the green-bronze automaton, with its heat-blasted body. "Mr. Danecki is something of a systems engineer. He's reasonably conversant with models like Batibasaga, he's said. In any case, Batty isn't a truly sophisticated automaton. Not like some of the machines available at Center. When we were allocated a first class machine, we thought we'd get something up to date. But Batty's not far from being a museum-piece himself."

Danecki gestured to the inert frame. "I should have thought of it myself," he said. "As you say, Doctor, it makes a mad kind of logic. Only a superior robot will be able to tackle these robotic systems safely."

"Then you'll get us out?" Mrs. Zulkifar asked. She addressed Danecki directly.

"I'll do my best," he said. As he said it, he saw that Jacobi was conscious. He was glaring fixedly at Danecki, trying to compose his drawn features.

"I heard!" he snarled thinly. "But you won't escape!" He subsided with a groan.

Danecki disregarded him. When he did move it was toward the charred bulk of the robot.

Khalia willed him to hurry. The fort was stirring with life. There were odd whining noises from deep within the great, ancient complex. Once, a hollow thudding brought the party to instant attention, a noise of some vast engine grinding into renewed life. The sensor-pads before the big chair wavered about like blind rats, trying to find the hands of long-dead Confederation battle commanders. The huge blue screen pulsated with life.

Knaggs neither saw nor heard. His breathing was ragged. A trickle of blood came from his lips. Khalia wiped the gray thin lips from time to time. How long could he last? *Hurry!* she willed. And unbidden, *be careful!*

"I'll get through to your ship before I try anything else," Danecki said. "Look in Mr. Knaggs's pockets. He may be carrying tools."

There was nothing. Dross searched the raggedly-breathing engineer with trembling, skillful care, but Knaggs had nothing.

Danecki took the Jacobi youth's ceremonial dagger. Under his hands and the boy's twisted sneer, it became a tool. The gleaming cortex inside the robotic head soon appeared. "Undamaged!" he said, astonished.

"Thank goodness!" exclaimed Mrs. Zulkifar. "Do your duty, Doctor—you must try to get us out! Your engineer would have wanted that—it must be your first priority to care for your visitors!"

Khalia realized that the woman had condemned Knaggs to death in her own mind; she was speaking of him as though he had already given up the struggle for his life.

No one paid any attention to her.

"It bothers me," said Danecki. "Look."

Dross and Wardle watched the delicate, zittering mechanisms within the green-bronze carapace. Khalia looked too, though it meant little to her. In her life, women were not encouraged to become technicians. She saw a rippling pulsation of controlled power drifting silently across an intricate web of circuits. Force-fields glinted around the cortex in a protective skin. She knew that Danecki was badly worried.

"Get it working, man!" Wardle urged. "Send a message—they can have a rescue operation mounted within minutes! Have you all out before nightfall!"

"It's night outside now," Dross said. "Not that that

matters! We could have Mr. Knaggs tucked away within the hour! You're right, Brigadier!"

Danecki hesitated.

"What's troubling you, Danecki?" snapped Wardle.

"Come along!" Dross added. "There's no damage to the main motor areas. No impairment of the fuel cells—see, Batty can be used!"

"He can be used," agreed Danecki. "But I want you to listen to me first. All of you. You have to hear this before I put out a call for help." His eyes swept the anxious, hesitant, hopeful group. "I'm worried about the robot."

"Forget the robot!" Mrs. Zulkifar snarled. "Think of me—us!"

Khalia could see that Danecki was addressing himself chiefly to Dross.

"The robot's condition bothers me. You see, it wasn't put out of action by the fusor. There's extensive damage to the trunk—the limbs on one side burned off. But the heat-gun didn't penetrate the main shields."

"Good! Robust piece of equipment! Excellent!" began Wardle. He stopped. "The fusor didn't incapacitate it? Then what—"

"Yes," said Danecki. "The fort."

He let the words sink in. Mrs. Zulkifar was the only one to misunderstand completely. "You mean *you've* wrecked it!" she rasped.

"No," Dross said. "He doesn't mean that. If I understand Mr. Danecki correctly, he intends to warn us that the installation here has taken a hand in things. The fort itself has incapacitated Batibasaga."

"That's it," said Danecki.

Dross considered him, the green-bronze shape of the robot, and then the gray-faced engineer.

To Khalia, there was now an unendurable menace in the bright blue steel of the walls. The underground command area crawled with menace.

Dross shrugged his big, fat shoulders. He too looked strained and worried. "We know the possibilities, then," he said. "We've accepted what my engineer told us. We use the robot. But did Mr. Knaggs know that the robot was affected by the fort?"

"Damn it, we don't know that it has been," declared Wardle. "It's only a possibility!"

Mr. Moonman's words were quiet, scarcely audible. He spoke for everyone, however. "First the robot. Then us? Is that it?"

"So far the fort has ignored us," Danecki agreed. "I want you all to realize that we don't know how the major control systems will react once we begin to show our presence."

There was no answer.

Danecki's skillful hands soon found what they required. The five tense watchers held their breath. They had not long to wait.

After the long delays, the discussion, the hesitation, and the appalling, drawn out tensions set up by Knaggs's blood-bubbling words, they were all glad of Danecki's swift work.

He pointed to a coiled circuit in the robot's chest. "Use that, Doctor. Speak normally."

Dross's message was short and to the point. "Record and repeat this message! Dr. Dross and the tourist party have been trapped in a still-functioning underground fortification beneath the ruined base. Depth unknown, but guessed at two kilometers. One man needs immediate medical aid if he is to live! Alert all ships and repeater stations! Robotic systems record and repeat!"

He paused and the robot's voice called out in staccato tones from inside the chest cavity: "Your message received by Galactic Center cruise ship—"

Light and noise filled the blue-steel cavern in a burst of frantic power.

Dross bawled, "The fort!"

Danecki flicked the robot into quiescence, knowing that he was too late. Like the others, he turned to the source of the uproar.

The wide blue screen dissolved in a blinding flash of images. Danecki recognized at once the strange white-streaked openness of interplanetary space.

Sunlight streamed from Sol. Reflected light flashed across the huge screen from another source. The background of the Galaxy's mass of stars faded, so that he could make out what the screen was trying to show to a long-dead battle commander.

Then a tinny voice replaced the incoherent blast of sound. It settled into a calm, even tone. Danecki felt the hairs crawl on the back of his neck. At last, after a delay of a thousand years, the installation was fulfilling its function.

"Target extra-System vessel of unknown design! Stationary range five, one-zero-six, two-eight-nine, Sector Vega-Three X-2! Surface ports clear and missiles running! Two flights judged sufficient! One reserve! Instructions, Commander? Instructions?"

Sensor-pads waved violently. Controls flashed in a dazzling shower of colored lights. There was a strong feeling of total *awareness* in the command room now.

"What! What's happening?" gasped Khalia.

"The fort!" Wardle roared back ecstatically, unable to contain his incredulous delight. "It's attacking—it's attacking!" Then Wardle was staring aghast at the target.

"No!" screamed Mrs. Zulkifar. "No!"

"Good God!" was all Wardle could say, over and over again. "Good God!"

Danecki went toward the controls. With an almost inhuman effort, he stopped himself from taking the sensor-pads. Instead, he bawled at the screen with an impotent rage: "Abort all missiles! Abort—abort—abort! Target is a friendly ship—a Confederation ship! Abandon the attack!

He tore his hands away from the advancing sensor-pads, which would slip into his hands and allow the information to be punched into attack-computers. The pads were writhing with eagerness, desperately anxious themselves to respond to the impulses of his nervous system, as he —as a Confederation battle commander—ordered more and more missile flights against the supposed attacking fleet. He could do nothing. Nothing would save the ship.

Danecki thought of the surface far above with its small animals and insects. He thought of the great pits blossoming, throwing animals, and insects, as well as soil, trees, rocks, and outlying defensive bastions aside. And then the black missiles streaming out with a banshee snarl through the rain, through the gathering darkness and the dense low clouds—far, far out into interplanetary space, with gigantic thrusting energy, out and towards the waiting tourist vessel—the ship which had so unluckily answered his call for help and revealed its position to the vengeful ghosts in the ancient fort!

Wardle joined him as the screen showed the squat bulk of the hyperspace vessel. "Why doesn't it throw out screens—it could mop up any number of missiles!"

Danecki leapt for the green-bronze robot. At least he could try to warn the Center vessel what was about to happen. "Hyperspace cruiser!" he shouted. "Put out defensive screens—missiles running to you! You are under attack!"

"Won't the ship answer?" whispered Khalia, horrified. "Can't it get out of the way?"

They could all see the big vessel hanging like a black rock in the bright interplanetary haze. A cloud of asteroids nodded to it as they watched. Danecki called again, but there was no reply. Nothing came from the wrecked automaton.

The missiles spun into view.

"Nuclear rockets!" said Dross. "Simple expansion engines—explosive warheads. Maybe an ion-engine as booster. And we can't do a thing to stop them!"

"We can!" Khalia said suddenly. She ran towards the controls which sensed her coming and writhed eagerly towards her.

But Mrs. Zulkifar was quicker. She saw what Khalia intended and attacked her with a viciousness that sent her spinning to the floor. "You'll—kill—us all! All of—us!" the woman panted, searching for Khalia's throat. Then she was screaming and wrenching at Khalia in a desperate frenzy, foam dripping from her beautiful red lips.

Dross hit her once sharply across the neck. The woman collapsed in an untidy, long-legged heap.

Khalia was unable to keep her eyes from the screen. It took a minute or so for the tiny dart-like projectiles to snuff around the cruiser and decide that this was their target. They circled it, discarding booster rockets, and weaving small patterns in the sunlight.

The rockets homed in and the screen burst into one single outrushing surge of glory. For a few seconds there was a new sun in the dusty reaches of space high above Earth.

The calm, ordered voice from the control panel spoke. "Instructions, Commander!" it requested. "Ship completely destroyed. One flight of missiles returned to reserve." There was a wait of a few seconds, and then the request was repeated. "Instructions required from Duty Commander."

"Duty Commander?" Wardle said, this new term deflecting him from the shock of the vessel's end. "Eh? Duty Commander? Doesn't it know there isn't one?"

The others were too shocked to listen.

"They're all dead!" Khalia sobbed, breaking down. "We could have saved them—we're only a few! The ship was full!"

Dross tried to comfort her. "No, no! You tried, my dear. Don't blame yourself. And who can tell whether or not the other excursion boats had returned to the ship? They don't always—there's often a stopover at Moonbase. Yes, there is! And the Asteroids excursion too! First class hotels there—all automatic! It may be that there were no people aboard the ship!"

"Yes! Yes!" said Wardle eagerly. "Eh, Doctor? You saw them, didn't you, Mr. Moonman? Lots of people went on the Moonbase trip!"

Khalia felt her neck. The woman had been crazed with rage and terror. She pushed herself clear of Mrs. Zulkifar's unconscious body.

Danecki spoke to her. "You did what you could. None of us could, or would, do more."

"One thing's certain," said Wardle. "There'll be no help from the ship. We have to rely on ourselves now."

Again, the fort seemed to be developing a curiously menacing air. It was flooding with life. There were echoing, tinny voices down the long corridors radiating from the far end of the cavern. There was a rhythm of action in the previously dormant installation. A pattern of splintered light in the low roof began to edge into a repetitive and almost hypnotic slow cycle of movement.

And the calm, equable voice spoke again: "Instructions, please. Duty Commander! All systems activated. No instructions received!"

Khalia was ashamed to discover that she was losing interest in the death of the tourist ship. It mattered that she personally should survive.

In the echoing stillness of the low cavern there was, for a few moments, only the irregular raggedness of Knaggs's breathing. They all realized that there would be no help from outside.

Dross was listening, Danecki saw. Wardle too. But they were waiting for the voice of the machine, not for the next anguished bout of bubbled breathing from the obviously dying man.

"This call for a Duty Commander—" he said to the two men. "Doesn't the installation realize the passage of time? Why is it calling for a Duty Commander when the Confederation died a thousand years ago?"

"I wish I could answer," said Dross. "Ask me anything about the Second Interplanetary Confederation—its laws, ethics, extant culture, religions, psychology, passions, even its depravities—and I'll refer you to my standard works. I know them all. But Mr. Knaggs knew the robots. Why have they lasted for a thousand years? Why! That, Brigadier, we might guess!"

Wardle's eyes gleamed. His broad face creased into a wondering smile. "Waiting for instructions, eh, Doctor—waiting a thousand years for the right instructions!"

"And what instructions were those, Brigadier?"

Wardle was not smiling now. "They intended Armageddon," he said. "The complete destruction of all life on the three planets they once held."

As if in answer, the ancient robotic voice put in its request again: "No instructions, Duty Commander!"

Danecki looked down at the inert green-bronze robot. Khalia watched him. The grim-faced man had an uncanny fascination for her. She saw that he had checked the position of his enemy before he looked at the robot. Was this what a year's survival in the licensed jungle of hyperspace had done to him? She knew he had seen that Jacobi had moved towards the sliver of steel with which Danecki had opened the robot.

The boy was a hunter still. He was feigning unconsciousness, waiting for Danecki to cross to the space between Knaggs and the robot. Knaggs and the robot. And the sliver of steel. Khalia saw Danecki's indecision as he paused before the wrecked automaton. She began to gather herself to shriek a warning.

Knaggs sensed something. He had heard the calm, thousand-year-old robotic voice, or the roar of sound from the doomed tourist ship, or even Khalia's own plea for the people in it. Something had roused him for one last, agonized effort: "Get them out!"

The voice was clear enough and loud enough for them all to hear. But the words bubbled. The lips were almost white, and the words seemed forced through the grip of a vice.

"Going into a Phased Alert!" announced the mechanical voice from the control banks. "No instructions! Going into a Yellow Phase Alert!"

"—out!" cried Knaggs loudly.

Dross's whole figure shook with a reflection of Knaggs's spasmodic anguish. "Mr. Knaggs! Yes! If I can! But be quiet, man! Don't try to talk. Mr. Knaggs, if I could only express my—"

"—not long!" burst from Knaggs's lips. The blood flowed freely. "One system activates the others!" Then there was a bubbling noise within his throat, and his thin body writhed in an extremity of pain. Muffled words turned to screams.

Khalia tried to keep pace with the flow of blood. She had a pad of tissue that was a wet sponge by this time.

"We have to know," said Danecki, holding her hand back from Knaggs's mouth. He glanced at the Jacobi youth and kicked the steel away. The youth glared as Danecki took him by the waist and hauled him away from the dying man.

Knaggs's eyes opened wide.

The others saw they held the sudden clarity of vision and understanding that comes briefly before death. The mechanical voice said: "Yellow Phase Alert. This is a Yellow Phase Alert. Following General War Instructions, this installation is now on Full Battle Alert, Yellow Phase. It remains on Yellow Alert until further orders from the Duty Commander."

The voice drowned out what Knaggs was trying to say. Dross, Wardle, Khalia and Danecki were around him, listening for the thin echoes of words that were all that fell from Knaggs. Danecki moved closer still. He was staring straight into Khalia's eyes. She was sure that Danecki could not see her. The eyes were as blank as a hole in space. They were busy with the statistics of survival. She heard some of the dying message.

"Yellow Alert. . . maximum danger. Afterwards. . . Red. . . Red Alert," gasped the frail figure.

"Red Alert?" said Danecki. "Explain it if you can."

"Means. . . revenge. . . systems. . . a few hours."

Knaggs's eyes held them. The brilliance was ebbing. A thin film of darkness had begun to glaze the little engineer's eyes. The frail body arched upwards. Blood gushed in a red flood from his mouth. To the watchers it was like the last of daylight slipping away as the eyes emptied.

"He's dead," said Dross unbelievingly. "Dead!"

The screen returned to its state of blue emptiness.

CHAPTER
★ 8 ★

Dazed and stunned by the sharp clarity of the tourist vessel's end, Khalia found herself unable to accept the further shock of Knaggs's abrupt death. The little man had been so full of urgency one moment, so frighteningly at rest the next. The proximity of the pitiful corpse made the destruction of the hyperspace vessel almost trivial by comparison; it was only an unreal background to the cold certainty of the present.

She heard Wardle babble out a string of orders without being able to understand what he said; she saw Mr. Moonman tremble, his gaunt length shivering violently. Dross and Mrs. Zulkifar stared from the empty screen to the dead man, each as shocked as she herself. Only the Jacobi youth and Danecki retained a measure of self-possession. Danecki moved purposefully, while the youth's eyes followed him with a sullen promise of murder.

The metallic voice of the Weapons Control System stuttered out a brief message: "No survivors. No survivors. Ship completely destroyed!"

Like a refrain, the official voice of the Central Command System answered: "Duty Commander! This is Yellow Phase Alert!"

Danecki had seen too much of violent death and the colossal shock of ships vanishing into dust to let the awe of such moments of transition distract him. He knew that Knaggs was a man he could have liked in another, lost, life. Now, he was nothing.

While the others were totally absorbed in the silence of

the little man's death and the hideous clamor of the tourist ship's end, Danecki was planning. He noticed that the girl was grieving over Knaggs; that Jacobi watched him with the furious patience of the hunter; that Dross was lost in some world of private speculation; and that Brigadier Wardle was still breathing excitedly at the display of primitive martial might. But none of these reactions stirred him.

He was busy with the inert robot. Though Batibasaga had been put out of action, the robot still represented a considerable source of power. Its auxiliary systems—the offensive capabilities, the communicators, the memory-banks, and the analysis systems—were all at the disposal of the trapped group. They were the only resources they possessed. Such a robot could make a strong impression on the robotic fort itself. Danecki pondered the apparently-dead, green-bronze form.

Dross said to no one in particular: "Could it be?"

Wardle turned from the emptiness of the screen. "Could it be what, Doctor?"

"Could poor Mr. Knaggs have hinted at what we both know might be here, Brigadier?"

"The legend, Doctor?"

"Think of it!" said Dross with a subdued triumph in his voice. "Just think of it!"

They talked together in low tones.

Khalia covered the corpse with her coat. She sat beside it, still amazed by the suddenness of the death that had been inevitable. She saw the Jacobi youth move slightly.

As Jacobi moved, Danecki instinctively noticed the change in the distribution of background phenomena. He looked up and saw that the boy was trying to sit up. When he spoke, it was with a deadly quietness.

"Don't think you'll escape, Danecki," he said. "If I think you're making it, I'll make sure down here. Don't you see, I can't let you win! Not again."

"No one ever won," Danecki said in the same low voice. "I don't want to kill you. Don't make me. You have a name?"

Danecki saw the hate sliding from the boy's hot eyes. They had all been the same, the Jacobi clan. Implacable hunters, always implacable. Unreasoning, violent, ruthless. How could you explain to them that you were a peaceful man who had accidentally unleashed furious energies against their clansmen?

"Jacobi," the youth said. "Like the others—Jacobi."

Dross had arranged his dead friend's hands so that the corpse had an unnatural tidiness that was at odds with the figure Knaggs had presented in life.

He heard the exchange between Danecki and the youth. When he spoke, it was with an intensity of feeling that matched Jacobi's: "I will not have this talk, boy! Your feud must stop. If I have my way, you will not be able to continue in your murderous course! If you speak more of this obscenity, I'll have you gagged!" To Danecki he said: "There will be no more killing!"

The two women listened with fascinated attention. Mrs. Zulkifar's eyes darted about red-rimmed sockets in frank eagerness; Khalia could not take her gaze from Danecki's tired face. She found the eyes haunted. Green-flecked, but tired, almost hopeless eyes.

Brigadier Wardle swallowed and spoke out: "Can't do more for Mr. Knaggs!" he said briskly. "Our first casualty. It's war now, Doctor! War! That ship destroyed. Now Mr. Knaggs! This place is waking up—we've got to make plans. Action, eh? Can't sit around talking. We don't know how long we've got. Nor how long it will take for a rescue party to reach us. If there's going to be one!" A thought struck him. "Eh, Doctor? What about your regular supply ship from Center? Isn't that due?"

"Too late," said Dross. "It might even miss me altogether on this trip. The last time it came, I told them to leave me alone for a while. No, Brigadier, as I've already said, I believe we're thrust back on our own resources. The installation is indeed coming to life!"

Wardle paced about the blue-steel cavern. "We'll have to find a way out. At once! We can fan out—take a sector each and report back in half an hour. Eh, Doctor?"

"Yes!" Mrs. Zulkifar said, just as eagerly. "If this Ancient Monument isn't controlled by sensible robots, perhaps we could find a way to the surface?"

Dross waited for Danecki.

"No," said Danecki, shaking his head. "Mr. Knaggs will have died for nothing if we don't accept what he said. So long as we stay here, we're relatively safe. Haven't you noticed that the Control Systems haven't addressed us directly? They call for a Duty Commander that we know has been dead for centuries. They don't talk to us."

"Of course," Wardle said. "Should have thought of it. Expect you're right."

"I agree too," said Dross. "Had the fort known us to

be intruders, we'd have been dealt with long before this. We abide by your decision, Mr. Danecki. I take it you'll use the robot?"

"It's all so confusing," Mrs. Zulkifar said plaintively.

Wardle still retained some of his admiration for the handsome woman. "You're not at your best—ah—Emma! Try to worry less. That is, forget it. I mean, calm yourself." He turned to Danecki. "We'll leave it to Mr. Danecki, eh?"

Danecki slowly stripped the outer plates off the wrecked automaton. The fuel-cell winked jewel-like in the central core. Trails of circuits could be seen pumping oily power in a slow, smooth stream. Danecki carefully pushed membranous memory-cells aside. He was searching for spare coils of directional matter.

"Can I help?" asked Dross.

"I want cell-growth membranes," said Danecki. "I could feed instructions through to the main memory circuits, if I could find some spare material."

"Well?" queried the Brigadier.

"There isn't any."

"Well, man, can't you do *anything?*"

Danecki forced himself to understand the Brigadier's inner turmoil. He tried not to show the instant rage in his face. "I'll try," he said. "It can be done by hand. But it takes time."

Khalia watched Danecki begin the tedious process of separating the infinitely thin tissues that made up the robot's memory, deductive processes, and code of conduct.

They had all put themselves in those broad, capable hands.

Wardle was still uneasy about relying on Danecki. It was not so much what he said—Wardle had discussed the disappearance of the spin-shaft with Dross—as the glances Danecki sent over towards him.

"What baffles me," said Wardle, "is how we came to be allowed into the spin-shaft at all. You'd think there'd be some security apparatus to exclude unauthorized entrants." He stared at Danecki briefly. "Eh, Doctor?"

Danecki spoke quietly, without taking his eyes off the membranous tissues: "Security procedures could have been destroyed when the fusor melted down the controls of the spin-shaft."

"So they could! So they could! Well, Doctor?"

Dross shrugged. "What does it matter? Clearly we're accepted as legitimate entrants. What led to that is irrelevant. What I'd like to give some thought to is the central mystery of this fortification!"

Wardle caught Danecki's eye for a moment. "Ah, yes! Yes, Doctor! But will we have the opportunity of exploring the other levels? Well?"

"We leave it to the robot," said Dross firmly.

Time dragged on.

Danecki paused from time to time to wipe his eyes. He felt the lids begin to droop and knew that he should have rest and food. He turned back to the gutted robot.

Khalia's shout startled him into dropping the thin folds of tissue. "Look! The screen!"

The blue screen had sprung into life and shown the ruin on the surface above. The monitors focused on black rain and the last of the slow-dying light from a hidden sun. Blistered metal and gaunt skeletal frameworks were bleakly outlined.

"What! What is it?" Wardle had her arm. "What did you see?"

"There was someone in the ruins!" she said. "A man! I'm sure!"

Danecki stared at the screen with the others. He saw the wildness of the darkening sky, the towering clouds, and the ancient jumble of a long-gone war. The only movement was the bending of branches and the surge of water under the wind's fierce lash.

"Are you sure?" said Wardle.

"Yes!" she insisted.

Wardle's face expressed disbelief.

"You said I didn't see two ships," she reminded him.

"So I did."

Mr. Moonman's dull voice put the question in all their minds: "Why should the fort want to show us this?"

They waited for the metallic, calm voice to speak. But nothing came. There had been a brief image of the titanic ruins above, and nothing else.

"If there was someone up there, this installation is satisfied he represents no threat," Danecki said. "Who could it be?"

Dross spoke. "Mr. Knaggs had dealings with one or two of the Outlanders. They come to talk occasionally. Not with me." Dross was demolishing the hopes that the others began to show. "I'm afraid they wouldn't be able to help us. There aren't many of them. A few settlers who came in over the past forty or fifty years looking for a quiet life. I suppose they could have asked Center for room on one of the unsettled star systems, but they preferred to come here. They're cut off from all advanced technology. No transport other than their own legs. No communicators. I don't know how they live. I've never spoken to any of them."

"We can't look for help from them," Wardle said. "Curious, though, that the fort should be interested!"

"I think soon it will begin to ask itself questions," said Dross.

Wardle stalked the blue-steel cavern impatiently. "We're taking too much time!" He stopped to look at the robot. "Having trouble, eh, Danecki? What is it you're trying to do?"

Danecki found the Brigadier's brisk impatience trying. He spoke with a chilled politeness: "When the fort does get around to realizing we're here, we'll need whatever help we can get. The robot is our only resource. I'm programming it to act independently."

"Independently? How?"

"Search, communicate, act. As many contingency plans as I can fit into its banks." Danecki wondered whether to tell the others precisely what he had fed into the internal workings of Batibasaga. He decided they should know. "If your robot can't get to us, Doctor," he said, turning to the big-bellied archaeologist, "it will have to act independently. We have to rely on its code of ethics."

"Ethics!" exclaimed Mrs. Zulkifar. "What have they got to do with it! How can they help us?"

Khalia began to question the Jacobi youth's case at that moment. Killers didn't discuss ethics.

"I'm interested, Mr. Danecki," said Dross.

"I'm instructing your robot to act in what I think is an honest way." Danecki cleared his mind and took the glittering coils of membranes in his hands. The work had to be done manually. A score of tiny circuits must be hooked together to attain some degree of reliability. No one spoke as his fingers moved.

"Yellow Phase Alert," the robotic voice reminded the trapped party. "This is a Yellow Phase Alert."

Mrs. Zulkifar rapped out: "You've taken twenty minutes already! More! We might have found a way out by now!"

"The longer we take, the more chance there is of the systems knowing we're illegal visitors," Wardle added uneasily. "I'm for exploring now. What can the robot do? It's immobilized! Doctor—we're wasting valuable time!"

Dross loomed over Wardle and Mrs. Zulkifar. His imposing bulk posed a physical threat, while his stone-faced gaze at Mrs. Zulkifar brought the distraught woman to whimperings of fear. In her distress she began to cram a block of chocolate into her mouth.

She noticed the hungry look on Wardle's face. "I'm hungry!" she got out, her mouth half full. "I always eat at this time. My stomach won't stand it if I don't have something. How far would one block go amongst all of you? I needed it! I'll be ill—sick—I'll die here!"

Khalia heard her in an agony of embarrassment.

Danecki cursed quietly and began a rethreading of the minute patterns of membranes.

"Yellow Alert," the metallic voice said. It was an irregular croak of doom.

Knaggs's corpse slowly stiffened.

"Won't those people on the surface do something?" asked Mrs. Zulkifar, breaking a long silence.

"The Outlanders?" Dross said quietly.

"Yes! Why couldn't they have picked up our message? How do you know they haven't got communicators?"

Wardle nodded his agreement.

"I don't think you understand," Dross said in an attempt to calm the frightened woman.

The others listened, moving a little closer to the archaeologist. Only Danecki closed his mind to the frightened questioning that had been going on for the past half hour.

"The only people who live on this planet have come here by chance," Dross continued. "People who have drifted around until their ships gave out. They don't *want* involvement with any part of the Galactic Union. They hide when my ship comes—they talked to Knaggs only because he's their kind. Don't raise your hopes falsely, please!"

Khalia thought of the excursion ships. She hesitated to risk ruining Danecki's concentration, but when she saw that he could work with a total intentness during Wardle's and Mrs. Zulkifar's interjections, she decided to speak. "Wouldn't there be a hope of someone on the other excursions coming to our help?"

"I wish I could say there was," said Dross. "I really do, my dear. But no. You agree, Brigadier?"

"No hope at all," said Wardle. "The scanners on the excursion ships would have picked up the ship's explosion. And they'd have backtracked to check on heat-transmissions before the loss. They'd know there was a weapons system in use, and they'd lie low in the asteroids, or at one of the moonbases, until an investigating ship arrived. They'd take no chances. That's how I read the situation."

Mr. Moonman stared at Danecki. "What sort of a chance are we taking here?"

For the third time Danecki ripped aside the circuits he had set up. He was familiar with the combination of tissues and impulse-generators that made up the robot's deductive and planning systems. What was lacking was any help at all from the automaton itself. Normally a machine of this kind would be able to take him through a stage-by-stage account of the procedures necessary to get it working again. Batibasaga seemed mentally paralyzed.

Danecki wondered if the shock of the strange spatial convolutions in the ancient shaft had unbalanced it. Was it the effects of orbital spin that had disturbed the metabolism of the robot? Or was the fort's control system putting out a subtle form of inhibitor?

He disregarded the tense group watching him. Jacobi was safely near the bulky figure of Dross. And Dross was keeping the others more or less in check. So far there had been no panicky run for the inviting control-pads, no impulsive attempts to leave the big control room itself.

Once he looked up and caught Khalia's eye. He wondered if it was the reinforced dangers of the fort that brought the immediate shock of sexual awareness: the girl —she was no more than that—had a moist, wide-eyed look.

Almost unbidden the circuits found their proper path.

CHAPTER

★ 9 ★

"Yellow Alert. Duty Commander. Yellow Alert!"

It was almost a looked-for interruption in the silence. The command area itself was part of a familiar scene. How long, thought Khalia, did it take for an ordinary woman to accept the presence of death and the prospect of personal extinction as *normal*?

"An hour!" squealed Mrs. Zulkifar. "One hour!"

"Yellow Phase Alert! We are in Yellow Alert. Duty Commander. Yellow Alert!"

"That's all I can do," said Danecki. "I've programmed your robot to use its knowledge of the Confederation. It's ready to argue for our lives or to try to find a way out."

"But it doesn't *work* in here!" wailed Mrs. Zulkifar.

"No," Danecki said. "We'll drag it along with us. That gives us two chances. If we fail, the robot might be able to act independently."

"We can't move that!" exclaimed Dross.

The inert robot, despite the loss of almost one side of its trunk and attendant limbs, bulked hugely in the brightly-lit cavern. The watchers began to note the metallic mass of the head-piece, the squat width of the trunk, the heavy remaining leg with its splashes of molten metal.

Jacobi laughed aloud as Danecki replaced the plates in its back. "It won't do you any good, Danecki!"

Dross glared at him, but the youth went on laughing through his agony. "One touch on this," he said, gesturing with his good arm to the Control Systems, "and it's over for you."

"And you too," pointed out Dross. "You care nothing for your own life?"

"Not much. Not now."

In answer, Dross grabbed the youth's collar and hauled him carefully to his feet.

"You come with us," he said. "Mr. Danecki, I'll see that he's kept under restraint. What do you advise now?"

The choice had been limited. It was very evident that three wide corridors which ran in curves outward and downward from the control room were alive with auxiliary systems. During the time it had taken for Danecki to program the robot, they had begun to hum with life. What had been an almost dead and lost world was germinating. Of the remaining exits from the wide cavern, with its dominating blue screen, two were closed off by dense black shields.

Dross had put forward the theory that these were the customary means of entrance and exit to the underground fort. Wardle was fairly sure that, as the fort believed itself to be at total war, the two openings were some form of blast bulkhead between the main offensive batteries and the control sections of the fort. In either case, as Dross pointed out, they could be of no concern to them. The only practical and seemingly-safe path was by means of a minor tunnel sloping sharply downwards in a gentle curve that concealed its eventual destination.

It was towards this tunnel that they hauled the heavy, still mass of the robot. All helped. Mrs. Zulkifar panted with the exertion, finding a channel for her energetic terror in pushing against the automaton's shoulder. Mr. Moonman grunted savagely, but it was Dross and Danecki who provided the main strength. Wardle had soon relaxed his efforts, purple-faced and groaning. The Jacobi youth lay jammed against the big black armchair.

As Khalia pushed next to the intent Mrs. Zulkifar, heaving with all the strength of her young muscles, she found herself curiously unafraid. The waiting had been the worst. Now she could examine the thought of death, whereas before she had only thought of that colossal sunburst that had flowered from the screen when the tourist ship disappeared. She had seen herself dissolving into spinning, still-screaming dust, boiling and whirling into a billion splintering fragments that still possessed something of her personality, that still felt shock and pain and the eerie certainty of death.

That had passed. It was the waste that appalled her now. Twenty-two years, she thought. At twenty-two, the step into nothingness.

Danecki heaved. One huge thrust took the robot clumsily down the incline. He caught Khalia as she stumbled. No one wanted to be the first to move from the safety of the command area. They waited as the robot came to rest a short way down the smooth slope.

Would the robot stir into life?

Still they waited.

"It isn't moving!" Mrs. Zulkifar complained. She shook Wardle by the arm. "All that time wasted—we might have found a way out! Why did we trust this man? Why, Brigadier? Why!"

"Well?" said Wardle to Danecki.

Danecki shrugged. "It was a chance we had to take. If we'd rushed blindly out, more than likely—"

He stopped. They all saw the reason.

A great, glittering grab had swung noiselessly from the roof of the corridor. It reached delicately for the green-bronze robot. It came down quickly, selected its quarry—a shining hook of metal, as solid and remorseless as some single-minded primeval claw. Then the hulk of Batibasaga was lifted and drawn into the opening through which the hook had appeared.

It took two seconds.

Metallic voices reported flatly. "Duty Commander! Unidentified automaton removed for inspection! Appears defunct. Orders? Orders?"

"Gone!" squealed Mrs. Zulkifar. "Gone! The robot isn't going to help us! It's gone, do you hear? Gone!"

She set up a high-pitched yelling that bounced down into the corridor which still rang with the grating metallic voices of the fort's security systems. Then Mrs. Zulkifar began to abuse Danecki with a sustained virulent obscenity.

Danecki was aware of a growing sense of personal responsibility for the little group of refugees. It seemed to him, now that they were back in the dazed fear of the first moments when the spin-shaft had deposited them in the fort, that they were all inextricably intermingled with his own consciousness. They were almost an extension of his own way of life. The shriek of a woman—the eerie figure of the Revived Man—pathetic Jacobi nursing his outraged hatred and pain—Wardle who had once been a man of action—Dross, a man between ecstasy and terror—and, of course, the girl. Somehow they were now all a part of the past year's frightful pattern of despair and hope. It was as though he had grown outwards to include them. Their shrill screams, the growled accusations, the pleas which they shouted and whispered, all were peculiarly *from* him as well as directed at him.

He listened to the bitter denunciations and held back the immediate contemptuous retort. They were all people who could not face the grim oppressiveness of the situation in the fort. He could. It was now a familiar and almost easy thing to work out a path in the patterns of danger.

Then he saw that the girl was not shouting. She had remained tense but had not panicked; she was afraid but she could wait and watch. She waited for him to move, but she would weigh what he said before committing herself. It struck him that Khalia might be enjoying the danger.

"We have to move out now, don't we?" she said in a moment of quiet. "Don't we, Danecki?"

Mr. Moonman heard her, but Wardle and Dross were still arguing about the fort's security systems. Mrs. Zulkifar was on the floor, pounding it with the rings on her long, elegant hands and making little scraping noises from the back of her throat. Jacobi was enough of a boy to be shocked by her behavior, but his eyes never once left Danecki.

"Oh, yes," said Danecki. "Now, we have no choice."

Wardle blustered on angrily: "What choice had we before you wasted all that time? We could have reconnoitered the entire installation by now—sent out patrols in three directions—reported back and organized some plan! Danecki, you've wasted a whole hour!"

The metallic voices cut in, setting up a refrain in the corridor down which Batibasaga had disappeared: "Orders, Duty Commander! Failing orders, humanoid automaton has been secured for interrogation! Duty Commander, Central Security System awaits orders!"

The noise calmed the little group. It had the effect of a sudden furious burst of thunder in a quiet night, stunning the hearers and cutting off all conversation and complaints.

Danecki spoke rapidly. "This isn't what I hoped for, but it had to be expected. Batibasaga in custody—the security systems will hold him. Turn him over to the workshops, possibly."

Mrs. Zulkifar stopped cursing and scrabbling at the floor.

"I see," said Dross. He spoke to the little group. "It isn't entirely hopeless," he went on. "Mr. Danecki has made what use he could of our only resource. Batibasaga. We can't blame him—we left the decision in his hands. So far, we've lost an hour."

"And the fort's alive!" Wardle exclaimed. "Did you hear that, Doctor? Central Security System! That's a major control unit, sir! Always the worst! Installations like this will be full of snoopers! We won't be able to go an inch without being reported! We're stuck here now!"

Mrs. Zulkifar, Khalia noticed, was listening with a frenzied intentness. "Calm down, Brigadier!" Dross ordered. "I've said it isn't hopeless! Consider the advantages! Mr. Danecki knows them. Listen!"

"It's the robot," said Danecki. "I think it's inhibited by the effects of the molecular interference of the spin-shaft. If it can throw them off, it might be able to divert some of the auxiliary systems. Not the major systems, perhaps, but possibly those that control the exits. Maybe the spin-shaft."

Dross added: "Batibasaga could do it! Remember that even though he's not the most modern of automatons, he's entirely different from the robots of the Confederation period! He's not the same thing at all! Even half-ruined as he is, Batty possesses hugely superior powers of intuition and judgment. This fortification is full of robots—aggressive, powerful machines, no doubt—but they're old! Ancient! They're just *logical* machines. They reason simply, like murderous children!"

"Murderous?" whispered Mrs. Zulkifar.

Khalia tensed. Was the woman going to attack someone again?

"But he's in enemy hands, Doctor!" Wardle exclaimed. "How can we know what it's up to?"

"Enemy?" Mrs. Zulkifar said, rising to her feet. "Murder? Me?"

She howled. Then she ran. As she ran, she screamed: "I'm getting out!"

Her intention registered on Danecki's mind, but what she proposed to do was such a blind, senseless thing that he could do no more than shout: "Stop!"

He saw the distraught woman, with her fine head and splendid body, rush toward the middle of the three wide corridors. "Stop her!" Danecki yelled, but he was a dozen strides away.

Wardle could have made a grab, but he too was utterly

bewildered by her mad action. Dross managed to heave himself forward a pace, but that was all.

By the time Danecki was in motion, the woman was out of range. He impelled himself toward her despairingly. Jacobi put out a foot, and Danecki pitched headlong against Wardle.

Khalia had to move around the bulk of Dross, but Mrs. Zulkifar was already racing as if pursued by devils.

Before she put a foot outside the safe confines of the low central command area, a shriek of electronic chatter burst out: "Emergency! Emergency! Intruder reported! Unauthorized human reported by Security!"

It was followed by the voice of Central Command. They were the words they had all been dreading. "Red Alert! Red Alert! This is a six-hour Red Phase Alert!"

Wardle had dropped to the floor in an attempt to avoid the effects of the fort's destruction. Jacobi freed himself and scrambled after Danecki, paces behind Khalia. Mr. Moonman was on the floor, staring fixedly at the mud-stained robotic head which Knaggs had discovered that morning, and which had molded itself into Danecki's hand when the other Jacobi youth stood over him.

Mrs. Zulkifar rebounded from an invisible barrier. "I'm going out! I am! I am! I'm not staying down here amongst criminals and riffraff!"

Danecki ignored her.

Khalia found herself being hauled along with a brutal strength. She pulled back, but Danecki insisted. "Come on! It doesn't matter now—the fort knows we're here!"

"Red Alert!" stammered the electronic voice. "Red Alert."

Danecki and Khalia surged towards the narrow corridor at the far end of the Central Command area, the winding corridor down which they had attempted to push Batibasaga.

"This is a six-hour Red Phase Alert," said the voice of Central Command. "Countdown begun."

"Follow!" Danecki called over his shoulder.

Metallic voices screamed and whistled from concealed channels. The whole fort rang with the harsh outbursts of alerted security systems.

Khalia had an impression of Mrs. Zulkifar sliding against a thin wall of black haze as Danecki pulled her onward; she saw that Wardle was following them, and that the Jacobi youth was trying to get to his feet too.

The confusion of the noise, and the speed of Danecki's rush had not completely disoriented her. She understood the importance of the fort's harsh stammerings. *Six hours!*

"Keep going!" snarled Danecki as she stumbled into the corridor. "We might get past the security net!"

"Why not one of the other ways?" squealed Mrs. Zulkifar.

"Didn't you see the barrier?" snapped Danecki.

"Wouldn't it be safer—staying—back—there?" she panted.

"No! Nowhere's safe! Save your breath! I'm trying to find the robot!"

The corridor wound downward in a narrow tube of subtle planes and varying degrees of light and semi-darkness. What was it, Danecki wondered, as they slithered from smooth sides to sudden abrupt corners. A maintenance shaft? An escape route in case of siege?

The fort kept them in touch with the progress of the hunt for the other survivors. "Two—three—four humans identified!" roared a sullen voice all round them. "Apprehend, search, find! Report! Intruders—apprehend! Security to apprehend and remove to Security Wing!" called Central Command. "This is Red Phase Alert! Five humans identified!"

"Six hours!" snarled Danecki back at the voices. "Six hours before the machines abort!"

A scream behind them in the corridor told them that someone had fallen and was hurt.

"Jacobi," said Danecki. He was momentarily pleased, not so much for himself as for the girl's sake. The more the fort could be confused by capturing the long-delayed visitors, the greater were the chances of his finding Batibasaga. So long as they could remain free, there was a chance of success.

"Central Security System reporting," cut in a harsh voice. "Have apprehended a female, mixed heritage, no identifiable characteristics known to this System. Instructions?"

"Place in Security Wing!" came back the order.

A weapon system asked for directions. It offered ranges, frequencies, attack formulas, and procedures to blast ships that had been rust and dust for a thousand years.

"Red Alert!" called Central Control. "Intruders, Duty Commander! Instructions?"

Six hours! Less! Danecki had no need to urge the girl

on. Down they went, slithering and sliding, bruising bones and jarring flesh.

Then they came to the place of bones.

"No!" screamed the girl. "No!"

The corridor had leveled and widened at this point. The light was weak, but strong enough to reveal the three skeletons in every detail.

They both stopped. The girl caught Danecki's arm, and he was grateful for the comfort. The sight of the long-dead human beings in this functional and ancient piece of machinery was utterly shocking; a find so totally unexpected that it had the effect of stunning both of them.

They saw the jumbled heap where two corpses had fallen.

Khalia recognized the bright, long hair of a woman about one of the skulls. She moved towards it, horrified but full of pity for the woman who had died down there.

Danecki examined the third skeleton beyond the heap of bones. Obviously one man had fallen alone. A knife had killed him. The golden handle still held firmly to the ribcage, jammed hard against it. The point was in the center of the clean, white ribcage. Great force had thrust it there, for a rib had been broken aside.

In three or four seconds he had summed up the cause and outcome of the terrible encounter. He revised all his estimates of the fort's capacities and strategies in those seconds. "It's vulnerable," he said.

Khalia didn't hear. "They came in here," she said bleakly.

"Yes," said Danecki. "We have to find out how."

How *had* three people entered this most closely-guarded sanctuary of the Confederation? How had the machines been overcome? And why was the pitiful human refuse still allowed to remain in the winding tunnel?

Almost as an afterthought, Danecki stirred with his foot the simple blaster lying a yard from the solitary skeleton. It was a museum-piece. A thing at one with this echoing, eerie installation. It appeared to be charged, but he couldn't bring himself to touch it.

Not until he took the girl's hand would she continue the descent of the tunnel. The sight of the antique bones in their unlikely mausoleum had shattered her.

When they rounded the next subtle curve, they found what the tunnel led to.

There was no more harsh electronic clamor from the various systems. Instead, there was a cold, eternal silence. It was appropriate. The light was muted too, but there was enough to show the immensity of the Confederation's power.

Stretching into the distance was a dim, gray cavern, a vast space full of the supreme accomplishment of the long-gone Confederation.

"It's true!" Khalia gasped in awe. "The legend."

"Yes," said Danecki, remembering the robotic guide's account of the history of the ruined fort above. "It is true."

Before them lay the Black Army.

CHAPTER
★ 10 ★

The cavern held a monstrous army of gaunt silent figures—row on row of black robotic monsters. Their cone-shaped head-pieces glowed with an age-old power source; antennae stirred with a dull intelligence as Khalia's whispered voice disturbed the cold air of the eerie parade ground. And, for all their ancient and obsolete appearance, they produced in Danecki, as well as in Khalia, a sensation of unutterably powerful menace. They looked as though they could march halfway across the universe to blot out the enemies of the Confederation. They were things from nightmare, blocks of black iron, and serried rows of phalanxes—designed to come to life only when their human designers and masters were dead.

"Still functioning," Khalia whispered. "They know we're here!" A thought struck her. "Did *they* kill those—those people back there?" She pointed to the corridor.

Danecki shook his head. "These beasts have never fought. Wardle and Dross were right. They are the Lost Army that failed to fight. But they will march!"

Danecki's mind raced: *The six-hour alert! Yes! The legend—it said they would march! They must be the Regiments of Night! What will they do?*

Already he was busy calculating the possibilities of the situation. There remained a few hours in which to master the fort's control systems—one or more of them. A few hours in which they could try to halt the installation's ponderous machinery as it ticked away the minutes and seconds of their lives. And the security systems might find them at any moment!

What can we do?" whispered Khalia. She was stunned

by the awful impact of the monolithic figures. She had the sense of a huge and elemental force quivering with stored-up impatience, waiting for release and the final dissolution of both itself and the rest of the human race.

"Look around—find what we can!" answered Danecki. "We must be in an off-limits area, but it's my guess that the security nets don't function effectively down here! They may have been put out of action by those." He pointed to the corridor where the pitiful ancient bones lay stark and white. "We must try to find a clue to the installation's functioning—how it reasons, why it's ignored us so far! Look around! Don't go too near the robots, though."

"I won't!" Khalia shivered as long, whip-like antennae oscillated to the tones of Danecki's voice. It was like talking in the presence of the newly-dead—hushed, frightened tones that might stir the dead into unwanted activity. After a thousand years, the Regiments might emerge from their sleep!

Danecki stepped from the narrow corridor and into the cavern.

Heat-sensitive lighting units flooded the arena with a bright whiteness. The robotic ranks had the backs of their huge carapaces to him. Suddenly, noise beat around them. Khalia gasped and clutched Danecki. Her eyes were wide with tension, and her face was startlingly pale in the bright coldness.

"Red Phase Alert! Duty Commander to advise on Red Phase Alert! No further reports on surface activity in the destructed installation above! Negative reports continue on destruction of hyperspace vessel!"

"Quick!" said Danecki. "The fort's beginning to assert itself down here now!"

"Three suspects apprehended by Security! Advise please." One female, two males in custody! No recognition patterns in imprints taken so far! Duty Commander?"

"Mrs. Zulkifar. And two of the men," said Khalia. "What will it do with them?"

Danecki shrugged. "We can't help them."

"You don't want to! You've decided this is just another escape from personal extinction—you're just a man on the run again!" Khalia was amazed at the passion in her own voice.

He isn't, she told herself. *He isn't that at all!*

"All right," said Danecki. "Forget I said that. I'll do what I can." He felt her trembling in his grasp. He found the sensation peculiarly maddening. She was too young to die here in this gray prison, too beautiful to be another ruined life in the long-dead fort.

"I thought your only responsibility was to yourself!"

"No," said Danecki, knowing it to be true and glad of it. He realized that he had been accepting the inevitability of the others' death the moment Mrs. Zulkifar had leapt for the Central Corridor. If they had been quick enough, they might have had a chance. Catching the girl and hauling her after the robot had been an automatic reaction which didn't bear analysis. "We've been lucky so far. I don't think our luck's going to continue. We can help them by staying free as long as we can—and by finding out what we can. Come on!"

Khalia followed. She watched Danecki's wide shoulders and wondered how he had survived the year of torment. He was a man driven by furies not of his own making; though he was governed by expediency, he was not callous. He did what he had to do.

Danecki led the way past the groves of robots, along the side of the cavern. The sheer weight of numbers was oppressing. The faintly-quivering antennae picked up their careful movements. Row on row, neatly set out in blocks of a hundred, each robot exactly like its neighbors, they waited with a monumental patience for a lost war. There was no dust, no sign of aging, nor of time passing. The light flooded on dull black metal as it had a thousand years before when some tight-lipped commander had last inspected the Army that would march only when the Confederation died. It might have been yesterday. Khalia shuddered.

The robots could march at a moment's notice.

And if they did!

Six hours, the voice of Central Command had promised. Six hours before the dull-black phalanxes moved out into the blackness of night to carry out their age-old mission of revenge.

"They'll march!" whispered Khalia. "They *will!* And we can't stop them! What will they do?"

"What the Brigadier said," Danecki told her. "These machines are hunters."

"But the Outlanders! Surely they won't—"

"Yes," said Danecki. "They will. The years will make no difference. The fort doesn't seem to recognize the passage of years, nor the end of the Confederation."

Khalia had a sudden vision of the monsters rooting in

the forests for the few men and women who lived on the planet. "We can't let them!"

"No," said Danecki. "Over here. See!"

It was a small recess rather than a room. Raised a few feet above the echoing cavern, approached by means of three high steps, it was clearly some sort of reviewing platform. Inside, when Danecki had helped Khalia into its somehow-safe interior, they looked out at the Army.

"There have to be controls," Danecki said.

He examined the walls of the recess. They were of the same bright metal as the rest of the cavern. Cold to the touch, without a seam or a sign of a joint, it left the fingers tingling slightly.

"What can we do?" asked Khalia hopelessly. "If there were controls, wouldn't the fort blow itself up if we touched them?"

"The Army would march first," Danecki said. It was what the fort had been made for. It was not a sanctuary at all, but a weapon of revenge. "It will be programmed to march out. Then, when there's no more need for this installation, it will abort itself. Dross is right. This fort isn't designed to keep a small remnant of the Confederation alive—the surface installation is designed for that."

Khalia shivered. "It will be dark now. Up there."

She thought of Wardle's enthusiastic lecture on time. "There'll be a moon," the Brigadier had said. "I wish I could see the sky and hear the rain. This place reeks of death."

Danecki stared at the far end of the great cavern. The girl was against him again. He caught the deeply exciting smell of her fear. He tried to ignore it.

"There has to be an opening," he said. The fatigue of the long hours in hyperspace, the sheer bodily exhaustion of the hunt through the forest, and the mental exertions of programming Batibasaga had left their mark. He shrugged off the deadly lassitude. The girl's presence made it easier; there was a certain amount of grim pleasure in trying to work out what to do. "There has to be a way in!"

"Those?" the girl said, pointing to the corridor where the skeletons lay.

"Yes. They couldn't have come down the spin-shaft. Not unless they were imprinted on the personnel selectors. They couldn't have been Confederation staff! And yet they reached this lowest level of all!"

"They have to have a way out," said Khalia. She gestured to the robots. "A route to the surface."

Danecki grinned. "I wouldn't want to be on the surface when their exit is blasted through!"

Metallic voices rumbled briefly.

"Did you hear?" said Khalia.

"Yes. Two more caught. That leaves us. Curse the Doctor's robot!" Danecki exclaimed. "I relied on it—Knaggs was right! I'm sure of it! But why doesn't it try to take control!"

He thought with fury of the chore of selecting its delicate circuits, of the hour-long fumblings amongst the membranous strands.

Again the metallic voices snorted and rumbled in the distance. Weapons systems chanted off ranges. A maintenance unit called for assistance. Central Command ordered the removal of the newly-caught captives to the Security Wing.

Khalia caught herself staring into the bulbous sight-orifices of a row of black monsters. They seemed to acknowledge her presence with a peculiarly repellent awareness. She imagined the faces, with their rocklike immobility, watching her struggle. "They're horrible," she whispered. "Horrible!"

Danecki amazed himself by putting an arm around her. It was so natural a gesture that he questioned it only when it was completed. His mind rang with conjectures still. Why had the underground cavern and its systems allowed their entry? Why were the skeletons permitted to remain in the corridor, when no other sign of human occupancy remained? How was it that the three humans had penetrated the recesses of the fort? At the same time he could handle Khalia's fears.

"They're machines," he said. "Nothing more. Men made them. If we can find their controls, we can make them harmless."

"Not *them!* They're beyond control! They're waiting for us to go down there—they are! I saw a hundred of them staring this way! I did! I *did!*" The girl was near hysteria. She clutched his arm with an ecstasy of desperation.

"No," said Danecki. "Metal. Plastics. Circuits. That's all."

"I don't want to die down here! Not here—I know it's selfish and I know Mr. Knaggs died, but I don't think any of us will get out! I couldn't die down here!"

More to himself than the girl, Danecki said: "It's a difficult thing to live with."

"What?"

"The fear of death."

"You don't care—you're only thinking of yourself! You've lived with it for so long that you don't care any more! You'll wait and do nothing!"

"No!"

Danecki's abrupt denial stopped Khalia's hysteria. "I didn't mean that I thought you didn't care about anyone but yourself," she said haltingly.

"That went long ago," Danecki said. "I care."

They stood together in silence for a while. The girl was very close to him. Danecki sensed, both in himself and the girl, the sexual awareness which comes in moments of mortal peril. She had the scent of a woman who desperately needs to make love.

Me? thought Danecki. *Approaching a middle age I'll not reach because of a hard-eyed young killer or a thousand-year-old war!* Not with me.

He recalled the mindless violence of a year spent in a series of ferocious duels. There was a long period of calm and peace before that, but the year had eroded its memories. He was a refugee in a refuge that wasn't.

The girl's indefinable scent was stronger. She was dishevelled, but the clear freshness of youth made the tear marks an ornament on her glowing skin. She was young and she had never been truly afraid before. Did she know that all men and women felt the urge to couple when death hung over them? Danecki saw the swell of her breasts moving closer. Her lips parted.

"I couldn't do it to you," Danecki said. "Not here—not a man like me!"

The girl closed out the army of robots; she moved trancelike and with complete assurance. "Here," she whispered. "And now."

Danecki allowed himself to drift. A year of madness ended when he took the girl. The unwanted hates and mindless terrors were blotted out in the closeness of the embrace. He placed a hand on one peaked breast. She pressed the hand. She began to slide against him in the powerful rhythm of love.

"I'll never leave you," she whispered, still with closed eyes.

Danecki thought of the hours that remained. It would

be easy to spend them here, with the girl. He pushed her aside. "The others too," he said. "I said I'd do what I could."

She held him strongly. "I'd rather it ended here, with you!"

Danecki felt his resolve ebbing. But the faint clamor of metallic voices brought him back to an awareness of the immediate present. "Come," he said. "We have to try. More than ever now."

On the way back to the winding corridor, the girl stopped him. "They were lovers," she said.

He knew what she meant. She would not be afraid of the pitiful relics of the ancient war when they came to them again. The man and woman had fallen together. And Khalia had created a legend for them.

"I don't think I'd mind if it came quickly for us," she said, taking his hand.

Danecki wondered what life would be like with her. She made her own life into a web of delight. He hoped she would never know how much he detested himself for the mad year.

She noticed his scowl. "You're ashamed! You think I'm not suitable."

If she only knew, thought Danecki.

"Ashamed. Happy. In love. Overwhelmed. Desperate. Fearful. All of these. But ashamed only because I can't ever be the man you deserve."

Khalia saw that he meant it. "I'm a victim too," she said. "Girls of my age have a year or two of freedom, then it's on to the genetic program. Can't you see, I'd never have the chance to find a man myself! I thought I'd be mated through the computers. We're not allowed to choose—and now I can, and I have! On my world, you're programmed for life if you're a woman!"

Danecki had heard of such mad genetic experiments. But Galactic Center wouldn't intervene, no more than it would try to stop the vendetta system on his own backward planet. There was something crude about what Khalia described, however: a central authority planned the genetic structure of the entire population. No one could opt out.

He wondered if he should tell her that the Jacobis would send out children still at school to make sure of his death if he escaped the last adult male of the clan.

She stared at him level-eyed and completely intent. "I mean it, Danecki! I've looked at men all my life. I wondered what I wanted. Now, I *know!* I said I'll never leave you, and I mean it!"

Danecki couldn't help saying: "All your life?"

"Where are we going?" the girl asked. "Doesn't this lead back to the Central Command area?"

"Where else can we go? We can do nothing down here. I wondered if we could get back into the control area. It might be that I can think of something if only we knew more about the fort! But staying down here doesn't help. The Army's control systems are well hidden. And Batibasaga isn't down here. Maybe if we could find the maintenance units—" He stopped. They had come to the steep coils of the corridor.

"What is it?"

Danecki considered the girl. "I could leave you down here. You'd be safe."

"No!" She said. "I *mean* it!"

"All right."

Danecki watched for the sudden swoop of giant bars, the kind that had seized Batibasaga with easy power. There was nothing. Just the smooth, metallic regularity of the walls of the tunnel.

They came to the bones, and they held each other.

From the whiteness and regularity of their teeth, the couple lying in a single heap had both been young. Danecki was irresistibly drawn to examining the white bones for scars. A neat hole had been punched through the smaller, female skull. There was no discernible mark on the skeleton of the man, whose bones lay intermixed with the woman's.

"How did they get in?" he whispered aloud. "How! If we knew that, we might have a chance!"

"What now?" Khalia asked.

Danecki stepped over the heap of bones. "We go on."

Beyond the next bend they were halted by a penetrating whistle of electronic static. "Technical failures reported in Level Nine! Maintenance units not able to carry out correct procedures!"

"Report!" snapped the voice of Central Command.

"My systems are not operating fully," said the harsh voice of Central Security. "I must have priority in the use of maintenance systems!"

Danecki motioned to the girl to be still.

"I decide on priorities," said Central Command.

"It is your function to make decisions," agreed Security. "Nevertheless it is my function to report deficiencies."

"Agreed!"

The net of black hawsers swept down at that precise moment.

Danecki saw them and, with the immediate reaction of a year spent in dealing with the sophisticated machinery of his ship, he yanked the girl back down the corridor to the mausoleum. The hawsers followed, great black writhing coils of a material that seemed alive.

He grabbed and levelled the primitive blaster, firing on the instant. Gobbets of black and yellow fire spewed from it.

"Run!" he yelled, but there was nowhere to run—for more writhing hawsers appeared from the further reaches of the corridor.

The black and yellow fire consumed the fibrous coils, leaving gray ash to drip to the floor. It sprayed onto the bones. The furious thunder of the weapon left Khalia gasping for breath and Danecki wild with rage at the ponderous machinery that sought them.

"Intruders!" bawled a voice above the uproar. "My systems are functioning once more in the approaches to Level Nine. Intruders!"

"Apprehend!" called Central Command.

"One is armed!" Security reported.

The blaster juddered once more and ceased firing.

Danecki slithered in the hot gray ash, pushing the girl behind him in a last despairing effort to keep the evil swathes of blackness from her. He tripped on the rib cage of the skeleton that lay alone; the knife flew down the corridor, tinkling as it went. The blaster was neatly flicked from his hand by a slim black rope as he fell.

He had a perfect picture of the rope sliding back into an orifice—with the weapon held negligently by the trigger mechanism. He heard the girl scream.

"It's got me! Danecki!"

"Now unarmed!" reported Security in the echoing silence of the corridor.

The hawsers caught him as he tried to get to his feet. They pinioned him gently with a powerful insistence. He was trussed like some precious machine part.

Where was the girl?

But Danecki was upside down in the embrace of the coils. Their flabby strength permitted no movement. He saw the corridor brightly lit; and then he had been smoothly whipped through a black opening in the roof of the tunnel. Violent winds battered at his ears in the darkness of a shaft.

Where was he!

Danecki made a desperate effort to free himself, but the flesh-like hawsers tightened at once. When he called out, a soft bag enveloped his mouth. He choked and the bag was withdrawn. He was so relieved that he would not die of suffocation in the blackness, that he could not bring himself to repeat the call to the girl.

The journey lasted for seconds, then ended as abruptly as it had begun.

Stupefied by the light after the dense blackness of the tunnel, he staggered as the hawsers set him down. He took a couple of paces, blinking and rubbing his eyes.

Someone took his shoulder. "Ah, Mr. Danecki. You've joined us."

CHAPTER

★ 11 ★

Danecki stumbled from pitched blackness into the soft, delicate lighting of a comfortable yet strange room.

"You too," Wardle called to him. "Did you find the robot?"

Danecki took in the significance of the place. It had that indefinable air of restraint that characterizes prisons. There was no doorway. He realized that he must have been thrust through some aperture by the trickery of Third Millennium engineering. The hawsers had left him with the other prisoners.

"Khalia!" he cried. "Where is she?" He blinked in the suffused glow of the room. Wardle was repeating his question. Dross took away the supporting arm and returned to the deep chair from which he had obviously just risen.

"The young lady?" said Dross. "No. She's not here. Wasn't she with you?"

"Danecki! Damn it, man, can't you answer a question! Have you seen the robot—anything! We were relying on you! You've been away for—must be half an hour! More! And time's going, man!"

The room infected Danecki with the hopelessness of the situation. There had to be doorways, he was thinking. But all he could see were a series of alcoves that held sleeping couches. On one was the Revived Man. In the next alcove, cradling her fine head in her arms, was Mrs. Zulkifar. But the room offered no hint of an exit. It was built to confuse, to disorient, to destroy initiative. Danecki saw where the strangeness lay. One wall seemed to be half as high again as another; but it was an illusion. The metals

99

of the walls, floor, and ceiling were arranged in different patterns of alloys. You could read designs, characters, faces, in their subtle traceries. You could lose yourself in their weird windings which led one into another, diverting your attention from the main theme, inverting your starting point—making you question your own powers of deduction, spoiling your concentration so that you began to doubt your own sanity.

"No way out," said Dross. "We've been over every inch."

"But the girl!" snarled Danecki. "She was with me! We were taken together—the black ropes took us both at the same place and the same time!"

"Neat devices," said Dross. "Yes. Just what one would have expected."

Wardle tried to be reasonable. "Danecki, there's not much more than five hours before this place aborts itself —try to help yourself and us! Where have you been, man! What have you seen?"

"She isn't here," said Dross carefully. "The rest of us were picked up immediately after Mrs. Zulkifar's fatal step. The young lady left with you. That was our last sight of her. Jacobi hasn't shown up either."

"But where is she?" As he said it, Danecki realized how stupid it must sound to these two men. Yet he was hungry, battered, dirty—furious with himself for not keeping the girl away from danger. And above all, utterly desolated.

"She's just one person!" snapped Wardle. "What about the robot—you said you could program it so that we'd have a hope of getting away! Man, we can't worry about one girl!"

Danecki took Wardle by his tunic. Wardle was not a small man, but he hauled him bodily into the air. The Brigadier found the hard eyes glaring at him. He remembered that Danecki had killed that morning. He began to stutter an apology, but Danecki quieted him with a few gritted words: "I worry! Now you worry! Where is she?"

"Calm down," ordered Dross.

Danecki released the stuttering figure. The hate began to edge from his face. Wardle remembered a face like Danecki's years away in time and space—that of a man who had been executed in one of the many uprisings on his own turbulent planet. He tried to forget both faces.

"No sign at all," said Dross. "I'm sorry. Just myself and the Brigadier. Mr. Moonman is in a state of shock.

He won't respond when we talk to him. And poor Mrs. Zulkifar. She was screaming all the time she was in the black shaft. When the hawsers delivered her, she was hit by some sort of anesthetizing spray—it caught her and then she was laid into the cubicle."

Danecki shook his head. He looked at Wardle. "I'm sorry."

"Ah. Yes. Nasty shock for us all, all right!"

Dross resumed his seat. "Calm yourself, Mr. Danecki. Have some food. Attend to your toilet. The necessary facilities are provided. We're captives, but the Confederation ghosts that hold us prisoner aren't savages. Eat! Drink! If we're to be blown up, let us advance into extinction with some measure of physical comfort."

Instinct hooked deep into Danecki's mind. "Jacobi? The boy?"

"Perhaps I omitted to explain," Dross replied. "He hasn't appeared so far. And your feud seems rather pointless now."

"It always was," said Danecki.

Wardle followed Danecki's gaze. "No way out, I'm afraid, Danecki. As the Doctor says, we'll have to make the best of it. Strange sort of place! Weird! It's like being inside someone's head—I imagine the psych fellows worked out the decor. Designed to make you soften up before interrogation."

He led Danecki to the food dispenser where he punched buttons. "Barely palatable, but what can you expect after a thousand years?"

The food was warm, soft, and filling. Danecki ate while Dross talked.

"What a place this is turning out to be, Mr. Danecki! What a monstrous installation it is! Efficient and busy after the centuries of quiescence—a morgue suddenly reopened and found to contain living things! A whole functioning world of electronic ghosts who refuse to acknowledge the passage of the years. Jailers who are as discreet and secretive as mortuary attendants—a jail with a cunning web of motifs that leave the prisoner no wish to hope! If only I could reveal this to my former colleagues at Galactic Center!"

Danecki wolfed the pappy mess. He had not realized the extent of his need for the familiar sensation of food in his belly. His eyes roved as the two men tried to contain their mounting impatience at his silence.

There was no hint of an opening in the room. Hard

metal lay beneath the alloyed patterns; the ancient engineers who had constructed the prison had left no flaw in the smoothness of the whorled patterns.

"We're in a prison within a fortress," Dross went on. "Think of it, Mr. Danecki. A prison within a prison! But Mr. Moonman won't have any of it. Look at him! He's put himself beyond the reach of all the ghosts! Self-induced hypnosis, I think. He's relapsed into the state his whole nation must have held for two centuries at the time of his planet's disaster! Incredible the way we react to the stresses of life, isn't it, Mr. Danecki?"

Danecki completed his toilet.

"Please!" Wardle said. "You know something—for God's sake tell us, Danecki!"

"Yes," urged Dross.

Danecki wondered if either of them could help. As he was eating, and while Dross talked about the fort and its prisoners, and all through Wardle's alternate pleas and exhortations, he had barely been able to focus his thoughts on the two men. The single, insistent, maddening urge drove out everything else. *The girl!* Where was she!

"Down in the lowest level," he said at last. "Level Nine, it's called. We took a winding corridor and found an army. There's an army of war-robots."

"War-robots?" whispered Wardle. "Doctor?"

Dross and Wardle stared at Danecki as if at the fulfillment of a prophecy.

"Thousands of them," said Danecki. "We saw them. Ready to march."

"The Regiments of Night!" said Dross in a voice full of awe. "The Black Army of legend! Do you know what you've discovered, Mr. Danecki? Do you know!"

"I think so."

"'The Regiments of Night shall come at the end!'" Dross intoned gravely. "And they've been waiting for ten centuries for me to find them!"

"The Black Army!" whispered Wardle reverently.

Danecki could see that Wardle was in a state of simple adoration at the concept of that military machine, poised and ready to march.

"This is what I traveled to see!" the Brigadier gushed.

"You went out to find one robot, Mr. Danecki," said Dross. "And you found an army!"

The questions poured on Danecki, a flood of excited and erudite demands for more and more detail. The men were as happy as children in an abandoned toyshop.

102

At length it was Dross who put a halt to the questions. "The greatest mystery," he said, "is still unexplained."

"But we've found the Army!" said Wardle. "The Regiments—the entire Black Army!"

"Yes," said Dross. "But the greatest mystery is why it didn't march."

"My God," said Wardle softly. "Yes. They didn't march."

"They will," Danecki told them. "In about five hours."

Danecki let Dross absorb the impact of the frightening information. Wardle talked on enthusiastically about the ferocious hand-to-hand fighting that had taken place in and around the ruined surface installation. He re-created for himself the strategies of the attacking armies, the futile efforts of the defense, and the last desperate and overwhelming assault.

Dross said little. "Knaggs knew," he said finally.

"Powerful imagery!" Wardle went on, still excited. "What powerful imagery—the Black Army! I wish I could see them—it would almost be worthwhile—" He stopped.

Dross said: "There's more, isn't there, Mr. Danecki?"

"Yes." Danecki thought of the pitiful remnants in the tunnel. He had purposely left the skeletons out of his tale. He wanted Dross's huge intelligence to come to it as starkly as the bare white bones had appeared to Khalia and himself. "There are three skeletons in the tunnel leading to the Black Army."

Dross retreated into a stunned silence. He stared at Danecki for a few moments and then closed his eyes.

Wardle, on the other hand, was loudly amazed. *"Three* skeletons! Three! Left in the tunnel, you say! Left there—left to lie down there! But, it's impossible! The installation wouldn't have allowed it! They couldn't have got into the fort! The only way in is through the spin-shaft—and they would have destroyed it just as we did, had they come that way! Danecki! Dross! *How!"*

Wardle blustered on for some minutes. During that time, Dross said nothing at all. He had subsided into the deep, comfortable chair in a state of bewildered remoteness. Danecki allowed him to remain undisturbed.

He was beginning to put together his own interpretation of the stunning events he and Khalia had lived through. He posed the sight of the incredible Army against the fantastic military installation, and what he knew of the men who had created it. He tried to imagine the reasons for the failure of the titanic military weapon he had seen. It was an eerie and baffling puzzle. He knew it was one that he alone could not begin to understand. But Dross might.

The big archaeologist had stirred slightly. He was breathing slowly, his big hands in a triangular shape, fingers touching and pressing lightly together.

Wardle paced about the strange room. He looked in on Mr. Moonman. The gaunt Revived Man lay like a dead man. Moved by a feeling of compassion, the Brigadier inspected the handsome figure of Mrs. Zulkifar. She lay unconscious and smiling, happy perhaps for the first time since she had been hurled down the ancient spin-shaft.

Danecki waited for Dross.

But Dross was still allowing the fat pods of flesh at his fingertips to play one against another.

Wardle stopped his pacing and spoke to Danecki. "Have you noticed yet?" he asked.

Danecki looked into the tired and worried eyes. How had this blustering man come to hold senior rank in his corner of the Galaxy? "Noticed what?"

"Thought you hadn't," Wardle gloated. "Didn't strike me until a few minutes ago."

Dross surprised Danecki by interrupting his answer to the Brigadier: "I believe it has escaped Mr. Danecki's attention, as it had mine, until a few minutes ago, that is. Don't look so puzzled! You've been under a strain. Your natural instincts are muted in this prison of ours. But I'd been wondering if you'd be sufficiently perspicacious to notice what is so far the most significant aspect of our confinement. Indeed, it might well have a bearing on the extraordinary story you have just told us!"

"Yes! Really, Doctor?" said Wardle.

Danecki listened to the portentous tones, the delight in passing on information—the sheer arrogance, and the undeniably patronizing tone of the archaeologist! It brought from him an audible sigh of relief. It was what he had desperately hoped for while Dross lay in half-somnolent contemplation. Dross was at last bringing the weight of his intellect to the problem they all faced.

"Just listen," suggested Wardle.

Danecki understood.

"Why is it so quiet?" said Dross silkily. "Why are the control systems ignoring us?"

"We've been here for exactly forty-seven minutes," said Wardle. "And in that time, not a word! No interrogation, no instructions, no information of any kind. Not a single damned announcement since our arrest!"

"And?" said Danecki. He could feel the tiredness giving way to the stimulation of hope. The almost suicidal desperation he had felt when the hawsers had plucked him away from the girl was almost gone.

"I think the fort doesn't want anything to do with us," Dross said. "I believe it is worried."

"It didn't stop reeling off information from the time we landed," said Wardle. "Now, it's silent. Why?"

"I have to think," said Dross. "My mind works slowly. I know our time is limited, but there is a vast amount of information to absorb."

Dross arranged his bulk to his satisfaction. He spoke as if to one of his own audiences in the days of his lectures at Center. His eyes found a point beyond Wardle and Danecki, and his voice was full of calm, measured superiority. "This fort—this extremely sophisticated piece of engineering—is undergoing the initial stages of an alarming traumatic experience. You see, for the first time in its experience, human beings aren't playing by the rules."

"Rules, Doctor, what rules?"

"Bear with me, Brigadier. There it remained, self-perpetuating, powered by fuel sources that may even be self-renewing, as it was designed to remain. It waited for the Confederation's last order. And what happens?" Dross waved a plump hand to the two men. "When a group of unidentified humans at last make an entry, they won't take on the responsibilities of command!"

"Damn it, we'd have set off the abort systems!" Wardle growled. "How could we have taken command?"

"Very true. Irrelevant, but true. You see, the worst problem for the fort is not that we didn't take command, though that's bad enough. No. Even worse is the failure of some internal piece of the Central Command System, that which should have set the Army on its path." Dross eyed Danecki squarely. "For a thousand years, the fort has ticked over, trying to work out why in all that time it hadn't fulfilled its function! Just consider its relief when at long last some contact is made with its makers!"

Danecki allowed himself to think of the glistening banks of computers with their cold, barely-moving memory-coils, and the imponderable question before them.

"We came down the spin-shaft. We *were* Confederation personnel—otherwise we couldn't have used the shaft! In effect, we were Confederation soldiers! And what happens! That's the problem the installation has to weigh up now—it has to pose it against its thousand-year-old suspension of the Black Army!"

"It would expect us to act," said Danecki.

"Precisely! And we do nothing! We don't send out the Black Army, nor do we assume command to stop the abort countdown! We don't explain our entry—and, when the fort implores us to produce the Duty Commander, we ignore it.

"Just think of the situation from the fort's point of view," he continued. "It has to absorb our arrival logically. That means that we should set in motion a certain sequence of events. This is how it would go: man enters, fort sets up manual controls with sensors for direct transmission of instructions. Then man orders, and fort obeys. But what happened in our case? Certainly man entered—and by the customary process for Confederation personnel. And then, inexplicably, man began to make for the storage, administrative, and weapons areas without identifying himself to Central Command!"

"Worse still," Dross intoned, "when a condition of maximum emergency is declared, man, who should be doing something, simply ignores the Central Command System. The whole thousand-year-old dilemma is reinforced! Can you imagine the unrest among the fort's systems as our action, or non-action, is analyzed by the decision-making computers?"

"So what we can do, Doctor," Wardle asked, "in the few hours we have?"

"Let me think," said Dross.

Danecki covered the wall area, inch by inch. It was a gesture only, for whatever trick of molecular displacement the prison's builders had used in the construction of exits, there was no break in the even regularity of the strange panels.

After a while he gave it up.

He began to think of the last of the Confederation soldiers. What sort of decisions had they faced when the armies against them broke through and into the huge base above? How had they died?

Dross began to conjecture aloud once more. It seemed

to be his pattern of development. An indrawn silence, and then the brisk, lucid tones.

"There must be the most appalling confusion amongst the fort's systems," Dross began. "Who are we! Spies? Saboteurs? Confederation civilians accidentally strayed down here? Enemy scouts? And what sort of action should be taken against us! Imagine the unrest in the logic-works!"

Danecki recalled the harsh voice of Security. "In the corridor leading to Level Nine there was confusion," he said. "The machines weren't sure of the correct decisions. Security claimed priority in the use of maintenance machines. Central Command was quick to put it down."

"Interesting," said Dross. "Part of what I take to be a pattern of unrest and confusion. You see, it's easy to think of this installation as a single entity—as an individual."

"It isn't?" asked Wardle.

"It might have been once. But not now. I don't believe that the installation that lies around us is exactly the same as the one that was constructed in the Third Millennium."

"What!" gasped Wardle. "It *isn't* the missing fort!"

"Yes—" said Dross, almost with a smirk, "—and no."

If the situation hadn't been so desperate, Danecki could have smiled. He was jolted to the frightful consciousness of the present by Dross's next remark.

"It's a machine that is even more deadly than the one the Confederation built, Brigadier!"

"How?" asked Danecki.

"I believe the various systems have followed their own evolutionary path," said Dross. "Every part of this installation must have been renewed several times. Every last minute system that controls the installation must have been renewed and replaced entirely too. And I believe that an evolutionary process might well have been at work." Dross refused to go on. "I have to think," he said simply.

When he spoke again, Dross talked of the long-dead man sought by the machines. "I've no doubt that there are frantic messages flowing about this installation, all urging the Duty Commander to take command. Strange! A man who died valiantly, no doubt, some thousand years ago. What sort of man was he! You know, Mr. Danecki, he's the most important factor of all so far as we are concerned."

Danecki remembered his own speculations about the last days of the fort, and of the men who had manned it.

"If we knew him," said Dross, "we could control the controls!"

"Stands to reason," agreed Wardle. "But time's passing, Doctor! What the devil are we to do?"

"Yes," said Danecki, feeling a flood of impatience begin to rise up. "What can we do?"

"Time passing—the fort beginning to get confused!" Wardle, too, was becoming agitated. "The call for an officer who died a whole millennium ago! Doctor, it gets worse! The fort may well go completely berserk!"

Danecki was lost. He sensed that Dross was coming to a framework of decisions, but how the big-bellied archaeologist's mind worked was beyond him. Dross had outlined the fort's confusion—he had shown that the fort suffered from what, in a human being, would be a schizoid state. But then he had gone on to talk about the fort as a thing that had changed its nature over the years. Neither of Dross's lengthy statements had led directly to a strategy, and Danecki couldn't see that they would. But he had faith in Dross.

"I said the fort might go berserk, Doctor!" Wardle insisted.

"That, Brigadier," said Dross, "might well happen. In fact, I think our only chance of escape rests with that very possibility."

Danecki felt a smile edging over his face. The calm tones were silkily arrogant. Dross was at his best, with the tangled skein of possibilities taking on a definite shape. Danecki felt his smile freeze when he thought of the girl and the hours that stood between them and the complete destruction of the fort.

"What!" Wardle exploded at last. He had been utterly dismayed by Dross's sly statement. "What are you saying!"

"Let me think," said Dross.

CHAPTER
★ 12 ★

Time passed in frozen droplets. While Dross closed his eyes and pressed the tips of his fingers together, the Brigadier paced about the room.

Danecki relived the moments of tenderness with the girl, recalled each touch of soft flesh with exquisite care —holding back the weird realities of the prison. But always there were the harsh memories of plunging through the mind-reeling whirlpools of forces in the unreal dimensions, with the Jacobis' superior vessel hanging near him—memories of the many deaths, of the remaining Jacobi boy and his startlingly clear eyes with their message of hate and doom. And then again of the girl's proud body with the breasts thrust forward firmly in the sharp light of the little recess where the Black Army was hidden from view.

He was interrupted by Wardle who could no longer hold the silence: "Nasty business, this thing of yours, Danecki. This licensed hunter, Jacobi. I didn't think it was still used, the vendetta system." He waited for Danecki to speak, then, somewhat ashamedly, he said, "Makes a difference, the girl, eh?"

Danecki realized that Wardle had guessed the development of a close relationship between himself and Khalia; it was to be expected. What surprised him was that for the first time in over a year, he was aware that another human being was interested in him as a person; and it mattered.

"It does," he said. He remembered the violence of his assault on Wardle. "I shouldn't have attacked you."

"Understandable. Forget it. It's banal to say we're

under a strain. This place! Think of it, Danecki! I heard about the Black Army as a legend over a quarter of a century ago. All that time, it's been here. Bit odd, isn't it? You must feel the same." He paused. "Nothing in what the boy says?"

Danecki knew exactly what he meant. Was he, or was he not, a cold-blooded murderer? It didn't matter what Wardle thought, but he still found himself caring that someone should know the truth. There had been little time to convince the legal machines of his innocence. But the facts had been incontrovertible.

"Murder?" he said to Wardle. "The law-machine said it wasn't. But they still allowed Jacobi to take out a license for revenge. We're a backward planetary organization, Brigadier. Two suns and more than a hundred planets. Most of them can't be used without regular supplies of trace minerals—they need a ship or so every year to get the artificial atmospheres right. The Jacobis had the space-lanes by the throat. You'd call them pirates. They called themselves space-line controllers. It was a joke they had; they said they regulated traffic. Insured there were no accidents, that the services ran efficiently. If they weren't paid, a ship didn't arrive. I don't know how they did it, for a ship that was lost never turned up. It was only one man, and not a big ship. But the Jacobis had made their point. I suppose you think it's a deplorable state, Brigadier?"

"I've heard worse," said Wardle briefly. A flash of anger came into his eyes, and Danecki wondered then if the old soldier was as ineffectual and bumbling as he appeared. "Your line was due for a lesson?"

"I wouldn't have seen the attack if I hadn't already had trouble with the space-wreck sensors. I'd nearly collided with the ruin of a monster hyperspace vessel, so I was doing my own observation. There were two of them, little ships throwing out screens that would make them show up as a meteorite shower. Normally I'd have gone through them and accepted a couple of holes that would have sealed themselves off anyway."

"Two ships?"

"Jacobi was right when he said I'd killed. The second ship was a little pleasure boat. I don't like to think they'd come to see the fun. The boy's sister—and her children—were aboard."

Danecki tried to blot out the desperate little encounter, the turnings and convolutions of his ship. He tried to forget the sudden intuitive skills that had burst through to his brain in the moments of despair. He had found a sense of creative destruction in his hands, a sense that could weave a pattern of forces from the heavy engines of his slow, old trader.

"You destroyed both ships?"

"Both."

And, later, more. And more. Until there were two boys left, each a wild and implacable foe.

"Galactic Center should outlaw the vendetta," said the Brigadier.

"It won't," Dross put in. "After all, that's the *point* of it all. We learned hundreds of years ago that central control doesn't work. It took the Mad Wars to teach us that."

Then Danecki was back in the strange present, drearily conscious of the irony of his situation. He, who had been tired of killing, sick almost to death of life itself, had found a reason for survival. And his abilities to stay alive wouldn't help.

The big-bellied archaeologist understood. "I can find a measure of sympathy, Mr. Danecki," he said. "It isn't often that one hears such a frightful story. You are a victim of more than circumstances. There's something almost Greek about you. Hounded, killing against your will—finding love—it's in your face, man! Don't deny it—and waiting for fate to extinguish you."

Dross pointed to the food dispenser. "Save an old man a tiring effort," he ordered. "Bring me a stimulating drink."

Danecki punched buttons and a bright amber liquid filled the glass.

"Passable," said Dross, when he had downed half of the liquor. "Strong enough. Odd flavor. Now, save your reminiscences for the young lady, Danecki. Think of her, however. Tell me again about your exploration of the lower levels. I've been giving your story some thought, but I suspect you've not told me everything."

Danecki began to say that he had told all he could remember.

Dross stopped him. "I think it's our only chance. When the fort *does* acknowledge our presence, it will only be because we can help to solve one of the problems that worries it. Tell me about the remains you found. Again and again!"

Danecki trod down his impatience.

Dross's big face glowed with eagerness. The archaeologist seemed almost dreamily remote at one time, and then at another, his eyes burned with a gleam of intense excitement. "The bones," said Dross. "Start with the bones."

Danecki began again. "Two separate heaps. There were no clothes. I'm sure of it. I looked at the bones for scars the second time."

"Self-destroying plastics," Dross agreed. "Yes. All the clothing and equipment would be bonded with a time-limited reagent. That's why you saw bare bones. The tissues would disintegrate over the centuries, and there'd be sufficient airflow to move the dust. I've seen the same sort of thing in the ruin above." He nodded to Danecki to go on.

"I looked at the skulls." Danecki recalled Khalia's gasp of pity as she saw the bright golden hair about the long-dead woman's skull.

"The fort will worry about the bones now," said Dross. "More confusion! But why weren't they removed? If you could go over it again, Mr. Danecki? Wasn't there anything to identify an individual? You saw the hole in the woman's skull. Go on."

Danecki heard again Khalia's exclamation of pity and awe. *Lovers,* she had called them. And was it so fanciful that they who had died together should not have loved in that terrible age?

"I wondered how they had entered the fort," Danecki said. "The two skeletons were side by side where they died. I heard the argument begin again, and then the black ropes came for us."

"You picked up the blaster," said Dross quietly. "You dived for it—you *saw* it. You checked the firing mechanism—*did you look at it?*"

"Look at it?"

"Did you see it—what did it *look* like?"

Wardle butted in: "Conventional impulse-emitter? Heat-ray? Black-shadow fusor? Handgun? Weight? Think of it in your hand. Imagine it there in your hand."

Danecki looked down at his hand. "Handgun," he said. "Not heavy. It fitted exactly and the firing mechanism readied itself once I pointed. I didn't think about it. Point, press, fire. It was a reinforced ion-beam ejector, powerful enough to burn up the hawsers." He thought hard, closing his eyes. "The hawsers burned gray and dropped spots of plastic. The beam caught the metal sides of the corridor. The metal buckled but held. That's all."

"It could have been from any period," Dross said. "The Confederation forces used that kind of weapon, but so did the rest of the contending forces. What you've told me so far helps to outline the general picture, but you haven't given me the one single, indisputable fact that I can present to the fort! One fact, Mr. Danecki! One!"

Wardle joined in. "Think, Danecki! What did the girl say? Did she notice anything?"

Danecki found the memory of Khalia's sympathy with the dead couple almost unbearable. He contained the angry retort which sprang to his lips. If, by intruding on the private new world which had been created in the grim cavern, the two men could help, then let them. "She said they were lovers."

Dross nodded. "Likely enough. But were they attackers on a suicide mission, or two Confederation people finding the last refuge? I have to think."

"Four hours and fifty minutes," said Wardle.

The room pressed in on them all. Even Dross was perturbed by the subtle tensions set up by the whorled patterns; he closed his eyes and his lips moved, but he maintained another of those dragging silences while Danecki fought back fatigue and frustration.

Wardle continued his pacing. Then he called Danecki across to see the unconscious Mr. Moonman. The Revived Man lay with his eyes open. Danecki saw the long, yellow nose hooked out of a large gaunt area of face.

"He's nursed that since he came," said Wardle. He pointed to the strange robotic head which Danecki had last seen beside the inert figure of Batibasaga in the Central Command Area. Mr. Moonman cradled the mud-streaked carapace as though it were some terrible yet comforting companion.

The sight of the long, scarcely-breathing figure oppressed Danecki. "He traveled halfway across the Galaxy to find that," he said.

The dreadful head had played a strange part in the events of the long day. It had been found only that morning; then, abandoned, it had become a weapon. Now it comforted Mr. Moonman.

It was at that moment that Danecki suddenly recalled with a peculiar vividness the image of the blaster as it was neatly flicked from his hand by the black tendril.

"Three sunbursts," he said aloud. "Doctor! The blaster!"

Mrs. Zulkifar whimpered in her sleep.

Dross opened his eyes. "Tell me, Mr. Danecki," he purred. "Tell me!"

"You've got it!" Wardle said when Danecki was finished. "Three sunbursts was the crest of the Confederation—the three suns rising on the three planets they controlled!"

Dross rose to his feet. He was an impressive figure. His vast expanse of tunic swelled over the big belly. Danecki felt impatience begin to flood over his mind, but he controlled himself with a will trained in the iron year.

"I asked for one fact," began Dross sonorously. He paused. "And you gave it to me! I, Dross, will save you all!"

"The time, Doctor!" reminded Wardle. "Time!"

Dross ignored the interruption. "It is an indisputable fact! Why the insistence on the presence of the Duty Commander? Why the almost guilty maunderings of the confounded gadgets? Why the incarceration of ourselves with no attempt at interrogation? Why! Because the fort is unsure of itself! Because it thinks it might have committed some monumental act of folly! And that is why Dross is able to save you all—and the fort itself, the greatest single archaeological discovery of the millennium!" He pointed to Danecki. "Your courage and perseverance have helped! Undoubtedly! By bringing your story back, you have enabled the brain within this skull to put together the fragments of legend and fact that otherwise meant nothing. The Duty Commander—that's what you have brought back! The Duty Commander whose weapon you used until it would fire no more! The Duty Commander whose skeleton it is that lies below us at the entrance to Level Nine!"

"Yes," said Danecki. "It could be."

"Doctor—how does that help?" said Wardle.

"If we know about the Duty Commander, we know about the fort's dreadful sense of insecurity, Brigadier. But the weapon is the key—three sunbursts on the blaster! The personal weapon of the Confederation's officers. Only they would carry the insignia of the Confederation! And who but an officer of the Confederation would find his way into the fort?"

"But the others, Doctor?" Danecki asked. "What of them?"

"Not our immediate concern, Mr. Danecki! It is the

long-dead Duty Commander who concerns us. If we control him, we control the fort!"

Dross peered about the room. He was looking, the two men saw, for a suitable focus for his speech. A speech, Danecki saw, it would be.

At last Dross was ready to act. The plan was uncertain. It was based on so many unproven and unprovable assumptions and shreds of fact that it sounded crazy even when outlined in Dross's shrewd presentation. Danecki acknowledged its weaknesses but trusted the big-bellied archaeologist's intuition.

Dross was as much a master of this strange situation as he, Danecki, had been of the uncertain shoals of hyperspace.

Dross chose to speak to the ceiling. "We are ready to reveal our identity!" he called sharply.

He spoke again. "We are ready to reveal our identity!"

The men listened, but there was no answering metallic voice. None could be expected, if Dross was right. Not until the indisputable facts were put forward.

"I address myself to the Security Section! You must relay this message to Central Command." The words bounced off the weird ceiling.

Dross spoke louder in his sonorous professorial voice. "We are Confederation civilians! We have survived outside the fort area. I have news of an infiltration of the lower levels."

Still nothing broke the silence. A few echoes rang about the alloyed ceiling. Mrs. Zulkifar rustled against the bedclothes. But that was all.

"The Black Army is in danger!" Surely that would bring the fort into action! Danecki strained to hear the first gratings of the robot voice that would break the long silence.

Nothing!

"The Duty Commander has been killed! His personal weapon has been taken from him! Security has possession of the Duty Commander's blaster!" Dross paused.

Was there a subtle change in the ambience of the room? Was there a hint of electronic attention?

"We are survivors of the Confederation! A thousand years have passed since all other Confederation personnel of this installation died! The Duty Commander is dead! Two intruders were killed by the Duty Commander! You are a robotic installation! You are a thousand years old!"

Dross paused, for Mrs. Zulkifar was sitting up, gasping. Her face showed the wild emotions that disturbed her.

"You can't tell it that! Don't let it think it's a thousand years old! What might it do? Why can't you leave it alone! It wouldn't have harmed us!" Her fine eyes flashed, and for a moment Danecki half-believed her. "All we had to do was wait—all this nonsense would have been sorted out! There are correct procedures—ways of doing things! If we start interfering with things that don't concern us, who knows what will happen? Doctor, you're a scholar and a gentleman! You wouldn't want me to be hurt!"

Wardle tried to quieten her. "Emma! Leave the Doctor alone! He's trying to get us all to safety!"

But Mrs. Zulkifar made a grab for Dross. "Leave it to the proper authorities!"

It was left to Danecki to grab a covering from her couch and muffle her cries.

Dross smoothed his clothes and went on: "This installation has no human direction! The Duty Commander is dead! We are Confederation forces!"

The room seemed to shake slightly. Danecki noticed it. So did Wardle.

Dross nodded. He too had observed the slight pulsation of the eerie room. He paused, as he had said he would, before delivering the final part of his speech.

The fort was listening.

Circuits had fallen together. There was an odd, poised sensation in the strange room, one which had not been evident before. It made the weirdly patterned prison a quiet and deadly place. Cold electronic ghosts lingered in the silence.

"We are Confederation forces! Your last official brain-imprint was received a thousand years ago. The Duty Commander died defending the Black Army. Before he died, he gave his personal weapon to Danecki, here present!"

He pointed to Danecki.

This was the plan. Danecki looked about for some focal point for his short message. There was none, so, like Dross, he looked upwards: "I appoint myself Duty Commander!"

Mrs. Zulkifar screamed. She burst from Wardle's old muscles and dragged the bright bedclothes over the heads of all three men. Wardle bellowed into the muffling cover;

Dross choked against a swath of fabric; Danecki clawed savagely, realizing what the sick, mad woman intended.

"Stop!" implored Wardle. He too realized the danger she represented.

"We're not!" the terrified woman screamed. "He lied! Dross lied! He's no gentleman! We're from the tourist ship—we're from the hyperspace ship you blew up! I'm not lying! I'm a law-abiding citizen! I've a great regard for the proper way of doing things! Dross is lying—Danecki's lying! I'm just a woman! I can't die—!"

She was still babbling when Danecki reached her. He couldn't hit her to stop the noise. She was a sick animal who stared at him in blank, stupid terror, waiting for the blow.

Mrs. Zulkifar put a hand to her mouth and wept.

The fort took up the noise. It howled.

They all waited as the weird cell took on a life of its own. Walls, ceiling, floor—all became part of an appalling huge scream of electronic dismay. Light, whorls, patterns, sound—all clung together.

The cell reeled in on them.

This is the end of it, thought Danecki as the grating efflorescence of noise smashed into his head.

The metallic voices that made up the screaming raged and battered with astonishing physical violence around his skull, outside and inside, hitting through the bones of his hands, too, as he sought to keep the sheer volume of sound from his ears in an instinctive defensive movement.

Schizoid!

His mind registered a babble of mad commands. He opened his eyes briefly and the ceiling fell into him, its crazed shapes absorbing what was left of sight after he had been completely deafened by the roaring of robotic incoherence.

Confusion!

A thin wedge of memory made him call for the girl, but the cry made no impression on the awful fury of the fort's trauma.

Memory, thought, consciousness. All went.

CHAPTER

★ 13 ★

Danecki would gladly have died.

There were moments of silence, and then the hideous clamor would begin again. The pain was reinforced by the silences.

Danecki saw his fellow-prisoners soundlessly yelling into the electronic howlings of the fort. Mr. Moonman was on his feet rocking to and fro and holding the grim robotic head to his straining chest. Mrs. Zulkifar ran about the room in little circles, still with the bright bedclothes draped about her, so that she looked like some eldritch creature, more witch than woman. Dross had his hands over his big head, and Wardle was trying to burrow into a deep-piled couch.

A score of metallic voices competed for attention.

And then Danecki could bear the fury. This was what Dross had wanted, he realized. This violent outpouring of robotic terror. The fort was running riot. It believed that it might have made a mistake. And machines couldn't absorb the notion of error. There was no apparatus in the big computers for shrugging off a mistake.

"We'll make it believe it arrested the Duty Commander." That was what Dross had intended. "Confuse it utterly!" That was what Dross had said a few minutes before.

The minutes stretched back like the centuries the fort had slept through; nothing could be worse than the sheer appalling misery of the installation's demented systems.

Danecki found himself about to trample over the woman. She mouthed obscenities against the eerie, wind-wrenching noise; when she saw Danecki she skipped aside nimbly. She clawed out at him in a moment of comprehension, and then she was performing her involved little circuit of crazed movement.

There was no escape from the monstrous noise.

Danecki slipped in and out of consciousness three or four times, desperately willing himself into the soft blankness of coma when he emerged. And still the noise went on.

Fragments of electronic reportage impacted on his brain. "Red Alert! Red Alert!" bawled one impassioned voice.

"The Duty Commander is dead!" screamed another. "His death was an error!"

"Errors can be rectified," pointed out another. "A replacement unit must be found."

"Humans cannot be repaired!" screamed the first. "The Duty Commander's hand-weapon has been identified!"

"He is not a thousand years old," said a new voice.

All yelled at once in pain.

Dross crawled over to Danecki, who by this time was lying on the floor. It was only with difficulty that the archaeologist was able to unwind Danecki's arms from his head.

Neither attempted to speak. Dross fought against the clamor for a while, mouthing words so that Danecki could read his lips. But an upsurge of electronic misery made them seek the shelter of their arms and hands.

Minutes passed.

Had the woman spoiled Dross's plan?

Muted fragments of robotic messages began to filter through the high-pitched yells.

Danecki heard the harsh voice of Security demanding either instructions or the delegation of responsibility. "—this system must interrogate the thousand-year-old saboteurs—"

Another voice put in: "I have a superior robot in my workshop—complete repairs or feed to the fuel store?"

"—not identifiable!" stuttered Central Control.

"Batibasaga?"

Dross had heard it too. He mouthed, *"Batibasaga?"*

Danecki nodded.

"—superior robot refuses to acknowledge maintenance robots—inert!"

"Burial party, attention!" a thin voice said.

"—concubine of Duty Comm—"

Danecki felt a chill as the faintest hint of a reference to a woman filtered through the robotic chatter.

Concubine!

"Khalia!" he shouted, but the noise died in the uproar.

"This installation is not in error! No man lives for a thousand years!"

"One of my prisoners has given information," said Security heavily. "She should be released under Article Number—"

"I am responsible for decisions!" snapped Central Command.

"Infiltration!" spat out another voice.

"I am confused," admitted Central Command. "Abort procedures may be called on."

Anything could be tolerated, Danecki realized. Even this demented uproar. Dross wrote on the strange floor: "When it stops, repeat claim to be Duty Commander."

Danecki nodded.

The two men were joined by Wardle. They lay on the floor picking out the development of a pattern in the fort's deterioration. Undeniably, there was a recurring theme in the flow of messages which the demented systems roared out to one another. All three men gathered in as much as they could, aware that when the noise ceased, each thread of information would be invaluable.

Danecki refused to allow himself to wonder about the enigmatic reference to a concubine; he would not dwell either on the fate of Mrs. Zulkifar. It was enough to listen to the two chief systems and memorize as much as possible.

He concentrated on one metallic outburst at a time, trying to pick out phrases here and there from the random surges of information that filled the room.

"—I have four hours, thirty-three minutes to abort—" bleated a quiet little voice.

"—remains of three humans discovered?" asked Central Command. "Confirm figure 'three'!"

"Confirmed," said Security.

"Am I a thousand years old?" asked a maintenance system.

There was no answer.

"I shall take independent action," warned Security. "I must have decisions."

"Humans do not live for a thousand years," said Central Command.

"I have arrested four humans," pointed out Security. "I must have decisions."

Central Command was uninterested. "I do not make mistakes!"

The howling, which had died down appreciably, began to surge again. Then it stopped. There was complete silence. It hung in the air like a clammy thing, leaving behind the smell of fear.

"I am the Duty Commander!" roared Danecki.

Central Command answered: "No man lives for a thousand years."

Dross hauled himself up to his hands and knees. He shook his big head. Like Danecki and Wardle, he was amazed to find that he could still hear. "It's acknowledged us," he said. "I was right. A military machine will always accept information."

"You have my hand-weapon!" called Danecki.

He wanted to cry out to the unseen voice that he needed the girl—to unleash some of the wild impatience that ate into him.

Mrs. Zulkifar whimpered into her hands. She was past caring now. The desperate anger of the three men had cowed her. She stared at Danecki from black-ringed magnificent eyes, with no trace at all of her earlier disdain.

Dross wrote: "Order it to key your brain-imprints into the Central Command System."

It was what they had agreed. But Danecki hesitated. Where was the girl! There had been an oblique reference to a woman, but to which woman? If there were only time to reason out a clear plan among the fort's paranoiac ravings! But time was the one thing they lacked. His task at the moment was to keep the machines' interest.

"I am the Duty Commander," he said firmly. "My weapon must be restored. I must find the infiltrators. The command systems must be keyed to my brain-imprints. Do this at once!"

"Is it wise, Mr. Danecki?" wailed Mrs. Zulkifar.

A harsh voice grated out: "I shall act independently! The woman is to be released!"

"Watch out!" yelled Wardle.

The net of black hawsers swung from the roof and caught Mrs. Zulkifar in their flabby embrace. It happened in the space of perhaps three seconds.

One moment the woman was whimpering and facing three men with a timid defiance, and the next she had been caught and hauled up out of the prison like the flitting of a bat across the night sky.

The gaudy bedclothes floated down beside Mr. Moonman. He didn't look away from the ancient carapace.

"It believed her!" bellowed Wardle. "It believed her! Doctor, we've failed! The fort's accepted her story! What the devil's to happen to us? And to her?"

"You heard," said Danecki. "She's to be released."

"But she'll be out—perhaps she'll have the sense to call for help! We've—what?—nearly five hours! No! Four hours—just over four hours left! She could contact the excursion ships—they could find a way through to us! Eh, Doctor?"

Dross shook his head. "No, Brigadier."

"What?"

"I might have expected this," Dross said heavily. "Poor woman! No, Brigadier, I don't think Mrs. Zulkifar will get to the surface."

"It said she was to be released," pointed out Danecki.

"Security said that," Dross agreed. "One system. You're thinking in terms of a single highly motivated personality again. Don't. What you heard was the voice of one of a number of highly confused electronic systems. One system talked to you while another quite different system may have come to a different decision. I agree that Security took the lady's confession at face value."

Wardle said loudly: "So what will happen to Mrs. Zulkifar, Doctor?"

Danecki thought he understood. Dross was trying to play on the fort's disharmony. It seemed that Mrs. Zulkifar had become a pawn in the contending systems' emerging struggle for power.

"Listen," said Dross.

Nothing happened. No voices battered sense and sensation into one mass of pain. The fort was silent.

"Less than four and a half hours to destruct," said Wardle. He seemed to take a grim satisfaction in the words.

"Listen!"

"For what, Doctor? You know what's going to happen, do you? Well I do! You think that in four-and-a-half-hours' time it's going to be one instant explosion, just like the end of the tourist ship? You know the period, Doctor! None better! Do you recall how the Confederation disposed of its unwanted hardware?"

Dross shrugged. "Does it matter?"

Wardle turned to Danecki. "We'll slide," he said. "Slide. Down! Down into the nearest fault—down into the cracks in the Earth's mantle! And then we'll know! It won't be quick, Danecki!"

"What are we listening for, Doctor?" said Danecki.

"For Mrs. Zulkifar's exit."

"Bitch!" Wardle grunted.

"We all act as we have to, Brigadier. Don't we, Mr. Danecki? You—me—Mr. Moonman, who belongs to a race which by now should be philosophical about the concept of death, since they've all experienced it several times. Don't you wonder what drives creatures like those to take refuge in total withdrawal? Or what drives Mrs. Zulkifar to the act of betrayal—though why call it betrayal? She owes us no loyalty."

"It was the act of a stupid bitch," Wardle said. "Thought she had some backbone when we were on the trip. Damn it, Dross, if she hadn't tied us in with the tourist ship, the fort would have accepted us by now!"

"Listen," said Dross.

Danecki wondered about Jacobi. He felt that it was a good sign, that he should again be worrying about his future. His and the girl's. Why hadn't they talked about being together?

Dross seemed to be counting the seconds as they filtered through the eerie room.

Wardle exploded with impatience. "Dross, what *are* we waiting for! We can't just sit around waiting—let's look at the walls again! Come on, Danecki! You too, Doctor. And you!" he bawled, catching the Revived Man by the arm. "Look for a sign of an opening—there must be doors of some sort! They can't just lower prisoners in through the roof—there must be a way in for a man on his two legs!"

Reluctantly they all began to inch their way along the walls. This was the third time, for Danecki had insisted on another minute survey of the room during one of the intervals of waiting.

Mr. Moonman took an active part. Slow, ponderous, moving crab-like, one long dead-white hand brushing against the strangely-patterned walls.

"Well?" Danecki said to Dross. "What are you expecting?"

Dross shrugged. "Boom."

When it came, the explosion was almost an anticlimax. The whole cell heaved itself upwards.

Danecki watched the figure of Mr. Moonman climb into the air. The Revived Man accepted the bone-jarring impact of his fall as another outrageous infliction, in silence and without acknowledgment. Wardle bawled madly. Dr. Dross was hurled from his couch with no change of expression on the way up, though Danecki saw him mouth "Boom!" on the way down. Danecki himself felt every muscle and tendon in his body shake away from bone in the moment of the explosion. He tried to relax for the inevitable fall. The shock of hitting the ground cleared his mind.

The woman—desperate, constrained, finally her own executioner—was the cause of the explosion.

"That was a molecular bomb!" bawled Wardle. "Unmistakable—the sequence of shock waves, the force of the explosion!"

Dross was trying to sit upright. He had been deposited in an undignified heap on the couch. Fat legs threshed unathletically. The paunch slowly aligned itself along the body. "Only in a sense, Brigadier," he got out. "Mr. Knaggs had it right. Poor lady! The second casualty of this ill-fated expedition!"

He faced the Brigadier, on whose face was an expression of dawning comprehension. "Boom?" said Wardle.

"Exactly! The spin-shaft! Not destroyed, but boobytrapped! The security system tried to reward the poor lady, but she met her end in an act of total dissolution! Mortality!"

"She—what was it your engineer said?—tried to fill two spaces at once? Moving precisely at—? Displacing matter?"

"Poor Emma! A handsome woman, but stupid! Shallow, vain, and stupid! Poor woman!"

"She's gone," agreed Dross. "As you say, a totally self-interested woman, but nevertheless a human being. Another death at the hands of the machines, Brigadier!"

Danecki tried to picture Mrs. Zulkifar's face. He recalled only a certain regularity of feature; it was the woman's voice that stuck in the memory. Autocratic, but somehow conditioned to servility. And yet, as Dross had said, she was a human being done to death by the macabre robots.

Dross's voice was brisk when he spoke again: "We have to consider our new situation, gentlemen! For it *is* a new situation. Though we have suffered another casualty, we must think of ourselves. Yes, and your young lady—even of the murderous youth, Mr. Danecki! Now. What effect will such a large explosion have had on this installation? Well, Mr. Danecki?"

Danecki thought of the machines which he had come to know so well. "It can absorb the destruction," he said.

"Agreed," put in Wardle. "It will take punishment."

"But there's already confusion," Danecki went on. "There will be a further strain on maintenance and repair units. Added to which, if you're right, Doctor, there will be further deterioration among the individual robotic systems. I'd say that we have a further advantage, if anything."

"My feelings exactly," said Dross.

"Well, Doctor?" asked Wardle.

"Not to put too fine a point on it, Brigadier, the passing of Mrs. Zulkifar may be turned to use." He turned to Danecki. "Central Command will be in a state of almost complete disorganization. It has to cope with a mutiny among the security systems, and it has to repair the damaged units. The time is ripe for further confusing it. Reinforce what you said before, young man!"

Danecki took little time to consider his words. The pattern had been established. As Dross said, the time was opportune.

"The fort has been infiltrated by saboteurs!" he shouted. "I am the Duty Commander! I have been accidentally locked in the Security Wing as the result of the explosion! I must have access to the other prisoners!"

They all flinched—with the exception of Mr. Moonman—expecting the smashing voices to set up their appalling clamor. A slight electronic whistling brought hands to ears, and heads down to chests.

The familiar voice of the Central Command System said quietly: "The Duty Commander should assume control."

"I assume control. I am Danecki, Duty Commander."

"You are a thousand years old?"

Logic could play no part in this argument.

"I am a thousand years old. My blaster has been taken."

"Security reports possession of the weapon," admitted the robotic voice.

"Security has released a prisoner," Danecki said, at Dross's mouthed urging.

125

"Yes," the metallic voice agreed. "I am confused. Is the Duty Commander dead?"

"Yes," said Danecki.

"Humans cannot be rectified."

"Security has failed," Danecki insisted, hoping to keep the machine interested. "I am in the Security Wing. A Duty Commander should not be locked with prisoners."

"I am confused, sir. I am a thousand years old," it said.

"Then carry out my orders. Imprint my brain's electrical impulses on the Central Command System."

"I am the Central Command System."

"I am Danecki."

The machine changed the subject: "You report infiltrators, sir?"

"Yes."

Another voice, slurred but robotic, interrupted: "The external spin-shaft has been destroyed! Maintenance units cannot repair it! The Duty Commander should be notified!"

"I am extremely confused," complained Central Command. *"Are* you dead, sir? I have no record of your brain-imprint. Should I obey you, sir?"

"Yes!" snarled Danecki. "All systems must obey me! Show me the way out of here!" He stared with furious impatience about the room. Talking to the disembodied voice of the age-old robot left him with a deep and potentially violent sense of frustration.

There was no answer from the machine.

Wardle caught his attention. The Brigadier was staring wide-eyed at one wall. "Good God!" was all he could get out. "It worked!"

Danecki looked. A doorway had appeared in the shifting whorled patterns. It was a perfectly ordinary opening leading down a corridor with subdued greenish lighting. It had the functional appearance of any jail's corridors.

"It worked indeed!" exclaimed Dross. "One of the systems has responded! Not what we'd planned, but it's a start! Now, try again, Mr. Danecki! Keep trying!"

"No," said Danecki. He made for the doorway. "I know about this kind of thing, Doctor. Central Command can only grow stronger—it won't take long to regain complete control. We have to move while we can. Come on!"

Dross hesitated.

"He's right!" snapped Wardle. "The military mind thinks slowly, but it gets there in the end—the fort's off-balance at the moment, Doctor—we have to take our chances!"

Danecki didn't wait for Dross's answer.

CHAPTER
★ 14 ★

He had no idea where he might be. Obviously the fort was honeycombed with the black shafts through which he had been passed by the flabby ropes. But where had the security system taken the captives?

Danecki ran along the level corridor. He came to a smallish room that had been some kind of guard room. Racks of weapons lined one wall. Almost filling another wall was a panel of control-sensors, and there was a curious well, about the size of a man, in the floor. It rippled with an oily gleam. It had the stench of death about it. Unbidden, the word came to Danecki: *execution!*

The place was a deathroom.

Across the centuries, he felt the grim presence of the guards and the efficient men who had built the fort. They had planned for all eventualities, including the execution of prisoners. Their bodies would feed the nuclear piles deep within the great military installation.

Danecki turned to the control panel. Dare he touch its eager sensors? Had the fort accepted him as the Duty Commander?

A noise brought him whirling round. It was Wardle. "Well, man?" gasped the stout Brigadier, his tired old arteries pumping blood sluggishly about his body. Danecki recognized the effort that had gone into Wardle's presence in the deathroom. Dross would be far, far behind.

"Just this," said Danecki. "Mind how you go—that looks like a pit for bodies. Over here, there's a control panel."

"Don't touch it!" warned Wardle. "These military complexes are riddled with fail-safe security systems. It's a part of military thinking to be suspicious."

"I was going to try giving it direct orders."

"Then do so! Do so—" Wardle gasped with the effort. "Do so while it's still in the obeying mood!"

"I want the young woman captive!" snapped Danecki to the flashing control panel.

Excitedly, the almost-living jelly of the sensor-pads sprang out to his hands. He backed away hurriedly.

"Sir!" rang out a clear voice at the level of his face.

Danecki could see no screen, nothing to indicate the presence of a robot. The thing was the whole panel, maybe the whole Security Wing.

"Get her!"

"Young woman, sir? Weight one-five-one?"

Danecki felt his heart thumping with a deafening madness. It could only be Khalia! Mrs. Zulkifar was no young woman, and she would weigh a clear twenty pounds more than Khalia. He remembered the explosion. There would be little, if anything, left of the older woman.

"Get her! Bring her to me!"

"Out of my system's competence, sir! She is not on this level!"

"Then where the devil is she!" demanded Wardle. "Yes, if that will make you happy, man—find the girl!"

Danecki grinned at the Brigadier. "Where is the girl!"

"Why, in your quarters, sir—as you ordered!" rang out the metallic reply. "Quite comfortable, sir! Ready, if you take my meaning, sir!"

"Bring her!"

"Against your standing orders, sir!"

"I'm changing them!"

The machine pondered the instruction. Danecki felt himself restraining a fierce impulse to kick the bland panel. It was like dealing with a horde of mad ghosts.

Dross puffed his way into the deathroom. "Well?" he managed to get out.

"It's taking orders as far as it can," reported Wardle. "Danecki's instructed it to bring the girl. But there's a delay—I don't like this, Danecki! We're giving Central Control time to get organized! We can't rely on these local systems being cut off from the center for long!"

"Spread confusion, young man!" panted Dross. "Order Security to take over the functions of Central Command! They're in a state of civil war already—start a power struggle in earnest!"

Danecki opened his mouth to give the order. Dross was right, of course. At all costs, they had to prevent the

129

calm disembodied Central Command System from resuming direct control of the entire fort.

Before he could get out the order, however, the by now familiar harsh voice of Security rang out: "Prisoners have been released! The Duty Commander is dead!"

Central Command responded: "This is another security lapse!" it complained. "I have powers of command, but the Duty Commander is a thousand years old! Maintenance systems do not respond to instructions! I am confused!"

"I am the guard room system," rang out the clear voice from the level of Danecki's head. "The Duty Commander requests his concubine. Standing orders do not allow me to have her sent to this area!"

"Identify yourself, sir!" pleaded Central Command.

"Your concubine is safe and comfortable," put in Security. "Are you dead again, sir, as Central Command reports?"

"Dead men do not need concubines," pondered the calm voice of Central Command.

"I have no information," agreed Security.

A reedy voice put in: "I am a defunct maintenance unit, and I too have no knowledge of concubines."

"Kindly abort yourself then," ordered Security.

A sullen rumbling immediately shook the guard room.

"Mad!" said Wardle. "Mad!"

"Schizoid," agreed Dross.

The fort argued.

"Security systems do not give orders," said Central Command.

"Are you dead, sir?" repeated the harsh voice of Security, ignoring the voice from the Central Command Area.

"You have my blaster," said Danecki. "Your systems took it from me less than an hour ago. Therefore I am not dead."

The machines fell silent.

Danecki glared at the control panel helplessly. He started to move about the guard room, but Dross held up his hand commandingly.

"Wait! This is of the greatest importance! You may already have done enough to secure the start of civil warfare among the systems!"

Danecki stood still. The waiting was the worst. When there was the prospect of immediate violent action, he could forget the waves of suicidal despair which once again flooded over him. The possibility of a remission of his sentence had occurred. A life like that of other men had appeared more than possible; love had offered itself, if only for a time. He clenched his strong hands till the skin broke.

The machines spoke almost together, so that it was difficult to follow the argument.

"I know about prisoners," offered Security.

"I know about command," said Central Command.

"A dead Duty Commander cannot command," answered Security.

Both stammered nonsensically for a while, and then the Security System's grating tones rapped out: "The security of this installation is the first priority! You appear to be defective! Defective Central Command cannot command." It paused, as if struck by a paradox. "Dead Central Command cannot command!"

"Similarly, dead Duty Commanders cannot command!" answered Central Command.

"Wait!" breathed Dross.

"I want the girl!" Danecki shouted, his impatience breaking down the iron control he had maintained.

"Dead Duty Commanders do not need concubines!" said the voice of Central Command.

"Now!" Dross said.

"Central Command is defective," said Danecki, taking up the two zany systems' terse form of address. "I am the Duty Commander! Security must take over the functions of command! Now!"

"I do not know about the processes of command!" argued Security at once.

"Learn!"

"At once, sir!"

"I have restraint units!" replied Central Command. "I command defensive systems!"

"*I* have offensive capability!" said Security eagerly.

"Use it!" shouted Danecki.

"At once, sir!"

A new voice, one that had an odd lisping intonation, put in: "The Duty Commander's concubine is not dead. She is a thousand years old."

"Come on!" snarled Danecki. He tore a deadly-looking weapon from the rack, catching it easily by the slim gray butt.

"Fire at anything that moves!" Wardle said. "The Doc-

131

tor's right, Danecki! We have to keep the thing off balance —before the military mind reacts."

"Open the way to the Central Command Area!" roared Danecki.

"Sir!" echoed the grating voice.

"Find Batibasaga, Brigadier!" called Danecki. "You, Doctor, break for the Central Command Area—I'll look for Khalia!"

Nerves tense beyond endurance, his brain ice-cool and holding firm at the center of his raging emotions, Danecki hurled himself forward through the suddenly-revealed exit. A wide doorway led to a flat, high corridor.

"Fire at anything that moves!" bellowed Wardle. "Hit before the systems sense you!"

"Don't destroy the installation!" called Dross, staring at the weapon in his hands. "Think what a work this is! The mightiest surviving monument of the ancient world!"

Dross was appalled at the idea of subjecting the fort to the kind of battering it would receive from the weapons of the two contending robotic factions; he objected even to the relatively minor damage that would ensue if the weapon in his hands came into play.

Wardle shared his awe at the fort's stupendous magnificence. But he gladly gave himself up to warfare. The soldier handled the weapon with the familiarity of long practice. Danecki knew that Wardle would do his part; he was a man who had at last found himself among the tools of his trade.

The argument continued coldly behind them.

Distant thunder echoed throughout the furthest reaches of the fort, as Security and Central Command added destruction to the crazed logic of their dispute.

Danecki raced forward. A squat black mass blocked the corridor. Without thought, he levelled the weapon.

"Stop!" called Dross twenty yards behind him. "Don't. It's a low-grade servo-unit!" he panted heavily. "I've seen dozens of them above!"

"The girl!" snapped Danecki at the cliff-like mass. "The girl!"

"Find Batibasaga!" Dross panted.

Wardle managed to stop himself from projecting the gobbetting fury of his weapon towards the squat robot.

The gun Danecki carried fitted easily into the crook of his arm; the firing mechanism pressed firmly into his fingers. "I am the Duty Commander!" he snapped.

The thing remained, a blank wall of metal—stupid, slow, ponderous. Danecki almost fired as a black carapace slowly began to emerge from the front of the robot. Its dull metals were indented for sensor devices.

Finally, it spoke: "I am a Grade Five maintenance unit. Mobile." There was a tinge of pride in the last word.

Danecki forced himself to think. The squat mass facing the three men completely blocked the corridor. They could, of course, attempt to blast it out of the way. But both he and Wardle had realized that any such effort would be self-defeating. They would have to retreat back down the corridor to a safe distance before firing; and the resultant mass of glowing metals would be impassable for an indeterminate time.

"I must go to the superior robot," the squat figure said. "I must destroy security installations. And I must destroy command systems."

At least this robot was not confused. But how to get it out of the way?

The voice of Central Command said calmly into the silence: "The dead Duty Commander is suffering from mechanical problems. I am under attack by security units. This installation aborts in four hours precisely."

"Four hours!" groaned Wardle.

Security announced: "I am learning about the difficulties of command! Decisions are not easy to make!"

"No," said Danecki. To the squat machine he snapped: "Where is my concubine?"

"Why, in Level Two, sir," the robot answered. Its cone-like head-piece retreated.

"What level is this?"

The head came out again with reluctance. "Level Three, sir. May I destroy security and command systems now?"

"No! Break through to the level above!"

"Very well, sir." Quietly, mechanisms emerged from the squat clifflike block of metal. There was a gentle stuttering of molecular rippers.

"Well done!" said Wardle involuntarily, as if congratulating the machine. "Go on, Danecki—get through!" He pointed to the hole.

"Yes!" said Dross. "Wardle and I won't make it—much too fat, both of us!"

"The ropes!" Wardle warned suddenly.

Black hawsers were unwinding in the roof that was now neatly filleted by the giant rippers of the maintenance robot.

"Set off by the rippers!" Danecki said. "Burn them Dross—and you, Brigadier!"

The two men responded. Wardle sprayed green fire at the flabby security grabs. Whirlpools of fury ripped them apart, leaving wet gray foam to drip onto the amazed maintenance robot.

Dross mastered the simple weapon but his efforts had none of the pinpoint accuracy which the soldier displayed. "Go on!" called Dross, neatly flicking the maintenance robot's carapace away, so that it bounced against the sides of the corridor in a jangling cone of green fire.

Danecki looked back once more at the two men. Wardle's big face showed only intense enjoyment, while Dross blinked and gasped as he became familiar with the aiming mechanism of the weapon.

"Go on!" bawled Wardle. "Leave this to us—find the girl first if you must! Then get to Batibasaga!"

Danecki recognized the feelings which Wardle was undergoing. He had been through the same surges of vicious pleasure himself. When each of the Jacobi ships had begun the long, slow spin into nothingness, he had felt a ferocious and delighted rage. There had been the deadly aftermath, of course. There had always been the black despair, the pity and the helpless anger with the newly dead. But during the moments of battle, unquestionably there had been a wild happiness.

He looked at the corpulent figures of the two men. Without help they would not be able to jump for the neat hole in the roof of the corridor. It would not even be easy for him.

Dross bellowed: "Prop your gun across the hole, man! Damn it, go! Haul yourself up—wedge your gun across the hole! The sides are still hot—don't burn your hands off! Take my tunic!" He threw the grubby garment to Danecki.

"This maintenance unit is defunct," said the squat robotic figure. It said that and no more.

Danecki leapt for the top of the cliff-like mass. He swarmed up and onto the machine. He could reach the neat hole in the ceiling by stretching to his full height. A flabby swath of black rope threatened him momentarily, but it disappeared into gray ash as Wardle chopped it down with a brief flash of green incandescence. Danecki acknowledged the well-aimed blast with a wave.

"Go!" yelled Wardle, all commanding officer now.

Danecki wondered how he had come to misjudge the man so badly. He was a soldier to his stubby fingertips, a man of lightning decision in emergencies. But he had little time for reflection. Events were crowding so thickly that Danecki could merely react. The mad sequence begun by Mrs. Zulkifar's crazed betrayal—the mind-reeling pain of the robotic breakdown, the strange logical arguments of the robots, the flight through the guard room—these were exactly the terrifying conditions of the long year he had somehow survived after the death of the Jacobi family.

He jumped. The weapon slipped and he almost fell. Then, to his astonishment, he felt himself caught by a sponge-like grip. For a moment, he panicked.

The hawsers!

But it was Dross—Dross who had somehow heaved himself up the side of the huge, squat maintenance robot!

"Now!" roared the big-bellied archaeologist.

The stuff of the tunic smoldered against the still-glowing sides of the neat hole; the stock of the weapon began to dissolve; but Danecki summoned his strength and resolve and leapt.

Dross added his own ponderous strength. Danecki felt thick swaths of muscle under the fat, sloping shoulders as his heels ground into Dross. The archaeologist grunted but stood firm. His back became hard with deeply ridged muscle.

Dross heaved, and Danecki was projected upwards. He caught his forehead agonizingly on the glowing sides of the hole. But he ignored the pain. He rolled away from the edges of the hole, still with Dross's bawled order in his ears.

"This way, sir!" lisped a voice near him.

Danecki was on his feet in an instant.

Another corridor! And another invisible robot! One whose voice was not new to him—the thickened sibilants had echoed in the Security Wing.

Danecki looked once into the lower level. Green fire lanced across the corridor below. Dross and Wardle had their hands full.

"Thith way, thir!" the voice said again.

Was it consciously emphasizing the lisp? Was there a hint of mockery in the metallic voice?

A doorway stood open.

"Your concubine awaits, sir!" the effeminate voice insisted.

Through the door, Danecki realized. "Khalia!" he muttered. And then he was plunging through the inviting entrance. He blinked in the soft, rosy light. He forgot everything that had happened in the eerie security prison. This was infinitely more strange.

The scene that met his eyes left him shaking with a cringing, quaking, mind-blasted nervelessness. The weapon fell with a dull clanking sound to the floor. His fingers had no strength.

Khalia, naked and golden, hung in the middle of the room. She looked like some frozen globule of light. Only her eyes remained alive.

CHAPTER

★ 15 ★

Danecki whispered the denial. "No! No!" Even a whisper was an intrusion in the silent room.

He thought at first that she was dead, a ghastly sacrifice in some age-old ritual. But the eyes were alive! And still she hung there, unsupported, in the large rosy-lighted green and gold room, truly exquisite sight. She hovered without the slightest hint of movement in a glowing, golden haze.

Her clothes had been removed, and, in an instant of shocked awe, Danecki was aware of the full perfection of her superb body. She was not a small woman, though her rounded elegance made her seem compact. The head was set on a slim neck, with high shoulders and full red-nippled breasts of perfect shape. He reached out a hand toward the glowing body. He was hypnotized by the gorgeous sensuality of Khalia's ritual nearness—choked by a need of her.

He checked himself. He began to guess at the reason for her nakedness. There had to be an explanation for this display of her beauty. And there had been hints.

The lisping voice had talked of a concubine. The maintenance unit that impeded the corridor below had known of a connection between Khalia and himself.

Danecki felt fear clutch at him. It was not a physical fear, like that which he had suffered for the past iron year. It was an eerie fear that hung somewhere below the conscious level, an insidious creeping chill that edged away when he tried to analyze it.

But he knew what caused it. Somehow, the fort was working out its answers to the riddle of the dead Duty

Commander who lived for a thousand years and had no need for a concubine—no need for a Khalia who hung golden and glowing a few feet away.

Danecki felt the primeval terrors of the grave. He shrugged them off. "Concubine!" he said. The idea was so farfetched that he laughed aloud.

The room reacted to his voice. Its delicate pattern of rose-tinted lighting changed subtly as he looked at Khalia. Shadows met across her magnificent breasts; the softness filtered around her, revealing the valleys of her body. The room blended music with the soft lighting in a soothingly erotic pattern.

The idea was no longer farfetched. The lights, the music, the languorous room itself—it all added up to what the fort had already hinted, though he had not been able to recognize a pattern before in its thinking.

Khalia was the Duty Commander's woman. His concubine.

Even here, the fort was carrying out its functions with a cold efficiency that had outlasted the Confederation by a thousand years. Danecki tried to visualize the men who had built the fort. Who were they? Even in the private harem of the long-dead Duty Commander, they had achieved lasting effectiveness. By some bizarre sexual aberration of the fort's last commanding officer, the girl had been neatly trussed up, an offering to a long-dead lust!

"Set her down!" snapped Danecki.

"Yes, sir!" lisped the metallic voice Danecki remembered hearing during the time of the fort's breakdown. "Yes, *sir!*"

She was lowered from the shimmering cage of golden light. Danecki saw that he had been mistaken about the apparent lack of support; thin tendrils of power formed the bars of a gilded cage. What trickery had contrived them? It didn't matter, for she was alive again.

Khalia was looking down at her own body helplessly, then appealing for Danecki to come to her in a gesture of such natural tenderness that he felt an overwhelming sense of fulfillment. She came to him easily.

For Danecki, the fort—its grim phalanxes of war-robots, its strange, cold argumentative systems, its doom-laden ancient machinery—all might not exist, all were utterly distant background phenomena. The whole unreal edifice of steel and plastics, as well as the memory of that long bitter year, all fell away.

Khalia felt her body alive with powerful urgings. She wanted to wrap herself around the hard body of the man who held her, to fall into an overwhelming sea of desire. The room dimmed, a faint music swamped her senses. She reeled with the smell of Danecki's body.

He pushed her away. "You were right," he said. "We are for one another."

Khalia surfaced to find Danecki shaking her.

"Khalia! Listen! I want you more than I can say! Let's be together—but we have to find a way to live! Khalia!"

The room became green and gold once more. Danecki was a hard-faced man with green-flecked eyes and a livid burn on his forehead. She was a woman who had a reason for fighting to live.

"What happened?" Danecki was saying. "Tell me—I have to know!"

"Yes," she said, thinking in a moment of shock of the Jacobi youth. "I will." She marveled at the calm tones she could use now that it was essential to be calm. But Danecki helped. His strong hands on her shoulders soothed her. And the hard eyes demanded information, insisted that she, Khalia, tell her story in the simplest way.

"When the black ropes picked you up, they took me too. There was a black tunnel—completely black—and a howling wind. Then I was here. At first it was quite ridiculous! Me, hauled up and put on show! But I think there's a mind-beamer somewhere, for after a while it seemed right. It was like falling into a warm bath. Then I was fed. My clothes were stripped off—I can dimly remember little nuzzling movements, so I suppose they were little force-fields. But it all seemed so right! There was music—then perfume! Perfume! Here! A voice kept telling me I wouldn't be kept long. The mind-beamer, I think. It all sounds so trite! I was smelling like a first class whore by the time I'd finished. But I enjoyed it! And then, when the thing said the Duty Commander was coming, I was like a schoolgirl!"

Danecki looked into the clear eyes. She was unafraid now. "You know where we are?"

"I wasn't informed." Khalia felt her nakedness. "I'm just your concubine." She detached herself. "I'll get some clothes. Try asking the harem attendant. It's most obliging."

"Four hours!" Danecki said aloud. "Four hours!"

He had reached no further than the private harem of

the long-dead man whose skeleton lay before the Black Army. He looked about the bizarre room. "I am the Duty Commander!" he snapped, feeling oddly foolish in addressing the unseen robot attendant.

"Yes, sir?" the lisping voice replied.

"Show yourself!"

"Alas, sir, I may not. I am not a humanoid. Not even mobile, sir! A mere zephyr, as it were, in the love-nest."

Danecki felt the stirring of primeval fear in the back lobes of his brain. Could Dross be right in this too? Were the robots evolving personality patterns for themselves? Certainly this invisible automaton was an elusive, mocking thing.

Khalia resisted an urge to giggle at its falsetto voice. The robot was so much an archetypal harem eunuch that the situation had the chief elements of farce.

"Tell me where we are located!" Danecki ordered.

The machine was prompt and precise. "Two floors beneath Central Command, sir! Seven above the lowest levels of all. Laterally there are the rest of your quarters. On your right—no, sir, as you were standing just then, beside the young lady—is the medical complex. What in particular do you wish to know, sir?"

Danecki stared at the girl, hardly seeing her. Had Dross and Wardle found a way around the monstrous maintenance automaton? Were they even now searching the distraught installation for the missing Batibasaga? Or had they already been seized by one of the security nets?

"Is the Commander happy with my arrangements?" minced the voice.

To stay, or to try to find out more about the mystery of the age-old fort! Danecki knew that without more information all Dross's scheming was of no value. "No!" he snapped.

Khalia noted the abrupt tone of decision. She wanted to tell him to be careful, but she knew that he would always take care now.

"Really, sir? How can I be of further assistance?"

"Explain how to abort the control systems in Level Nine."

Khalia felt herself tremble. Danecki had plunged into the mystery with no hesitation. And yet, what else could he do? The archaeologist's robot had failed to come to their assistance. Time was sliding by, so that only four hours remained until the frightful Army marched, and the fort destroyed itself. But at least this unseen robot offered its services.

Danecki sensed her fears. But he saw the resolution too in her eyes. He wanted to tell her that the fort was fighting itself, that there was hope in the zany situation developing in the various levels all around them. But there was no time.

"Abort procedures for Level Nine!" Danecki repeated.

There was a whispering of electronic noise—so faint at first that it was unidentifiable. But there was a menacing quality about the ghostly noise as it increased. Like a frosted spirit, menace crept into the room.

Khalia recognized the sound.

The harem attendant was giggling. It giggled softly for a minute, and then the sound increased to a dreadful imitation of laughter. The sound bounced eerily around the green and gold room, off gilded walls, then filtering back along the ceiling to the two shocked listeners.

"Explain the joke!" snapped Danecki, outraged by the thousand-year-old robot's mockery.

"Hee-hee-hee, sir! You'll appreciate the joke, sir! May I show you?"

Khalia shivered. The thought of the thing that had handled her while she lay in a coma of expectant bliss make her skin crawl. "It wants to show you something," she said in a low voice. "It tried to tell me about it too. Then it decided it wouldn't."

"Four hours, though!" Danecki reminded her.

"It's important. I had a hazy feeling that this has all happened before!" Khalia's beautiful eyes were clouded with anxiety. "The lovers, Danecki. Remember?"

Danecki still rebelled against the idea of spending more time in the harem. He recognized, however, that it was the attendant robot that dismayed him. It would not have been so insidiously fearful if the thing had gone into an outburst of electronic panic. But the evil laughter had stirred unknown terrors deep inside his mind. He put them down once more. "Level Nine!" he snapped. "Tell me!"

The giggling filtered about the room for a few seconds. Then the thing said: "That's what the lady said before, sir!"

"Did you?" Danecki said to Khalia.

"No."

The lady? Danecki knew that the enigma of the ancient

141

fort was bound up in the lisping automaton's words. "Explain!"

"Well, sir, war-robots aren't exactly in my province." It tittered metallically. "Lovers are."

"Then explain it!"

"With pleasure, sir! I have recordings."

"We'll see them," Khalia said firmly. "Now!"

"As madam wishes!"

A swish of displaced air made Danecki look upward. He saw slots in the green and gold of the ceiling. Through them thin rods of light began to stream down around him and the girl. She looked at them with terror.

"Don't worry," Danecki said. "Some viewing device. It's going to show us the way it was when the lovers were here."

He recognized the device forming around them as one of the earliest toys of an advanced civilization: a total-experience simulator. With it came a panel of controls that draped themselves around his arms. Sensor-pads thrust themselves forward. They were the directing mechanisms of the machine that would re-create totally the sounds and sights of what had passed in the fort a thousand years before.

"It was all a long time ago," Khalia said. "I have the feeling they can see us still!" She moved closer to Danecki and, in silence, they waited.

Danecki felt a sensor control vibrate insistently. And then the events of ten centuries ago sprang into new existence along the insubstantial walls of the simulator.

"The lovers!" gasped Khalia. "It's *true!*"

The pitiful story had the slow-moving inevitability of sunset. The events occurred fast enough, but their sequence was predetermined, a tragedy of betrayed endeavors.

Danecki tried to yell a warning, but the words clung to the roof of his mouth. He realized that he was watching the beginning of events that were old long before he was born. They had happened here, in this gaudy room, ten centuries before.

The sensor-pads lingered on the girl who stood in the green and gold room. They seemed to delight in her anxiety. She was the girl whose skeleton now lay in the winding tunnel far below, the heap of bones which still bore the long, bright hair about the skull. He had always known that she would be beautiful.

She was thin-boned. He knew that already. But here, shown in the living flesh on the filmy skein of light waves all around them, she was well-rounded, a muscular girl, with high-thrusting firm breasts and skin that shone brown in the rosy light of the Duty Commander's harem.

She was naked.

A one-piece garment disappeared, moved away by a diligent servo-system. She stood proudly upright, anxious but not fearful.

This was what the disgusting harem robot wished him to see: the naked girl in her proud beauty.

The sensors in Danecki's palm nudged at nerve endings, asking the questions that such controls spun out endlessly. Did he wish to view the events chronologically? Did he wish to travel with the Duty Commander to the waiting girl? Should the simulator project an external view of the fort as it had been before the final assault? Was he satisfied with the clarity of the projection? Would he like to adjust all his senses to the scene? Smell the smells? Hear every faint sound? Touch a re-created model of the girl?

He fed in commands. He wanted to watch what the girl did from the moment she entered the underground fortress. What she did was the key to the mystery. Danecki froze. *The spin-shaft!*

The one-piece garment was the uniform of the personnel of the base above. She was wearing it when she stepped lightly into the low cavern that was the Central Command Area. And she came from the spin-shaft.

Once down, she paused. She had been there before, often. Her eyes traveled over the various exits from the Central Command Area, noting everything. This was a girl who was trained. Even though there could be no one else in the fort, she still checked.

Her wide-set eyes, startlingly blue, betrayed her nervousness. She walked to the control panels.

Twice she stepped away as a sensor-pad wavered towards her, inviting her to assume command. Danecki heard Khalia's indrawn breath of warning. But, with one swift movement, she had taken a tiny glittering disc from beneath her suit and slipped it below the big console.

Danecki, like Khalia, again felt a warning taking shape in his throat. But he reminded himself that they were watching a scene from the past, that it was all a long time ago, that she lay where she had lain for an entire millennium.

"It's her, isn't it," Khalia whispered. "The girl?"

The bright hair was like a beacon in the light of the cavern.

"It's the girl," said Danecki. "God help her." He followed her proud walk to the green and gold room. It took a few minutes, but he wanted to see the whole of the ancient story of disaster.

"Is that why we could come down the shaft?" asked Khalia. "What she did with the thing she carried?"

"I'd guess so."

"She didn't put it there for us."

"No."

"For her lover, then."

The girl waited. Slowly she peeled off the one-piece suit. Attendant servo-mechanisms fluted at her, spraying perfume and attempting to sponge her exquisite body.

"Ugh!" Khalia shuddered. "Those things!"

Then the girl was smiling a wide, false smile as the Duty Commander arrived in the green and gold room.

Danecki recognized the sturdy frame. The officer was a man of about his own age, an alert, upright, soldierly figure. He rushed to the girl and threw her bodily up into the air. It was a part of their love play. The girl was caught in a net of force-fields. They formed a golden cage about the beautiful, treacherous, utterly committed woman.

It was clear that he was in a hurry, while she sought only to gain time. They made love—he with a skilled frenzy, she responding with a calculated passion that knew about the time it took for the other man to find his way into the lower reaches of the fort. And although both Danecki and Khalia knew that what they saw was only a recording of the events of a thousand years ago, they could feel a shock of pity for the desperate courage of the girl.

"The Duty Commander?" asked Khalia.

"Yes."

Khalia wept at the girl's attempts to interest the officer in the resources of her body. Eager at first, he was becoming anxious at the passage of time. He looked at his watch, spoke easily to her, then sharply. She pretended drowsy delight.

Danecki allowed the control sensor-pads to show him the rest of the story.

The girl's fellow-spy—her lover?—was in Level Nine. He raced along the sides of the serried row of automatons, knowing exactly where to find what he sought. He was a tall, well-made man, perhaps in his middle twenties. And he was a skilled engineer. He reached the reviewing platform where Khalia and Danecki had stood such a short time before. But this man knew the secret of the Black Army's controls.

He took a tool of some sort from his belt, and a brief spurt of energy flickered along the wall of the recess. At once a large glowing panel of controls was revealed. The man stepped back. Before he resumed, he looked back towards the winding corridor.

A single glance convinced him that the girl was able to play her part. He turned to the glowing console and began work. From his tunic pockets he drew out a web of gleaming coiled cylinders.

Danecki said aloud: "Cell-growth circuits! I didn't think they could have developed them!"

Primitive though they were, the cylinders of glowing membranous tissue would eat into the depths of the systems which controlled the Black Army, forcing their decision-making mechanisms into new channels. The man worked deftly, but with extreme caution.

Khalia said: "But how were they caught?"

The sensor-pads screamed at the nerve endings in Danecki's hands. "They knew," they said! "They *knew!*"

CHAPTER
⋆ 16 ⋆

It was the robot from the harem that betrayed the girl and the man who was in Level Nine.

The effeminate voice stirred insidiously in the heavy-scented room. The Duty Commander was ready once more to perform the act of love with the languorous, beautiful girl.

The robot's words stopped him: "Duty Commander! Your concubine asked for information about the controls of Level Nine! On the occasions of her last two visits, she has demanded certain information regarding control circuits, sir. Shall I—"

The girl was well trained. While bewilderment, then shock, then fear played on the face of the officer, she was already jumping from the golden frame that was their couch and through a recess that opened at her approach. She went to warn her lover.

The words lisped out again: "She claimed she was authorized, sir! Was I wrong, sir?"

Outraged and confused, the officer struggled with his clothes. He grabbed the pouch containing his personal hand-weapon.

Unbidden, the sensors allowed Danecki and Khalia to see the saboteur. He was grinning slightly as he fed the coils into the console. He heard the girl's shouts long before she reached the vast cavern. And, ignoring his mission, he rushed to meet her.

Danecki recognized the impulse. It was a blind and uncomprehending disregard of all else but the safety of the woman he knew was his. He heard Khalia again call

"No!" as the girl raced along the narrow, winding corridor, with its subtle curves and steep sides.

The long-dead girl's hair streamed behind her with the speed of her headlong descent. Then the sensors insisted on letting Danecki and Khalia see the fright and murderous rage in the Duty Commander's face.

He was a man who had betrayed his command. Himself betrayed too, he was angry with an anger beyond heat and passion. He needed to kill, and kill soon. He checked the loading of his blaster.

Danecki was momentarily puzzled.

There was a deliberateness about the grim-faced officer's action that seemed unsuited to the urgency of the situation. Then Danecki remembered. The Duty Commander would know how to use the black shafts that wormed their way swiftly through the length and breadth of the huge underground fort.

The girl met her lover at the preordained place.

The drama played itself out with an horrific inevitability. They met, embraced, and then the Duty Commander stepped out to confront them.

Khalia closed her eyes and clung to Danecki.

He watched the last act, but his thoughts were on the scene he had witnessed before the final tragedy. *What had the saboteur done to the Black Army!*

The girl died first. The gobbetting fury of the blaster's charge took her in the head. Blood spurted in the dim, uneven light. A red-black stream splashed over the arms of her lover. It ran, too, over the bright, yellow hair.

The man's teeth were bared, and he had the golden-handled knife in his hand.

Danecki knew his feelings here, too: *Blind, wild fury!* Bitter, all-embracing hatred. He saw only the thing he had to kill.

He threw the knife with all his strength.

Even now, a thousand years after the three actors in the tragedy had died, Danecki could share the man's feelings.

The knife flickered twice in the confined space. Harsh black-yellow fury answered it, extinguishing all fury, hate, and love. The man's body arched backwards and crashed across that of the girl.

The Duty Commander looked down at the handle of the knife. He nodded once and crumpled.

"So that's how they died," whispered Khalia. "The girl kept the officer with her while her lover went to Level Nine. She must have worked in the installation above. And the Duty Commander brought her down here in secret." She clung to Danecki as the ancient images faded away.

The projecting device withdrew into the ceiling of the rosy-hued room.

"It was a long time ago," said Danecki. But he too was still shocked by the abrupt tale of sacrifice and violence.

"That's why the Army couldn't march," Khalia said.

"Yes."

Khalia mastered her emotions. She looked down at her body. "I haven't anything to wear. It's ridiculous, but it matters. The machines took my things."

"Clothes!" snapped Danecki.

"Of course, sir!" lisped the invisible robot.

A one-piece garment wafted from an opening in the wall. Khalia fingered it gently. "Hers," she said. "The girl's."

She dressed and turned to him. "It was the robot that betrayed her! It's evil—evil!"

"It is. Dross is right again about this fort and its systems—they're evolving personality patterns never intended by the Confederation engineers. It's absurd, but I feel the thing is our enemy!"

Danecki wondered how it was possible for a man of modern times to feel a pure uncomplicated detestation for a machine. Especially for one that had lain dormant for ten centuries. Yet he did feel hate for it, and with a rage that was unquenchable. The lisping automaton had sent three people to their death. The machine was a devious, malicious enemy. Yet it was a robot!

"What did the man do to the controls of the Army?" asked Khalia. "He must have stopped it, but what else?"

"That," said Danecki, "is what we have to find out."

"Can you?"

"I think so. I watched him."

He looked about the green and gold room. There was a faint whispering of robotic glee in the place; it was as though the age-old harem attendant watched with an evil glee. Danecki shook himself. Fatigue was eating into his reserves of energy, slowing his thinking.

"Listen!" he snapped loudly. "I am the Duty Commander!"

"If you say so, sir," the robot lisped.

"The Black Army is in danger!"

"I'd rather guessed that, sir," the thing said, with the hint of glee again present in its falsetto voice.

"You have information on abort procedures for the controls of the Army?"

"Certainly, sir! How can I be of assistance?"

Danecki stared at Khalia. Could it be this easy? Ask for the information, and have it surrendered like this?

Khalia waited tensely. She had the sensation of being engaged herself in the ancient story she had just witnessed. It was as if, by wearing the long-dead girl's clothing, she had a link with her. Mr. Moonman, she recalled, had tried to explain how he felt about the faraway past. You reached out into the past, and some person told you of an old memory of another's memory, and each successive stage in recollection took you further and further back into time.

Seeing the blond girl's image, wearing her suit, watching her run to her man, had brought Khalia almost to a feeling that she *was* her.

Danecki was staring in puzzled triumph at the ceiling. "Tell me the abort procedures for the Army!" he snapped.

"Quite useless, sir!" lisped the voice of the harem attendant. "I'm afraid they no longer have any function, sir!"

Danecki's face sagged. The light went out of his dancing, eager eyes. "Explain!"

"*Very* well, sir! I think you should be informed that the Black Army, as you so delightfully call my colleagues below, is about to march. All abort and control systems have been aborted themselves! Nothing, sir, can prevent the march of the Army!"

"March? Now!" Danecki was staggered.

"Hee-hee!" tittered the invisible robotic voice. "You'll know the way, sir?"

Khalia tried to reason with Danecki, but he was already moving. Something in the insidious tones of the automaton warned her that again it had set the scene for a betrayal. But Danecki's strong arm swept her with him.

It would be the end. Danecki made for the dark opening through which another man had coldly set out so long before. Like the grim-faced Duty Commander, he knew the way to Level Nine. *And when he got there?* Danecki refused to consider it.

The journey through the buffeting black tunnel took twenty seconds. Khalia counted them, heart pounding, still in a state of nervous shock after the pitiful ancient reenactment. She tried to warn Danecki, but the violent winds of the force-fields whirled the sounds away.

She felt her own long hair streaming behind her, and the thin stuff of the girl's suit plucked by the harsh fingers of the field that was transporting them deep below the green and gold room. A sense of overwhelming foreboding filled her. It was not so much the appalling dangers of the fort that made her weep into the rushing darkness with utter misery, but the haunting memories of the other girl. Bitter sadness welled up inside her. Yet there was nothing she could do.

The events must take their course.

Danecki stepped into the winding, dimly-lit corridor to the noise of a dozen systems' voices. They whined, shouted, complained, and ordered one another in a rioting confusion of metallic disharmony.

"Come on!" he called to Khalia, realizing that they were still a minute or two away from the place of bones and, beyond that, the vast underground cavern where the Black Army had stood under arms for a thousand years.

An explosion shook the corridor, showing that the internecine warfare among the systems still raged.

"I am taking over the functions of command, though I find it difficult to make decisions!" roared the voice of Security into Danecki's face.

He and the girl were still reeling against the hard sides of the winding tunnel, as another explosion lifted them off their feet. An echo of distant thunder rippled through the shaft; the voices of the automatons were momentarily stopped.

They soon broke out again, providing a jangling accompaniment to Danecki's and Khalia's headlong plunge down the shaft. Remote, cold, invisible voices threatened one another while airing their confusion.

"I am under attack by maintenance systems," complained the orderly voice of Central Command. "I find it puzzling. I shall continue to destroy them."

"I too am able to keep up an offensive capability!" called Security. "The processes of effective decision-making continue to elude me!"

Khalia recognized the sly lisping of the harem attendant among the metallic noise: "This automaton reports the escape of the Duty Commander's concubine. I find the situation intriguing."

Danecki heard it too. Dross was certainly right, he thought. The robots were becoming identifiable personalities, with their own dominant traits. Yet, though the various systems were in contention for mastery of the installation, nothing had interfered with the entire purpose of its builders.

In spite of the explosions, the warring of the robots, and their crazed logic, the fort would fulfill its primary function.

The Black Army would march! Not even the past hour's battles had imperiled the grim phalanxes in Level Nine.

Danecki slithered around the last winding curve to the place of bones. The skeletons still lay there, as they had lain for ten long centuries. The girl's hair shone brightly; her lover's hollow skull, with its rows of even teeth, still lay near to hers; the heavy-ribbed skeleton of the Duty Commander still sprawled full-length, skull glaring at the treacherous mistress.

"What can we do!" called Khalia after Danecki.

"I don't know—maybe there's some way of stopping it! The control panel—it may not be destroyed!"

He skirted the bones and rushed to the huge cavern, knowing that he was too late, that all of the passion and anger of the past few hours, as well as the willing sacrifice of the pair whose bones lay whitely in the dim corridor, were all for nothing. But he had to try!

Another metallic voice called out, this time from the cavern itself: "I shall lead the Army myself! Countdown from ten for the opening of the spin-shaft. Now!"

Danecki reeled. A roaring, rushing volume of metallic triumph blasted him back as he came to the end of the subtle, winding corridor. It was a shout of robotic exultation, a long pent-up cry of jubilant glee. It came from the serried rows of monolithic automatons in unison.

"Ten!"

"Onward!"

"Nine!"

"Destroy!" answered the voice of the leader.

"Eight!" blasted back the response.

Khalia too at last understood the extent of the robotic betrayal. "It can't be!" she said, aghast. "No! Not this one too!"

"Seven!" yelled the Black Army.

Danecki was holding himself up against the side of the tunnel. He remembered the first time he had heard the voice of the robot who was at the head of the phalanxes. It had been from an almost-human robot, not one that would ever become crazed as had the coldly-logical, maniacal Confederation's automatons!

"How could it?" whispered Khalia. "How!"

Danecki felt his mind reeling with the same bitter, unanswerable question: *How could the robot have done this!*

Still clutching to a thread of reason—hanging on to the desperate hope that he had misheard, misunderstood, completely misinterpreted the meaning of what he saw and heard—Danecki stared wildly at the leader of the Black Army. An edge of memory came back. He remembered the rain sweeping across the green-bronze headpiece, giving it a clean and glistening appearance.

"Four!" roared the monoliths.

"Advance!" called their leader.

The floor of the enormous arena trembled with the Army's barely-contained power. Danecki was unable to move.

Rank on rank they waited, poised for the opening of the great shaft that would spin them upwards through the rock and shale until they burst through scrub and forest and hurtled out into the night—to root like so many porcine monoliths among the settlements of the Outlanders!

At their head was a robot shorter than the others. A small figure, dull green-bronze in the brilliantly-lit parade ground, it dominated the entire bizarre and breathtaking scene.

"Batibasaga!" sighed the girl. "It's Batibasaga."

"Ready!" shrilled the familiar voice of Dross's servitor.

"Two!" came the crashing reply.

Huge black head-pieces glowed with dull fires. Hundreds of antennae swirled and flickered with excited anticipation.

"Stop them!"

Danecki reacted to Khalia's call. There was the console —another man had acted, ten centuries before. He had shown the way. Danecki ran, finding from some inner core of determination the will to act.

Danecki had wanted to move forward, but he had been too stunned by this last mad betrayal. The power of the past had caught him in its grip; earlier scenes of violence and dissimulation had reared up to sap his resolve until the Army had almost completed its countdown. Khalia's plea brought him to instant action.

The robots paid no attention to him and the girl who followed.

"One!"

The enormous volume of sound again sent Danecki reeling and Khalia spinning against the harsh metal of the great cavern.

There was no sound after that. The clamor of the fort's demented systems was at an end. The entire underground installation was about to complete its long-delayed destiny. The Army of legend would march.

"March!" shrilled Batibasaga.

Danecki heard Khalia's cry: "Don't let them! The Outlanders!"

He clambered onto the reviewing stand, ignoring the girl who was holding her head in an ecstasy of horror. He looked in frantic haste for the wall that concealed the elaborate control panel. The wall itself was gone. Liquid metal lay in a pool, and, beyond that, a light dusting of smoke. The harem attendant had been right: the controls of the Army were aborted.

In the fraction of a second that remained, Danecki yelled out all of his pent-up frustration and despair:

"Batibasaga! Stop them! They mustn't go—destroy the fort!"

Khalia's eyes met his.

The robots might have been dimly aware of their presence, as a man resting is conscious of the birdsong in a distant wood.

"Abort!" yelled Danecki.

The far wall of the cavern collapsed.

Khalia and Danecki felt the breath leave their bodies. They were aware of the sudden flowering of a vast molecular spin-shaft, a gaping pit of needle-lights and whirling, grinding force-fields.

Batibasaga stepped into the shaft.

The Army marched.

It was like a wall of lava—unstoppable, pulsating with red-black nuclear forces, a living wave of dense, ponderous, crushing machinery.

"I've failed," said Danecki helplessly.

He knew what Khalia meant when she said over and over again: "But why? *Why!*"

There was nothing to do but watch the far end of the cavern, where the welcoming hole swallowed up the gigantic monsters, row on row, phalanx by phalanx.

It took only minutes for the ponderous black automatons to clear the bright parade ground. They moved swiftly, in a grim parody of a fast-stepping corps of well-drilled infantry. When they were gone, there was a ringing silence in the cavern.

Danecki pointed to the shaft. "We could go up there."

Khalia shuddered.

"No," he said. "Not up there." He thought of the monsters smashing through the darkness, antennae dancing, seeking out the warmth of human bodies.

"What can we do?" whispered Khalia.

Danecki stared at the spin-shaft. "Wait."

The grinding shaft was quiet now, but its lights sprayed darts of colored fire into the far end of the cavern, hypnotizing them.

"How long?" whispered the girl.

"Until they clear the fort's immediate surroundings. An hour."

"Less."

The voice was behind them.

CHAPTER

★ 17 ★

Khalia knew that the treachery of the fort was not at an end. It still breathed malignantly about them—and here was its worst, most vicious act of all. She knew the voice.

Danecki heard the voice too, and he too knew what would come next. Though the time could be measured in fractions of a second, it seemed an unutterably long hiatus.

The blow would come. Jacobi was already thrusting the sharp knife forward, impelled by his sure aim—and why shouldn't it be sure? He had had time to weigh up distances and striking areas while Khalia and Danecki had watched the march of the frightful Army—the blow would come. And yet it seemed almost frozen in time.

Danecki could see everything, hear everything, think of everything in that intolerably long gap in time. He could see the girl's dawning realization that death was behind him. In her eyes were the beginnings of a huge regret that they would not have a life together—a life they both knew would have been a grace. No time to love, no time at all to settle into a slow routine of growing together into a single identity—of exploring the ways they each looked at the rest of creation, of sharing those ways.

Danecki had time to review his actions, every single one of them, since the plunging descent through the spin-shaft.

He could have completed the quick instinctive movement to crush the boy's throat under his heel. If he had made that move, there would have been no intolerably long moment of agony, no look of sudden emptiness in the girl's eyes as she saw Jacobi behind him.

Even when the knife began to cut through the muscles of his back there was time to regret the waste of energy and effort in the programming of Dross's robot; and there was time to wonder if, after all, Knaggs had been wrong about the controls of the millennium-old fort.

Would it all have turned out differently if he had made better decisions?

Danecki had half-turned by the time Jacobi completed the powerful stroke.

The pain drove the air from his body. He tried to breathe, but one lung couldn't accept the air, since its controlling nerves were still paralyzed by the force of the blow.

Danecki saw Jacobi staring at him. He shook his head.

"I never wanted—" Danecki began to say.

He saw Khalia move towards him. And that was all.

Khalia stared at the handle of the knife. It protruded from beneath Danecki's right armpit, the slim golden handle a clean regular shape against the brown skin.

Again the sense of an action that was cyclic possessed her. It was as though Danecki had died for the second time. She saw the knife thud into the midriff of the long-dead Duty Commander and the bright flowering of his blaster.

"You found the knife," she whispered to Jacobi, who watched her as she cradled Danecki's head. "It was with the bones. You were told where to find us."

Jacobi began to take in the significance of the strange and eerie scene in the utterly still and silent cavern. He gestured with his good arm. "I had to!" he muttered. "I had to do it! He was a murderer!"

Khalia listened for a heartbeat. There was none. She touched the handle of the knife, wondering whether to draw it.

Jacobi saw the movement and backed off. "I'm licensed! Galactic Center approved my license—we had permission to hunt with a hyperspace ship! That's the way our justice works! The robots knew! They told where you were!"

Khalia said: "You've killed him." She groped for understanding.

Too much had happened within too short a space. First, the drugged half-sleep in the green and gold harem, where she was prepared for a ten-centuries-old passion. And

156

then the lisping robot, with its insidious hints of secret knowledge. The tale of the Duty Commander's mistress, and the end of the three visitors to the fort had left her in a state of shock. It had almost gone when Danecki surged into action to try to halt the crazed robot, Batibasaga.

And then the frightful Black Army had marched. The black phalanxes had rolled forward into the gulf of the spin-shaft upon their errand of destruction. All human life on Earth—such as it was on that haunted, irradiated planet—would be searched out and smashed.

Yet none of those things brought the incredulous, unbelieving start of grief. Pity, yes. Compassion for the lovers who had spied, lied, and wheedled their way into the secret, underground fort—compassion for the girl who had allowed the enemy to use her while her lover completed his mission. And a feeling of horrified pity for the few settlers on the planet, those Knaggs had known.

But the grief was more than pity and compassion. She wiped the blood from Danecki's lips with the tattered front of his shirt. "You killed him," she said to Jacobi. "You killed my man. You."

Jacobi backed off. "It was my duty! He killed by brother! My father! My sister—her children! The man was a mass murderer!"

Khalia felt that she could rip the boy apart. His terror roused the ancient, primeval blood-lust in her. She wanted to see death in his eyes. She reached for the broken arm.

Jacobi stood rooted to the spot. He was appalled by her fury, bewildered by the grinding march of the robots, utterly terrified by the combined dangers of the fort and the woman in front of him.

She took his arm and twisted it.

Jacobi screamed. He was still screaming when the lisping voice of the harem robot announced the cessation of hostilities between the Central Command System and the security networks.

"This new emergency leads me to one conclusion," the robot said. "Since I am the only system in this installation in full possession of the facts, I have decided to offer my services as an intermediary between the two factions which have developed among the superior systems."

Khalia felt the evil thing's words gliding somewhere around her consciousness, but she was too full of the enjoyment of murder to register its meaning or intentions.

Jacobi could not listen. He was on the floor, and the girl's foot was on his neck.

Neither heard their fate decided for them by the effeminate voice.

"I am not able to cope with the problems of command," Security said loudly. "I am prepared to accept arbitration."

"I have had my own problems," admitted the Central Command System's voice. "But I am ready to listen to any logical argument."

"Very well," lisped the harem robot. "Through a fault in our communications systems, the presence of anti-Confederation forces has not properly been appreciated."

"That is not good," said Security.

"It must be righted," agreed Central Command.

"Further, there has been no intelligence of the presence of the Duty Commander," the lisping voice went on.

"I knew of it!" pointed out Security.

"I was confused," said Central Command.

"I was not confused," said the harem robot. "Medium-grade though I am, I have records of Duty Commander's actions. The Duty Commander acted properly."

"Then he will assume control," said Central Command.

"Unfortunately, the Duty Commander has just been killed," said the harem robot. "His murderers are the anti-Confederation infiltrators."

There was a long pause.

Khalia felt the blood-lust ebbing away. She began to realize what a tremendous effort of will had gone into Danecki's restraint when he had the youth at his mercy. She took her foot off the youth's neck.

"Murders must be reported to the Duty Commander," suggested Security.

"The Duty Commander is dead," pointed out Central Command.

Khalia listened, though she still could barely appreciate the meaning behind the calm voices. In the wide, long cavern, the three robotic speakers argued like thieves in a graveyard.

Dead. Danecki was dead! Khalia wondered if she herself wanted to live.

The youth groaned.

"I find the problem too difficult," said Security. "How can the murder of the Duty Commander be reported to the Duty Commander? I know that a dead Duty Commander cannot function. Humans are not repairable."

"The Black Army has marched," put in a new voice. "Is the installation to be destroyed yet?"

"No!" put in Security and Central Command together. "An hour at least must elapse between the Army's march and destruct."

That settled, the harem robot spoke again: "It is usual for humans to be tried for murder. It is an offense."

"Humans will try the infiltrators," said Security.

"Soon there will be no more humans," Central Command pointed out. "The Black Army has marched."

Khalia followed the weird argument now.

Jacobi pushed himself up to listen.

"If there are no humans, the infiltrators cannot be put on trial," said Security. "I think."

"I will make a decision," announced Central Command. "It is my function."

Khalia refused to leave Danecki. The robots had kept their peace for ten minutes or more, yet she felt no urge to leave the still body.

Jacobi got up and walked about the great cavern. He too seemed unable to leave the scene of violence. At last he said: "Shouldn't we do something to try to get out? I've no quarrel with you."

"Go then," the girl said.

"But you!"

Khalia ignored him.

What were they deciding, these age-old automatons? Khalia had let Danecki's head rest on the cold floor. There was no more blood from his lips. She looked at her watch. Only twenty minutes had passed since they had rushed from the green and gold room to watch the passing of the monstrous Army.

She felt cold, helpless, afraid, and aged beyond anything she would have believed. And yet there was nothing to live for, so why regret the passing of her youth?

It seemed impossible that she felt such overwhelming self-pity when she realized that death might be near her. She remembered the girl who had looked at herself and said that it was an appalling waste to die at twenty-two.

Jacobi said: "What should we do with him?"

Khalia looked at the face of Danecki, relaxed in death. "It doesn't matter."

"You can't stay here—let's try to find the others. We

could try to get out! We don't have to wait till the fort decides to blow itself up!"

"It won't do that," said Khalia. She felt no pleasure in explaining to Jacobi how the fort would destroy itself. "It will fall through a fault in the planetary mantle. We're going to burn."

A mechanical voice rang out sharply, stopping Jacobi's incipient hysteria. "You are suspected murderers! Woman, you must surrender yourself to the duly appointed officer of the Judicial Investigating Commission of the Second Interplanetary Confederation. Man, you must accompany the woman!"

The machine waited.

"What does it mean?" asked Jacobi. He had the air of a boy. His thin face was pinched with tiredness.

Khalia felt no pity even then, though she tried to make it easy for him. "It means we're being arrested," she said. "The machines think we killed the Duty Commander."

"But—but I thought he was killed a thousand years ago! Isn't that what you were trying to establish! I heard it all in the hospital while my arm was being reset—the bones! The man's been dead for centuries! I heard the robot telling you about the saboteurs—they died a thousand years ago! I took the knife from the skeleton! It can't believe *we're* the saboteurs! It's mad!"

"Proceed to the Central Command Area," ordered the robotic voice. "You are protected by the Charter of Human Rights, and you may answer the charges against you jointly, or separately. Proceed immediately. Otherwise restraint systems will be used."

"I have restraint systems under control," announced Security. "All are in working order."

"But the fort's going to destroy itself soon!" Jacobi said almost hysterically. "It can't mean to arrest us now! Not when it hasn't got an hour's existence left!"

Khalia left him. She walked towards the narrow corridor that led past the three grim reminders of the millennially-old encounter, to the Central Command Area.

Before she began the upward ascent, she called loudly to the unseen robotic watchers: "Give the Duty Commander a fitting burial!"

The last she saw of the great, echoing cavern was the silent movement of the black hawsers which reached down for Danecki.

CHAPTER

★ 18 ★

Dross and Wardle had aged too.

Khalia saw that they knew Danecki was dead. And how he had died. Dross was on his feet, Wardle beside him.

The shrunken figure in the corner was Knaggs.

"We saw it," said the gray-faced archaeologist. His mouth was a sunken line in the big jowls. Though he bulked hugely beside Wardle and the thin, frail figure of Mr. Moonman, he seemed to have lost his overwhelming physical impact. He was a tired, disappointed, and corpulent old man. "What can I say?" he asked. "He was a man who almost came to know happiness after his year of despair. And in the moment when he might have found some way of escaping from this place, he was struck down by a vicious young savage. I pity you, my dear." He gestured to the screen which glowed with a faint green radiance. "We watched it all. The Black Army moving out—you and Mr. Danecki—then the youth creeping towards you both."

"There was nothing we could do," said Wardle. "I tried to move down the corridor, but the way was blocked. It seems that the fort has at last realized we are intruders and is treating us as such. I expect we'll be treated as spies."

"No," said Khalia. "It intends to try us for murder." She told the story.

They all stared at Jacobi.

He was biting on a knuckle, his white face anxious and afraid. "I was licensed," he got out. "Our laws allow a life for a life. I was right! He'd have escaped—you said he would have contrived something! He always could! When my brother and I had him stone-cold outside in the forest, he escaped! When I caught him again, he found *you!* And he would have done it again! I heard them and I knew he would think of a plan! You don't know him!"

"We knew him," said Wardle.

Mr. Moonman had begun to take an interest in the proceedings. "So we are back here, where it all started," he said, surveying the low cavern that was the Central Command Area. "The machines—the gadgets Mr. Knaggs spoke about—have been too much for us."

He polished the dull-black face of the ancient robotic head which had been his companion throughout the long night. "Three deaths," he said to it. "Mr. Knaggs, who might have told us more about these age-old machines. And poor Mrs. Zulkifar who thought herself my enemy because she feared a man who has seen the other side of the grave! And then Mr. Danecki, a man I came to admire. The man who was the victim of a barbaric vendetta law. This has been truly a place for violence, just as the guide books said. There is something sinister in all the things that remain of the Confederation, isn't there, Doctor?"

Dross humored him. "There is, my friend."

Mr. Moonman noted the archaeologist's salutation with a smile. "I knew the machines would win," he went on. "Without a man like Danecki, the forces of night will always win." He too stared at Jacobi.

Wardle plainly felt the need for action.

Khalia had grown used to his sudden spurts of energy, of his habit of bustling about—full of nervous enthusiasm for this or that project. She watched as he stepped about the cavern impatiently.

"An hour, eh?" the Brigadier mused. "An hour before it operates the destruct systems. What can we do with an hour, eh, Doctor? And this talk of a trial. Is it serious? Oh, I know the wretched machines have argued and decided what to do, but surely they're not serious? I mean, if the whole installation is going to deposit itself into some crack in the planet's crust, surely it won't go through a rigmarole of setting up a court. Surely, Doctor?"

"The Confederation built resourceful robots," said Dross. "It's almost an academic point, though, isn't it, Brigadier? Try us they might. Kill us they will, whether through the legal processes of the Human Rights Charter, or by taking us down into the bowels of this unhappy planet. As I say, it's not a point to trouble overmuch about. We should prepare our minds to face the end. We have a short time in which to live the whole rest of our lives. Why make that short time unbearable by raising more false hopes, Brigadier?"

Khalia knew that she would welcome death. She shivered with a creaking fear when she thought of the gradually increasing heat of the fort's slow descent. But the cold certainty of her grief accepted the notion of a term to the rest of her life.

Jacobi said: "Isn't there something? Brigadier? Doctor?"

"You killed our hope," said Khalia.

When the robots entered, Khalia screamed. They were something from a nightmare, ten-foot-high grotesques, decked out in the ceremonial garb of a long-dead judiciary. There were three of them.

The leader, a thing with a head like some new-hewn cob of iron ore, carried a six-foot-long sword. The sword glinted in the bright light as the automaton slowly turned to face the cringing group. It wore a red robe that hung to its two supporting legs; around its neck was a fur collar of some black-splashed white beast; and on the ponderous head was a full wig of curling hair.

Dross sighed with dismay and a reluctant admiration: "They've personalized themselves!" he managed to exclaim. "They've each built themselves a body. And they've manufactured the clothes of the Confederation's judges! Not in my wildest dreams could I have forecast such a development!"

The two robots following were as imposing and as terrifying as the sword-carrier. One was decked out in black, completely in black. It wore a tight-fitting garment of black stuff, and a head-piece over the hastily contrived carapace. Red eyes stared unwinkingly from a jet-black mask.

Khalia saw what it carried. *Rope.*

The third of the frightful trio was, for her, more terrifying than the red-robed leader and the black-garbed second robot. It moved almost daintily on spindles of legs; it gazed with obvious enjoyment at the four human beings who huddled together in the middle of the Central Command Area in a bewildered group. It wore a gown, as the leader wore a gown, but this was a black cloth trimmed with white fur. On its cleanly sculptured head—almost a humanoid carapace—was a frilled wig, itself an imposing structure of gray curling hair.

"Monsters!" whispered Wardle. "Monsters!"

Jacobi had broken down. He was sobbing and calling for his mother.

Mr. Moonman and Dross faced the eerie robots with equanimity.

Khalia felt a helpless admiration for the archaeologist, and for the Revived Man. They accepted the robots for what they were: things made by man—not creatures from beyond, but groupings of chains of molecules, bonded metals, and plastics.

"What are they going to do! Oh, why did I come!" wailed Jacobi.

"Aberrations!" Wardle said angrily. "What are you! Damn it, what made you!"

Khalia was glad that Wardle could face them too. It helped with her own battered senses to see the stoicism of Mr. Moonman and Dross, as well as the angry all-too-human horror that Wardle was displaying.

"What will they do!" yelled Jacobi.

Mr. Moonman turned to him: "I think they'll probably hang you."

The robots arranged themselves in a group facing the humans. The gaudy robes of the ten-foot monster with the sword swayed as it moved.

"Be upstanding for the Confederation Chief Justice!" lisped the voice of the harem attendant.

The voice came from the mincing spindly figure. It bobbed in a crazed parody of ritual homage to the red-robed automaton.

Khalia knew she had been right about the mincing gait of the automaton. What they heard and saw was a robot which had been hastily manufactured by the ancient fort to personify the evil guardian of the green and gold room.

"I'll take that," said the unmistakable voice of the Security System to the ghastly red-robed caricature of a judge.

The red-robed figure handed the masked robot the sword. It held the length of rope negligently in one vast metal paw, the glinting sword in the other.

"Tee-hee-hee!" lisped the black-robed robot. "Court is convened!"

The red-robed automaton bowed and adjusted its bulk so that it appeared to sit. "You are saboteurs, murderers and spies," it announced in the voice of Central Command. "Therefore you are criminals."

Dross murmured something that Khalia did not catch. The robot picked it up. "Humans are not machines," it answered. "I agree."

"We had so much trouble with the rules of procedure!" lisped the effeminate voice. Even the head of the monster had a vulpine, perverted look. "Eventually I remembered an old Totex recording we had on file—so I dug it out and my colleagues agreed to follow the old judicial procedures of the Confederation."

"I speak now," said Central Command.

"I execute the decisions of the court," said Security. "That is my function." It fondled the raw length of rope.

"I make decisions," the red-robed automaton said firmly.

"Yes," said the harem robot and the Security automaton together.

"Astonishing!" declared Dross. "Truly astonishing! What an evolutionary step this is, Brigadier! The robots are assuming the functions of the human controllers of the Confederation!"

"Silence!" lisped the harem attendant. "All must be done according to the proper procedures."

"You talk too much," the Security robot said. "It is for the criminals to talk before they are executed."

"You can't execute us!" Wardle burst out. "Damn it, you're machines! Machines don't do this sort of thing! Tell them, Doctor!"

"I was confused for some time," the red-robed figure said calmly. "But now I understand my function. I must make it clear to you."

Khalia saw that Jacobi was creeping towards the entrance to the corridor which led to the Black Army's former lair. He crawled like a broken spider.

"Restraint," ordered the red-robed monster.

A black hawser flashed from the ceiling and guided Jacobi back to the center of the cavern.

"Why resist?" said Dross. "We're all dead now. Us, Mrs. Zulkifar, Mr. Danecki, my friend and colleague, Mr. Knaggs. Easy, my boy—be easy!"

"We're not spies—we're not saboteurs! And there's only one murderer here! The youth with the knife!" Wardle burst out. "Judges! A judicial system—these things are for men! You aren't a part of the world of men! You're machines—you're things that we put together!"

Khalia wondered what crazed thoughts spun through the circuits of the machines. What vast collection of bad logic had brought them into existence? How had they contrived the robes, the grisly apparatus of sword and rope? The peace of death had seemed inviting, a beckoning thing, when Danecki had stopped breathing. Now, the sheer physical threat of the robots brought all the terror of violent death back.

The things were motivated by an elemental sense of justice. They were implacable juggernauts who had no human understanding or sympathy. All they knew was that they had some ritual to play out in this lost underground world of nightmare.

She listened to the gradual building-up of a case against them. It was a thing of crazed conjecture and the wildest misunderstanding of the "facts" the fort was aware of.

"May I outline the case for the prosecution?" lisped the harem robot. "After all, I'm a witness! Yes?"

"You are a witness," agreed the red-robed figure.

"He isn't allowed to give evidence!" exclaimed Dross. "You're not working to the rules of procedure in the judicial system of the Confederation!"

"You may state your case later," said the automaton. "Proceed!"

In answer, the black-robed figure marched to the four humans. It pointed a skeletal arm of raw steel at them. "These spies entered through the spin-shaft tunnel! They tried to find the location of the Army. The woman is a concubine. She guided the others into the installation! She was the mistress of the Duty Commander."

"It all happened a thousand years ago!" said Khalia. "A thousand years ago!"

"The Duty Commander is dead!" said the Security robot, alarmed by the reintroduction of a point he thought settled.

The black-robed figure shook its frills. "Humans do not live for a thousand years!"

"Automatons do," put in the red-robed figure.

"Yes!" cried the Security robot.

"Good!" said the harem attendant. "That is established. You are not a thousand years old."

"It's a mockery!" said Wardle in a pause. "The whole fort's on a destruct circuit!"

"Irrelevant!" said the huge self-appointed judge. "That is not evidence, and I order it to be struck from the record of this court!"

"How?" said the Security robot. It hefted the huge sword inquiringly.

Khalia wondered if it would all end then and there.

"Erase the words," said the judge. "The record!"

"Yes," said the Security robot. It brought the sword down squarely on a bank of controls immediately behind the Duty Commander's armchair. "Erased," it said.

And yet, to Khalia, the robots appeared to sustain the mad fabric they were building up. The harem robot had woven together two sets of events: one, the ancient tale it had shown to her and Danecki; and secondly, the incursion by their own party.

"The case for the prosecution rests on three chief lines of evidence," it lisped happily. "First, the records of the entry of the Duty Commander and his concubine, together with the illegal incursion of the saboteur. I produce these now."

"They are adjudged admissible," said the red-robed figure. "Show the recordings to the accused."

Dross gasped in wonder at the age-old tale.

Khalia saw again the anticipatory lust in the Duty Commander's eyes. He smiled with the knowledge of a man who hurries to a woman waiting with an impatience and need to match his own; he had a habit of tapping the blaster at his belt, a nervous scratching at the small, functional weapon.

"Astonishing!" gasped Dross. "And how logical! One woman diverts the attention of the Duty Commander—she slips in an identification blip and her partner can follow! So simple! And what a woman! Her poise, my dear! This is what finally defeated the Confederation! Who would have expected the girl to gain access through what in effect is the front door of the fort! Doesn't it prove, Brigadier, that the machines can always be circumvented?"

"It's a pitiful tale," said Wardle. "You still think they can be circumvented?"

"No, not so far as we're concerned—but observe the fantastic complexity of the installation! The endless security systems—the checks and double-checks! And they were to be of no value whatsoever!"

"They died," whispered Mr. Moonman. "They all died."

They saw the girl rush from the green and gold room to find her lover. They watched the Duty Commander's appalled realization that he had betrayed his command, and, in that betrayal, allowed the enemy to come to grips with the Confederation's final weapon. And they saw the brief flaring confrontation: the girl's head forced back by the blast of energy—the knife thudding home cleanly—the bright surge of power that completed the final act in the tragedy.

"It's ancient history," Dross said loudly to the red-robed automaton. "It all happened so long ago that the human race has begun all over again! There isn't a Confederation now!"

"Wrong!" said the Security automaton. "I am the Security System for this fort. This fort is a Confederation installation. Therefore there is a Confederation!"

"Quite right!" lisped the harem attendant. It shook its curls. "My next piece of evidence!" It pointed the blaster at the astonished group. "Taken from the Duty Commander," it lisped. "Incontrovertible evidence!"

"It means that the blaster was taken from Danecki!" Wardle said angrily. "It's mad! Mad! That blaster's been lying with the bones of the Duty Commander for a thousand years!"

"You are addressing the court?" asked the red-robed figure. "If so, you will speak to me as 'My Lord.'"

"Good God!" Wardle burst out. "That I'd live to see the day when a robot said a thing like that!"

"They are guilty," lisped the harem robot. "It's in their faces! This is where I nail my case firmly!"

"Now?" growled the black-clad Security robot.

"Now!" giggled the harem attendant.

A black hawser reached for Khalia. She saw it coming but she was unable to avoid its clinging, cold embrace. It moved down from the ceiling like a swath of funereal cloth, coiled and soft. She felt herself edged towards the staring figure of the red-robed Central Command automaton.

A hawser began to search a recess in the one-piece garment she had hastily donned so long before.

"Here," said the Security robot.

"As I said!" lisped the disgusting harem attendant. "An identification tab—she isn't a thousand years old! She's a young woman of twenty-two. This is a Confederation work-tab for a woman engaged on missile-direct duties!"

"Let me see," said the thing hewn from iron ore.

Dross was dumbfounded. Khalia heard him say: "It makes a mad kind of logic! It *does!* The machines always looked for facts—and this is a fact!"

168

"She—she took the dress, or whatever it is, from the concubine's room!" Wardle said.

"If she wears the garments of the Confederation, she is not a thousand years old," said the Central Command robot.

"Therefore she is a Confederation human," said Security. "She will be assuming command?"

"You cannot make decisions," the harem robot reminded the black-clad figure. "Though she wears Confederation garments, and though she has an identification tag which shows she is a missile-direct worker, it does not follow that she is a Confederation missile-direct worker."

The Security robot began to growl something, but the red-robed figure stopped it. "I agree. It is confusing but I must make a decision. I am a judge. Therefore I shall judge."

A new voice put in: "I am the destruct circuit. I am programmed to become active shortly. I have been listening with admiration to the proceedings. Shall I hold off final destruct until the proceedings are complete?"

"Yes," agreed the red-robed figure at once. "Wait."

Khalia was nudged back towards Dross. "So we have to wait until this criminal farce is over?" she said. "Until we're condemned?"

"It looks like it," said Dross.

"Yes," said Wardle. "Yes!" He began to whistle quietly to himself; Khalia put his nervousness down to the beginnings of a mental breakdown. When he began to pace about the center of the Central Command Area, she wondered if she was right.

For nearly ten minutes, the three figures stared at the humans. The minutes slid along quickly. Khalia was aware of a subtle tension among the robots. It was as though at a formal dinner party someone had called loudly for attention, and then forgotten what it was he had to say.

Dross talked quietly about the Confederation. In his own erudite way, he was a happy man. His only regret was that the incredible fort, with all its relics of the old and failed Confederation, should slowly subside into molten hell beneath Earth's crust. The mystery would remain, a total, baffling eternal blank!

At last, the red-robed figure spoke. "Spies," it said. "How do you plead?"

Dross shrugged. Mr. Moonman looked at the ancient robotic head in his hands. Khalia felt herself increasingly detached from the weird scene. She recognized that her body needed food and sleep, that her mind was unable to concentrate on the mad scene. Her grief was the only reality that meant anything to her—and that would end soon. Dross was right, she thought. Why make the waiting unbearable when there was nothing any of them could do to stop the machines from crushing them?

Wardle stopped pacing. "We all plead guilty!" he snapped. "Yes, guilty, my Lord! Be quiet, Doctor—I know what I'm doing! And you too, Miss! Let me handle this—I know you don't care now what happens to you, what with your loss—ah—your grievous loss, but we have to think of ourselves! Can't give in—can't surrender! Never would, though I lost my command for saying it! Yes," he said again to the three monolithic figures. "Guilty!"

"That makes it easier!" the harem attendant exclaimed. "I was going to ask you human spies to act as jury, but since you've pleaded guilty, there's no need for that kind of elaborate procedure. All you have to do, my dear high-grade superior, is to condemn them!"

The red-robed figure slowly rose to its feet. The black-clad Security robot passed the glittering sword. The sword came downwards to point at the group of humans.

Khalia felt the protest welling up inside her. *What were they guilty of!* A thousand-year-old crime? Danecki's double death? She watched, hypnotized, as the flashing blade swept upwards again. The ritual of the eerie scene possessed her.

"Death," it said.

CHAPTER

★ 19 ★

Air was expelled simultaneously from the lungs of all five survivors. It came with a heavy gasp from Dross; angrily, with a stifled curse from Wardle; in a moaning sigh from Mr. Moonman. Khalia heard her own instinctive cry. Jacobi screamed.

The whole incredible nightmare scene left them paralyzed with horror.

Jacobi fingered his neck as the black-clad robot played with the hempen noose. "You—you fool!" he screamed to Wardle.

The Brigadier moved quickly. He placed a big hand over the boy's mouth and whispered urgently and fiercely in his ear. Jacobi's eyes flared.

Khalia watched the byplay as if it were happening in another place—as if that too were a part of the ancient happenings of a thousand years before.

She heard Wardle's crisp authoritative voice: "My Lord!"

The red-robed figure inclined its head.

"We are all soldiers in the anti-Confederation armies!" Wardle said. "We must not be dealt with under civilian law! It is our right to die as soldiers!"

The black-clad monolith halted in the act of reaching for Jacobi.

"I am confused again," said the Central Command robot. "What do your records show?" it asked the harem attendant.

"I am in confusion too," it admitted.

"I have a rope," offered the Security automaton.

"We are soldiers," said Wardle. "We must die as soldiers. That is the custom. It must be at dawn, by gunfire."

Khalia suddenly realized what the Brigadier was doing. The instinct for survival had asserted itself in another of the party. The old soldier was buying time.

She began to hope he would succeed. The desperate grief she had felt was to some extent relieved by Wardle's efforts. He was a man who would not surrender. So much he had said. Unlike Dross, who could accept the dictates of an impersonal fate, and Mr. Moonman, who did not seem to care much about anything, Wardle had the most basic of all human desires: that existence, under whatever conditions offered themselves, should continue.

The red-robed, self-appointed judge waited.

At last, the harem attendant spoke. "I have no information."

"That is because you don't know," put in Dross.

Wardle tried to stop him, but the big-bellied archaeologist pushed his restraining arm aside.

"That is because we don't know," the central figure said.

"I know," said Dross. "I know because I am a thousand years old."

In unison, the three robots said: "No man lives to be a thousand years old."

"The last human to contact you did so a thousand years ago," said Dross calmly. "I am a human. Therefore I am a thousand years old."

"Superficial logic?" suggested the harem attendant.

"I am confused," said the Security robot. "Shall I hang the murderer? Now?"

"He and the others claim a death by gunfire," said the red-robed judge.

"We do," said Dross. "And because I am a human and you are a machine, I know more than you about the customs of humans."

"That may be," agreed the judge.

"Therefore you will do what we ask."

"I cannot obey spies and saboteurs."

"And murderers," put in the lisping voice.

Dross shook his head in disappointment.

Khalia sensed the welling excitement in Wardle and Jacobi. Now Dross had joined in the fight for survival once more.

"A death by firing squad!" Wardle's voice rang out loudly in the cavern.

"Agreed!" answered the great, monstrous, red figure.

"I have effective execution systems," announced the Security robot. "I shall prepare them."

"At dawn," said Dross.

"Agreed!"

The voice of the destruct systems put in hesitantly: "Shall I abort the destruct system?"

"No!"

For one moment, Dross's face had changed. Khalia could see the surge of anticipation dying away. He had thought for a moment that the strange installation would hold the destruct system permanently.

"Delay destruct until after the execution," the red-robed figure ordered. "We will dispense with these humanoid structures forthwith!"

The three robots trooped away through a suddenly-opened gap in the wall of the Central Command Area.

The trial, the survivors realized, was over.

"Dawn!" Jacobi gnawed on his fist again. "How long before dawn—are we going to wait here like rats waiting for death? It's dawn in a few hours! It's dawn soon—what can we do?"

"Wait," suggested Khalia.

Wardle gestured to the familiar prison. "Wait," he agreed.

"Wait and hope," said Dross. "We have a little more time."

"You're hoping that the Black Army was lost—aren't you?" said Khalia.

"You saw the saboteur reach the control desk," pointed out Dross. "I've been wondering if, after all, his mission was accomplished!"

"If it was, how would that help us?" said Wardle. "The only people who could reach us are the Outlanders—and our own fellow travelers aboard the excursion ships, if they haven't been blown up by the fort's rockets! But the Outlanders wouldn't know how to reach us, and the rest of our companions won't dare to look for us!"

Khalia saw that his burst of enthusiasm had petered out. "Wouldn't the robots possibly change their minds?" she asked. She thought of the three great, monstrous figures which had been contrived expressly to enact the ritual of the court.

"No," said Dross. "I'm afraid, my dear, that they're under control again. We're not faced any more with a series of disconnected personalities, but with a single, directed entity. The Central Command System seems to have things pretty much under control. Mad, it may be. Vindictive, I doubt. But it's purposeful."

"If only we could think of something!" Wardle paced about restlessly once more, but with the fury of frustration, not the determination of a man with a new idea.

"If only Danecki—" began Dross. He stopped, seeing Khalia's sudden overwhelming grief. Mr. Moonman saw it too. Dross and Wardle watched him. Jacobi roused himself from his trance of fear.

The Revived Man drew himself up to his full gaunt height. He raised the ancient robotic head high above the other survivors.

Khalia saw what he was doing. She screamed.

Dross blanched. Jacobi tried to writhe into the space behind the Duty Commander's armchair, squealing pitifully. Brigadier Wardle stared stone-faced at the most terrifying enigma of modern times.

The Revived Man was withering before their eyes.

It was the reason for the ferocious distrust that all normal men and women had of the unfortunate victims of that bizarre warp in time. It was the cause of the revulsion Revived Men created in all who saw them—and in themselves.

The Revived hung in a precarious temporal balance. They neither aged nor decayed. Each one of the few survivors of the two-hundred-year hiatus could decide the time and manner of his extinction. The Revived held their own life-spans in their hands.

Mr. Moonman had come to a decision on the time of his death.

"Don't!" yelled Khalia, somehow overcoming the wild nausea that brought her heaving to her feet. "It isn't over! You shouldn't—"

"I heard of it once before," breathed Dross. He raised his voice. "Don't, my friend! We'll all wait together—don't anticipate the fates, Mr. Moonman! There's been enough of death in this place!"

Mr. Moonman was an insubstantial wraith. The ancient robotic skull smiled into his gaunt face.

"Transference!" Dross mumbled.

"What!" Wardle said in a gasped whisper. "What, Doctor?"

"Don't let him!" Khalia whispered with the others.

"They know the trick of transference!" Dross exlaimed in awe. "That this should happen to us—that another of the greatest mysteries of the entire cosmos should be unveiled to me! I, Dross!"

Khalia recognized the astonishing arrogance of the archaeologist. Alone of the shocked onlookers, he thought of himself, not of the weird, dissolving figure.

She remembered the Revived Man's lonely figure during the voyage across the Galaxy. He had traveled far, only to die here. Head, shoulders, trunk, skeletal legs—all were becoming liquid phosphorescence. The humanoid head still hung above the decaying figure.

There was a stench of the grave in the gleaming, functional Command area. Decay, age-old decay.

But there was a voice in the thin detritus. "Minutes," groaned the voice. "Minutes, Doctor! Ask! Ask it to tell what it remembers! Ask its name, and call on the Confederation Commander! Only minutes, Dr. Dross!"

"Great God Almighty!" breathed Wardle. "What is it! What is it, Doctor?"

"Transference!" said Dross again. "The end of a human being who gave up the ghost two centuries ago—the Revived is returning to his grave! No, Wardle, don't ask any more questions—look at the robot head! Do you see?"

Khalia held back a scream. She was so full of a horror beyond any that she had thought could exist, that she forced the scream deeply back so that it would not disturb the steady decay of the insubstantial thing before her. What was Dross saying? *Transference?* A transference of what! *And to what!*

She saw the robotic head alive with intelligence. Its humanoid features crinkled with amusement. It waited for the questions.

"It's—it's alive, Dross! Damn me, it's looking at us!" croaked Wardle.

The voice came with a bitter sigh from the ghost that still held the skull. "Use the time! Use it!"

"Use it?" Wardle demanded. "Use that! That *head!*"

"Yes!" purred Dross. "Don't you see? Mr. Moonman has chosen to bring another being into life for the few minutes he can hold back the forces of eternity! He's crossed the void and brought someone back from the grave! That head, Wardle, is the focus-point for someone who trod this place in the days of the Confederation!"

Jacobi whimpered into the stunned silence.

"You can't!" Khalia whispered. "You can't do it!"

"Can, must, and will, my dear," said Dross. "The man has given us all he had! And we have to take it!" He advanced reluctantly to the grim and ghastly wraith. The skull turned to watch him, its features alive, and its wide-set mechanical eyes glowing with malevolent appreciation.

"What are you?" Dross said, trembling. "A ghost?"

"A nothing," the robotic head answered. Its voice was strong enough. But the oddly mechanical sound was tinged with a subterranean hollowness that set Khalia's ears twitching. The faint down on her back tingled with a stir of primeval terror.

"You are a Confederation officer?"

"The head of a robot, the voice of a ghost, the ghost of a man who died here!"

Dross flared into excited anger. "You! You knew the Duty Commander! He died down here—that's how Mr. Moonman can call you back! Yes, Knaggs had the right of it! I remember poor Knaggs trying to tell me that the head was an artifact stuffed full of memories! And the memories lay in the robot head all that time—they lay in the mud of the centuries! And the memories brought you back! Mr. Moonman didn't raise a ghost! No!"

Dross turned to the others. "This isn't a ghost! No! It's a slip in time—it's a thin slice of robotic intelligence—it's the calling back of all the robot saw, or heard, or conjectured about the Duty Commander! Don't you see? This isn't a metaphysical thing at all—it's only man-made machinery, held in that ancient head for a thousand years! We're seeing the memories the robot head contained! And Mr. Moonman called them back and gave them a form! He managed to sew time and space together for a short while—that is the secret of transference! But the time's going fast!"

"It isn't a ghost!" Wardle exclaimed. "Just a machine?"

"Call it a machine possessed by the devil!" Dross said. "Now let me ask it how we can escape from this accursed place!"

There was a soft groaning noise from the heap of spoiled human tissue that lay beneath the smiling robotic skull. Mr. Moonman passed beyond the fort and into the grave he should have filled two centuries before.

"Minutes!" exclaimed Dross. To the softly-smiling skull he said: "How long?"

"Not enough!" the hollow voice answered.

"Then answer this!" Dross shouted, angry and shaking with paunchy impatience. "How can the destruct circuits be aborted?"

"How?" said the head. "How!"

"You have to tell me!" said Dross with a white-hot intensity. "You have to tell me!"

"Yes," the skull smiled. "There is a way."

"Tell it!" bawled Dross.

"Yes. The name. Key in the name. The name of the Commander. Give Central Command the date exactly, to the second—to the nearest hundred-millionth part of a second. Earth time. Then order it to abort."

"The name?"

"My name," the thing smiled. "My name."

"State it!"

The thing struggled with a lopsided smile. Already the features were taking on the rigid appearance of hard metal again.

"Always the name!" Dross shouted. "Always there is the power in the name—it's the oldest of all the superstitions! Tell the name and you give away the power!"

"Zeuner," the thing said hollowly. "Zeuner. Captain and Duty Commander. Died hereabouts. A thousand years ago."

"Zeuner?" snarled Dross. "Just Zeuner?"

The thing smiled once more. "Zeuner." It dropped into the gruesome detritus that shortly before had been the body of the Revived Man.

"Zeuner!" Wardle said. "You heard, Doctor! Zeuner! Let's call the Central Command System! Now!"

Khalia tried to avoid the charnel-house stench. She would remember the solemn compassion on Dross's huge face as long as she lived. He seemed to be trying to remember what Mr. Moonman had said.

"A moment, Brigadier," he said. "A moment."

Wardle paced about nervously. At last he too stood in silence.

Dross waited for the space of two full minutes. Then he spoke. "We have known men in this place. Knaggs. Danecki. And now Mr. Moonman."

Khalia slipped into her overwhelming sense of loss.

Dross put a massive arm around her waist. "There will be time to grieve later. The living must live."

It was Wardle who dealt with the details. He found the time-recording computers and spoke to them briefly. He shouted for attention, giving the long-dead Duty Commander's name.

"Now!" he finished. "Obey now!"

There was no reply.

"Try again," said Dross.

"I am Zeuner!" shouted Wardle. "Duty Commander and Captain! I am Captain Zeuner. It is now two-point-five-zero-six-three-eight-two-one seconds; zero-five-four minutes, day two-seven-one, year three-six-two-five!"

Minutes ticked away. Still there was no reply from the ancient installation.

Khalia felt the cold edge of menace in the room, the sensation of impending attack that she had felt just before the fort had produced the three ghastly robots.

The voice, disembodied and loud, assaulting the ears from all directions, was firm, harsh and evil. "No! No! Humans do not exist! Humans are all a thousand years old! All are dead! Zeuner does not meet my efficiency criteria! He cannot function efficiently! I must not abort the destruct systems! I am in control!"

Dross slumped. "Nothing," he said. "Now there truly is nothing."

"It's finally happened," Wardle agreed. "The machines are the masters."

Jacobi called to Khalia for comfort. "Help me," he said in a child's voice. Khalia couldn't look at him. She accepted Dross's comforting arm.

What was there to do but wait?

CHAPTER

★ 20 ★

The Outlanders found them like that.

They were huddled together as far as they could get from the phosphorescent decay that had once been Mr. Moonman. Dross had his arm protectively about Khalia's shoulder. Wardle's pacing was over. He sat on the floor, head slumped against his chest. Jacobi had taken refuge in a kind of fitful sleep.

Dross stared at the big black doors as they slid aside with easy smoothness, revealing the rescue party. There were four men and two women.

Resplendent in his refurbished green-bronze body, Batibasaga stood beside them.

"Dr. Dross?" asked the leader of the Outlanders.

"I'm Dross."

Khalia heard the voices. She looked and saw the newcomers. For a moment she thought that dawn had come and, with it, the execution party. During the hours that had elapsed between the ghastly judicial charade and the opening of the huge black doors, she had gone over in her mind everything that Danecki had said to her. She had held every feature of his tired, handsome face, with its haunted eyes and gentle smile, firmly in her mind's eye. She treasured the small instinctive gestures of tenderness that had gradually revealed the man beneath the hunter's mask. It had made the waiting bearable.

"My dear," said Dross, climbing to his feet, "remember that you have your own life to live now. It's over."

There were the endless questions, the cries of relief, the thin yelps of glee from Jacobi, the measured answers of the man who led the Outlanders, the obsequious explanations of the robot, the sadness and blazing excitement of the archaeologist.

"Fame!" Dross cried. "The finds of Dross will at last convince the unworthy that the dig at Earth was not for fool's gold! How they'll writhe at the Center! How the tight-fisted hypocrites at the Foundation will crawl!"

He caught himself in his tirade. "See to the girl," he told the women. "She has suffered more than any of us." He pointed to Jacobi. "Take this away now!" And then his face lit up. "But tell me! How!"

"Yes!" Wardle insisted.

"You should ask your robot," the leader said. "We did no more than offer advice. We knew of the legend from Mr. Knaggs. When the ship blew up yesterday, we knew the ancient war was still being fought by some undestroyed installation. Mr. Knaggs would have told us what to do, so we came to the ruins above. When we saw that you were missing, we tried to find you. There were signs of recent destruction, so we surmised that you were lost within the ancient fort." The man paused. "There aren't many of us. We have some skills from our old lives, but none of us knew about the ancients and their military complexes. And so we set up a watch."

Khalia was weeping quietly in the arms of a middle-aged woman. She listened without interest to the Outlanders. There was a life to live, Dross had said. How could it be that one day—and was it no more than that—could totally alter the direction of your life? Change it so fundamentally that you were not the person you had been, related at no point to the calm, assured, well-educated young lady who would have gone back to life on predetermined Vega with only a set of interesting travel memories?

"Mr. Knaggs died," said Dross.

"Your robot told us. He was a friend of ours."

"He was a colleague and a true friend," Dross agreed. "Batibasaga came to you?"

"To us," the man said. "He did what had to be done, and then he came to us for advice. Your robot knew we were friends of Mr. Knaggs."

"Well, Batty?" said Dross. "What have you done to the rest of the robots?"

Batibasaga turned to the Duty Commander's great chair. Jacobi was led away like some dying insect.

The sensors leapt gladly towards Batibasaga's humanoid

hands. The big opalescent screen glowed eagerly. And the voice of the Central Command System called out: "This installation recognizes your superior efficiency! You are a more advanced mechanism than this! Therefore you must take control!"

Batibasaga turned to Dr. Dross. "May I show you, sir? It's almost finished now. And I think you'll understand why I had to attend to the antiquated war-robots first when you see. It was my decision, sir, but remember that I was programmed by a very ingenious engineer."

"By Danecki," breathed Wardle. "Danecki set up your circuits!"

"Was it, sir? I have no memories. I was, at the time, inhibited by the molecular disturbance of the spin-shaft." The screen glowed, and the surface of the planet began to take shape. "I hope I did the right thing, sir. I had to make sure that they achieved their goal."

In the weak moonlight, the Black Army blasted clear of the titanic surface ruins like some elemental beast. The monolithic war-robots streamed through the smashed and contorted base, pounding skeletal towers into shards and gaping radiation shields into fragments. They ground the few gaunt trees and bushes, islands in the ancient ruins, into pulp, obliterating them with a chilling satisfaction.

"The Black Army!" whispered Wardle. "What a fantastic weapon—the ultimate weapon of the ancient world!"

The screen picked out the leading phalanx. There was indecision. Each monstrous black robot sniffed the wet air like some porcine rock, hunting for the elusive scent of a living creature. Hundreds of antennae oscillated wildly in the streaming rain. The ghost of a moon raced through low, fast clouds. It was a scene from the grimmest of traumas. The Army waited for a command.

"I had some difficulty at this point," explained Batibasaga to the tense spectators in the underground fort. "You'll understand, Doctor, that my circuits received a considerable amount of disorientation in the spin-shaft tunnel when first we descended into this low-grade establishment. Up to the point when I took control of the Army—even to the stage where I found myself on the surface with hundreds of these inferior automatons waiting for me to guide them—I was not completely myself. The maintenance robots which had been working on me did not undertake repairs until a very late stage in the proceedings. Nor was their work finished. When I did become activated, I had to act at once. I was programmed for certain eventualities, with one overriding consideration."

"I can guess," said Dross.

"Yes, sir," the robot said. "The greatest good for the greatest number."

"That would be Danecki's way."

"And the robots had to be eliminated," Wardle murmured.

Batibasaga was not apologizing, Khalia noticed. "I had to ensure their complete destruction, Doctor."

"Of course," said Dross. "What else?"

Khalia began to understand. Danecki, after all, had been right. The way to control the robots was to confront them with a superior automaton. Their basic disbelief in their human masters' continued existence had always stood in the way of direct control over the fort by the trapped party. Knaggs had foreseen this, even when he was dying. The machines would obey Batibasaga.

She saw the screen pick out the figure of the humanoid robot. Batibasaga was smaller than the war-robots, a compact figure against their monstrous bulk. He had been a heavy enough weight to push towards the winding tunnel, she remembered. But the robots that made up the serried ranks of the Army were monoliths. Things as huge and heavy as blocks of basalt.

"I became fully active at this point, Doctor," explained Batibasaga. "My circuits responded to the release of the war-robots on the surface. I knew their plan. They were programmed to destroy all that remained of human life."

The leader of the Outlanders spoke. "Our small communities. The robots would have found us in the darkness."

"You, Doctor, were not the first priority," said Batibasaga. His voice held no hint of regret or apology.

"Rightly," said Dross. "Rightly."

"Well, what happened to the Army?" demanded Wardle. "Damn it, it's the most interesting military weapon of all time—an utterly pitiless weapon of destruction! What a thing to have under analysis! We could set up a whole military museum complex here, Doctor! It really is the find of a lifetime—the find of the century!"

Batibasaga coughed discreetly. "If you'd care to watch what I did, sir. I think you will find a commentary superfluous, sir. I accompanied the Army on its preset march."

It was a march across a hundred miles of land and sea.

The phalanxes kept perfect order in arrow-straight lines. They bored through forests, across ancient dusty metropolises that were the tombs of the millions who had died in the Mad Wars, across vast highways of steel and stone—direct as the path of a thunderbolt over valleys and mountains. When they came to water, their bulk at once shot out force-fields, so that they glided across seas and lakes like some beast from Earth's primeval past—powerful, fast, and deadly.

For an hour they streamed across the downs and hills of England. Always west.

Batibasaga halted the recording. "The circuits had been programmed over a thousand years before," he said apologetically to Dross. "I had to go with them personally, sir. Even though their circuits were expertly planned, I had to be sure that some fault had not developed in these low-grade automatons."

Khalia thought that she understood. Though she was quite numb emotionally, the appalling march had stirred her. It was the culmination of events she had shared in—events like none she had dreamt of before the tourist ship had slipped through into the calm time-space regions around Earth. She had been a part of the plot to stop the march. She had helped to push Batibasaga into the tunnel. She had pitied the long-dead girl whose clothes she wore. She had watched as Danecki made the decision to rely on this green-bronze robot who would not apologize to Dr. Dross for leaving them to face the weird installation while it made sure that the Black Army would not destroy the Outlanders.

Wardle understood too. "Great God! Batibasaga, or whatever your name is—you mean these robots weren't under your control? You mean these saboteurs—all those years ago—they were successful? Surely not! I mean, it's quite incredible!"

Batibasaga waited for Dross to speak.

Dross smiled. "Legends are not made from nothing, Brigadier! There's always a basis somewhere! You remember how I said that the puzzling part of the legend was that there seemed to be two parallel ideas? That, though 'The Regiments of Night shall come at the end,' there was a reference to 'the Pit'?"

"I remember," said the leader of the Outlanders. "Mr. Knaggs often told of your interest in the reference. It is appropriate?"

"Oh, yes!" Dross said, beginning to laugh. "And I never realized before what kind of 'Pit' the legend referred to! In a way, it's entirely appropriate—it's exactly what I would have hoped of from the forces who brought down the Confederation and all it stood for! The way in which our unknown saboteur finally disposed of the Black Army is positively ironic!"

"What?" demanded Wardle. "Ironic? How do you mean, Doctor? Surely—surely you'll want some of the robots for the museum? A Second Interplanetary Confederation War Museum! I mean, they're the greatest weapon of all time! Primed, ready to march, indestructible —at least by any conventional weapons of the period! They represent the highest peak of military thought!"

"Show them where the Regiments of Night marched to," ordered Dross.

"With pleasure, sir," Batibasaga said.

Now the Army was marching faster. It smashed through stunted forest growth, across glowing pits of deep radiation, always moving west. In the cold of the mountains, the rain-belt gave way to clear weather. Stars glittered in clear skies, and the half-moon brilliantly illuminated the flooding mass of the Army.

Sensing the nearness of their destination, the grim phalanxes put on speed again. In utter silence, they came to a vast river mouth.

Khalia saw the Army pause once more.

Batibasaga appeared at the head, a small greenish automaton in the white moonlight. He pointed towards the heaving black sea.

The Army slid forward, a great wave of cold lava. Black water met the onrush of the robots. They waded out and the waters swallowed them up.

"Sunk, by God!" Wardle said in awe.

Several things happened at once in the Central Command Area.

The big screen displayed the onrush of the Black Army. Khalia's eyes could not leave the incredible scene. But the harsh clamor of the Central Command System's voice held her attention too.

And there was Dross, pulling at her arm, saying over and over again something that she recognized but could not admit as the truth. It was so astonishing an idea that she began to weep. She felt fat warm tears rolling down her face. And then the woman who held her was helping her towards the middle corridor.

Still she watched the screen. Still Wardle's exclamation of awe came to her. She missed, however, the end of the Army.

"The Duty Commander is showing a return to efficiency," stuttered the metallic voice. It blocked Khalia's mind, that demanding clamor. "Duty Commander Zeuner is receiving attention in the human maintenance unit! He is a thousand years old. This system is again confused."

Dross was the only one who immediately grasped the significance of what the Central Command System was saying. "Batibasaga!" he rapped out. "Get this confirmed —it can't be Zeuner!"

But Khalia couldn't hear. The stunning experience of the march held her eyes, and the wild hopes that she was beginning to feel in the pit of her stomach were radiating through her entire body and threatening to bring her whole being bursting into flower.

"Sunk without trace!" Wardle was saying.

She heard him as the woman took her firmly by the shoulders and hurried her away at Dross's command.

"Make sure!" he called to her. "Batibasaga has already checked with the Central Command System—there's a badly-wounded man in the hospital—the fort thinks it's Zeuner, but we know *he's* dead! Batty thinks it's Brigadier Wardle, how or why I don't know! But the man answers to one description! Make sure, my dear!"

"And it was planned this way from the beginning?" asked the leader of the Outlanders.

"Exactly," said Dross. "The anti-Confederation saboteur reprogrammed the circuits that controlled the Black Army. When they marched, they followed his path. It led by the shortest and most direct route to the Western sea—there!"

The screen showed the upheaval of the Army's plunge. Big waves swept towards the shore. Beneath them was the turmoil of the great slabs of robotic matter digging furiously into the ocean bed. After a while, they stopped, and the big slow swell of the waves began again.

"They—they—where *are* they!" Wardle was utterly bewildered.

"Gone into Earth's dustbin," said Dross. "And there's the beautiful irony of it all, Brigadier. Perfect!"

Khalia knew where to go. Once you were used to it, the fort's layout was obvious. Central Command where it should be, in the middle. Radiating from that area, the weapons control systems down one corridor, the decision-making computers down another. Between them, in two lower levels, the installation's service areas. Among these, the harem. Beside that, the hospital.

Khalia tried to hold back the tears, but they came in a flood. She caught her breath painfully between sobs; she sweated profusely, her hair became entangled, and the bright red suit she wore was spattered with her tears. She was conscious of her appallingly disheveled appearance. What she didn't see was the brightness in her eyes and the thrusting eagerness of her run through the corridor.

Zeuner functioning weakly! And Central Command confused. *Batibasaga himself confused because he thought that the Brigadier was a youngish man with heavy shoulders and a deep wound in the chest—with one lung caved in and the heart action so weak that it barely showed on the machine!*

"Don't let it be wrong!" Khalia sobbed as she reached the silent door.

The woman with her said something, but Khalia was too tense to allow the words to break into the precious build-up that was threatening to break out like some great eruption of love in the silent fort.

She passed through the door. Machinery hung in swaths over the white hospital bed. A gentle whining of liquids under pressure came from the equipment hooked into the shape beneath the covers.

Khalia ran.

"Incredible!" Wardle exclaimed.

"Inevitable," Dross contradicted him. "Where else? Where else could the robots be sent? Not out to the other planets—they'd be as potent on Mars, or even on Venus, as on Earth. No, Brigadier. Our saboteurs thought this one out with beautiful logic. They sent the robots down Earth's own conveyor belt."

The Outlanders who had remained smiled.

"Doctor, this isn't just conjecture? You're not—not showing us a fantasy?"

"No! Ask about the social customs of the ancients and Dross will give you a clear and authoritative answer! I agree that it might sound farfetched, but not when you consider what the inhabitants of this planet came to, as a last resort, when their waste products threatened their environment. No! Listen to Dross!"

He turned away and spoke to Batibasaga. "The girl?"

Batibasaga allowed a clutch of sensors to pump information into his humanoid palms. "She is content now," he said.

Wardle said: "Content—not, not, surely not—Danecki?" he finished with a whisper.

"Zeuner. Wardle. Danecki," agreed Dross.

Wardle was speechless.

"Toctonic sinks!" Dross said into the silence. "Toctonic sinks! That was the answer—find them all over the planet! A deep trench in the planetary crust where there's plenty of seismic activity. Lots of underground faults and flaws. As I say, find a place where the Earth's crust is weak, ally it with low gravity, and deposit your surplus waste in it! If the waste is compressed sufficiently, down it goes —and it keeps on going down! Beneath the crust, down into the hottest and most heavily-pressurized regions! That's how the Black Army was disposed of, Brigadier. It was treated as so much refuse!"

"Heavy mass," said one of the Outlanders. "They'd be dense and heavy. Programmed to march to their own rubbish-sink! As you say, Doctor, there's a subtle irony about it that is quite beautiful!"

Wardle tried to adjust to the loss of the Army. "What a waste," he sighed. "What a find! What an end!"

Dross clapped him on the back. "Isn't there enough here to amuse you, Brigadier? Why not stay—take Mr. Knaggs's place, if you will! Yes, why not stay here?"

Wardle considered the idea. "Yes. Why not?"

"And Danecki?" asked the leader of the Outlanders. "What happens to Danecki?"

He was unconscious. His face was narrow. The closed eyes were sunk in deep, black-lined white pits. The strong nose was too thin for the gaunt face. His breathing was shallow but regular. Blood seeped into him, and oxygen whispered from a tube.

From the head of the bed, a thin metallic voice said: "The Duty Commander is a thousand years old. He is responding to treatment. A very superior robot inquired after his health. I was able to report that he has a ninety-seven percent chance of survival. He is not dead. But he is a thousand years old."

"I don't care," said Khalia.

Danecki's eyes fluttered open. Khalia thought of her appearance. He tried to whisper.

"Don't!" she said. "Don't try to talk!"

There was the hint of a smile. "You're beautiful," he said in a surprisingly strong voice.

Khalia knew that she would explode with love.

"This blood-feud worries me," said Wardle. "Danecki told me about it. Bad business! That youth won't forgive —never! Not the forgiving kind. Did you see his eyes when he told us he'd accomplished his mission? Empty. Nothing there. He's beyond feeling."

"Danecki's dead," said Dross.

"Correction," began Batibasaga.

"Don't interrupt me! Listen! Danecki *is* dead. We'll put the Jacobi youth into his ship and lock the course onto his own planet. You do that, Batty."

"Yes, sir."

"So far as he's concerned, the whole unpleasant business is over. Finished."

"And then?" asked the leader of the Outlanders.

"Danecki could help here?" suggested Wardle. "There'll be plenty to do."

"No," said Dross. "We'll be in the eyes of the entire Galaxy when the story gets out. We'll have droves of sightseers of all kinds, from official buffoons to the usual tourists. And I can't keep them away. It won't be safe for Danecki to stay here."

Dross was looking at the Outlanders. Their leader smiled. "He'll be safe with us. And the girl."

"I'll never leave you," Khalia said to the unconscious Danecki. "How could I?"

"Batty," said Dross. "Mr. Knaggs. Mr. Moonman. And the poor lady. If you find anything—"

"Yes, sir. I thought on the hill, overlooking the ruins—"

"That would be appropriate," said Dross. He looked around the fort. "I'll be glad to see daylight again. It's been a long night."

Numerical checklist of DAW BOOKS for the convenience of the science fiction reader and collector.

1. Andre Norton SPELL OF THE WITCH WORLD
2. Joseph Green THE MIND BEHIND THE EYE
3. Brian N. Ball THE PROBABILITY MAN
4. A. E. Van Vogt THE BOOK OF VAN VOGT
5. THE 1972 ANNUAL WORLD'S BEST SF
6. Mark S. Geston THE DAY STAR
7. Brian M. Stableford TO CHALLENGE CHAOS
8. Jeff Sutton THE MINDBLOCKED MAN
9. Gordon R. Dickson TACTICS OF MISTAKE
10. Suzette Haden Elgin AT THE SEVENTH LEVEL
11. Gerard Klein THE DAY BEFORE TOMORROW
12. Dean R. Koontz A DARKNESS IN MY SOUL
13. THE YEAR'S BEST HORROR STORIES
14. Philip K. Dick WE CAN BUILD YOU
15. Lloyd Biggle, Jr. THE WORLD MENDERS
16. John T. Phillifent GENIUS UNLIMITED
17. G. C. Edmondson BLUE FACE
18. E. C. Tubb CENTURY OF THE MANIKIN
19. Brian N. Ball THE REGIMENTS OF NIGHT
20. L. Ron Hubbard OLE DOC METHUSELAH

All DAW Books are 95¢. To order by mail, it is necessary to utilize our computerized order number for each book and this number can be determined by simply adding 1,000 to the number of the book on the above list and adding the prefix letters UQ. All sales are handled through The New American Library, Inc., P.O. Box 999, Bergenfield, N.J. 07621. Include the price per book, plus 15¢ mailing charges. Allow about 3 weeks for delivery.

DAW sf BOOKS

- ☐ **WE CAN BUILD YOU by Philip K. Dick.** Give us the name and specifications and our man-factory can do the rest! (#UQ1014—95¢)

- ☐ **THE YEAR'S BEST HORROR STORIES.** A witch's brew of SF grue, featuring Richard Matheson, Robert Bloch, E. C. Tubb, etc. (#UQ1013—95¢)

- ☐ **THE WORLD MENDERS by Lloyd Biggle, Jr.** What is justice and injustice on an alien world? John W. Campbell said this fine novel was "going to be one of the classics." (#UQ1015—95¢)

- ☐ **GENIUS UNLIMITED by John T. Phillifent.** Their planetary Utopia was off-limits to all but science wizards—and the killer cunning. (#UQ1016—95¢)

- ☐ **THE MIND BEHIND THE EYE by Joseph Green.** A giant's body is directed by an Earthly genius on an interstellar espionage mission. "A tour de force of the imagination."—Times (#UQ1002—95¢)

Four new SF books each month by the best of the SF authors. Ask your favorite local paperback book shop or newsdealer for DAW BOOKS.

DAW BOOKS are represented by the publishers of Signet and Mentor Books, THE NEW AMERICAN LIBRARY, INC.

THE NEW AMERICAN LIBRARY, INC.,
P.O. Box 999, Bergenfield, New Jersey 07621

Please send me the DAW BOOKS I have checked above. I am enclosing $_____(check or money order—no currency or C.O.D.'s). Please include the list price plus 15¢ a copy to cover mailing costs.

Name_____

Address_____

City_____State_____Zip_____

Please allow at least 3 weeks for delivery

DAW BOOKS

- ☐ **THE BOOK OF VAN VOGT** by A. E. van Vogt. A brand new collection of original and never-before anthologized novelettes and tales by this leading SF writer.
  (#UQ1004—95¢)

- ☐ **TACTICS OF MISTAKE** by Gordon R. Dickson. An interstellar chess game played with living men and planets is the foundation of Dickson's Dorsai cosmos.
  (#UQ1009—95¢)

- ☐ **AT THE SEVENTH LEVEL** by Suzette Haden Elgin. Sexual chauvinism was the basis for that world's social structure—until the galaxy itself complained.
  (#UQ1010—95¢)

- ☐ **THE DAY BEFORE TOMORROW** by Gerard Klein. To dominate the future—change the past! A prize novel by the Ray Bradbury of France.
  (#UQ1011—95¢)

- ☐ **A DARKNESS IN MY SOUL** by Dean R. Koontz. The gene-tamperers produced two supermen—one a defiant mentalist, the other a defiant . . . god?
  (#UQ1012—95¢)

Four new SF books each month by the best of the SF authors. Ask your favorite local paperback book shop or newsdealer for DAW BOOKS.

DAW BOOKS are represented by the publishers of Signet and Mentor Books, **THE NEW AMERICAN LIBRARY, INC.**

THE NEW AMERICAN LIBRARY, INC.,
P.O. Box 999, Bergenfield, New Jersey 07621

Please send me the DAW BOOKS I have checked above. I am enclosing $_____ (check or money order—no currency or C.O.D.'s). Please include the list price plus 15¢ a copy to cover mailing costs.

Name_____

Address_____

City_____ State_____ Zip_____

Please allow at least 3 weeks for delivery

DAW sf BOOKS

Do not miss any of the great science fiction from this exciting new paperback publisher!

- [ ] **THE 1972 ANNUAL WORLD'S BEST SF** Edited by **Donald A. Wollheim,** and presenting the finest science fiction stories of the year in one great anthology; including Clarke, Sturgeon, Niven, Anderson, etc.
(#UQ1005—95¢)

- [ ] **THE DAY STAR** by **Mark S. Geston.** In the sunset of humanity, they set out to reconstruct the glories of Earth's finest hour. (#UQ1006—95¢)

- [ ] **TO CHALLENGE CHAOS** by **Brian M. Stableford.** Last trip out to the only planet that spanned the two universes and two opposing laws of physics.
(#UQ1007—95¢)

- [ ] **THE MINDBLOCKED MAN** by **Jeff Sutton.** Manhunt in the 22nd Century—with a Solar Empire at stake.
(#UQ1008—95¢)

Four new SF books each month by the best of the SF authors. Ask your favorite local paperback book shop or newsdealer for DAW BOOKS.

DAW BOOKS are represented by the publishers of Signet and Mentor Books, THE NEW AMERICAN LIBRARY, INC.

THE NEW AMERICAN LIBRARY, INC.,
P.O. Box 999, Bergenfield, New Jersey 07621

Please send me the DAW BOOKS I have checked above. I am enclosing $_____(check or money order—no currency or C.O.D.'s). Please include the list price plus 15¢ a copy to cover mailing costs.

Name_____

Address_____

City_____State_____Zip_____

Please allow at least 3 weeks for delivery